Back in Belmont

by

Maria Paoletta Gil

Dedication

For Tafari and Elijah

Chapter 1

"Papa! Come get me. I want to go home."

Day Danese flipped shut the phone and peered out the apartment window, half expecting to see her father's Buick round the corner and double park on Broadway. It had only been seconds since she'd called him, but Papa could work miracles, and this morning Day needed a miracle more than ever.

She was going to miss the rumble and stink of the Upper West Side delivery trucks, car alarms, fresh dog poop, and frying bacon from the Athenia Coffee Shop. She adored Manhattan. Small towns and dense, incestuous little neighborhoods bored Day. Every time she found a new man, part of the attraction was where he lived. She'd pack up and follow her new paragon to Chicago, Atlanta, Baton Rouge, settle in and a few months, sometimes even a few weeks later when it all went sour, would pack up and go back to Papa.

In the past twelve years, Day had been the erudite sounding board of a Memphis attorney, the muse of a wannabe LA director, first mate to a Seattle ferry pilot, and concierge for the proprietor of a Miami boutique hotel. None of them had worked out. Maybe she'd worn the wrong clothes, decorated the new love nest too soon, ignored the signs instead of addressing them, but something always happened. The lawyer married his high school sweetheart, the director wanted Day to get implants and make porn, the pilot sailed away, and the hotelier decided he was gay. Day never achieved a longed-for future of excitement and passion, or even one of peace and contentment. So far, the future always turned out to be the same as the past: Papa and Belmont.

Whenever Day called Papa after yet another disaster, she half-expected him to say, his Italian accent still thick after nearly forty years in New York, "*Basta*, Deanna! You on you own. I no come no more!"Day wouldn't blame him. Why shouldn't Papa be fed up? Her twenties were a distant memory, and she was sliding toward forty, still chasing dreams.

Day checked the time. Where was Papa? She was eager to sit quietly, sulking in the Buick, arguably bigger and certainly cleaner than her dreary furnished sublet. She'd even endure the usual lecture: *This time you stay home and marry a nice Italian man.* Day had once dated a Papa-approved paragon by the name of Bobby Leone, gone out with him for an entire summer after high school, liked him a lot too.

Bobby had a quick temper, but he was fun and cute and spent money without complaint. Day would never body-shame anyone, but it did bother her that he was short, barely her height, while Day was tall and liked to look up to partners, at least figuratively. Moreover, Bobby made no secret that he planned to live with his mother until he married. Most of the boys of Belmont married their mother's clone and moved next door. Strong, independent women with a yen for adventure were trouble. It was okay to sleep with Talia or Tiffania with tats and a tit ring, just don't bring her home for dinner.

Day leaned out the window and scanned the street. The dog walker's arms pinwheeled. Mr. Abbas unlocked the metal gate of Athenia Coffee and the meter lady circled a delivery van.

"Come on, Papa," Day breathed. "Where are you? I need to get away from here."

Papa was her prince, her rock of Gibraltar, always responding when she called, never balking, never betraying. He sent money for airfare and except for a woebegone look and the *When You Marry?* lecture, Joe Danese kept his mouth shut. Still, everybody in Belmont knew that Deanna Maria Danese, Joe's only child, his *piccina,* little one, no matter she almost topped six feet in her Jimmy Choos, was a fuckup.

Day checked the time again and began to pace. The smell of frying bacon was starting to upset her already roiling stomach. Generally, Day didn't eat breakfast, and to her father's discontent, could get through an entire day on avocado toast and two Almond Joys. Yet her figure was full-breasted, broad-hipped, and slightly overweight from Thanksgiving through Christmas. The truth was, Day liked to gorge late at night. Her stomach started rumbling around eleven o'clock and by midnight she was cooking dinner or sending out for *pad Thai*, six H & H everything bagels, and a quart of chocolate milk. You could do that in big cities. Every restaurant, corner deli, rib joint, and bistro from San Francisco to Key Biscayne employed a guy who delivered your three-course meal, complete with napkins, dipping sauce, and a two-liter Coke in the middle of the night. But if Day craved a slice with anchovies from Enchanted Gardens, she had better call it in before the evening news was over. Papa's

3

restaurant, like most of the Bronx, closed at nine.

The doorbell rang. Day rushed to the intercom. "Papa?"

"Is no the pope."

She grabbed the handle of her rolling suitcase and slammed the door behind her. Mercifully, the elevator was waiting.

Chapter 2

Joe Danese stood by the Buick, dressed as always, winter and summer, in black pants and a white, polyester short-sleeved shirt. He gave Day a quick once-over.

"You look like hell."

"Thanks, Papa. Want me to drive?"

Joe frowned. "You crazy?" Then, getting the joke, grinned broadly.

The Buick was Joe Danese's mistress, dependable friend, the son he never had. No one leaned on it, fooled with the radio, or dared sit behind the wheel.

He bowed to Day. "Your limousine, *Signorina.*"

Day scooted in and clicked her seat belt before Papa reminded her, sat up straight, faced front, and tried not to leave fingerprints. Joe hit the ignition, checked the rearview mirror, and shifted into *Drive.* He rolled forward an inch, shifted into *Reverse*, rolled back the same inch, and moved forward into *Drive* again. Rocking back and forth several more times, Joe finally eased into traffic, nearly decapitating a cyclist.

With the speedometer locked at 40 mph, he progressed glacially up the middle lane of the West Side Drive, ignoring nasty honks and irate middle fingers.

Half an hour later, on the off-ramp for the Cross Bronx Expressway, he glanced briefly at Day. "You eat breakfast?"

Day shook her head. "You know I don't eat in the morning."

Joe said nothing for a moment, and then, "Another guy no work out?"

"No, Papa, he didn't."

Joe took one hand briefly off the wheel to touch the side of his nose. "I no say nothing before, Deanna, because you a big girl, but right away I smell a rat. You send photograph and this man,"—Joe's finger moved to his earlobe— "earrings! *Per la miseria*, like a pirate."

Day leaned back against the headrest and closed her eyes. "Lots of men wear earrings, Papa."

"You have to be more smart," Joe countered with a hint of exasperation. "You past thirty now, no job, no graduate college. By the way, when you going to do that?"

Day cringed. Her last love hadn't been the Miami hotel owner as Papa thought, but a professor at NYU where she'd enrolled to complete a bachelor's degree. She hadn't known it, but the flamboyant English Department Chair had a fan club. Female Lit majors queued up for his legendary lectures that could switch an entire trailer park of romance readers to James Joyce. The man was handsome in a matinee idol way, had a lifetime membership in the Downtown Racquet Club, a ten-speed bike, and a Museum Mile Premium Pass. He referred to starry-eyed Day as his warrior goddess and the only Viagra a sixty-year-old libido required. Day, of course, thought she'd found the Paragon at last, an older man with no hang-ups and a floor-through on East sixty-eighth, until she found out he lived there with his wife. Feeling dumb as a trout, she had licked her wounds, dropped out of NYU, and called Papa.

Joe exited the expressway without signaling and crept down the access road, hitting every light in the process, and parked in the loading zone in front of Enchanted Gardens, his pizza restaurant. For a long moment, neither he nor Day moved. Finally, Joe turned.

"You stay home now, no more run, okay?"

Day surveyed the scene. A clutch of women sat on folding chairs underneath a spindly tree with plastic bags hanging from its branches. Several men lounging in front of Optimo Cigar bestirred themselves to leer at a buxom teenager pushing a stroller. Pigeons pecked at greasy pizza crusts. The air smelled of garlic and tomato sauce, and passing cars blared Frank Sinatra and Bad Bunny. With a sigh, Day met her father's gaze.

"Yes, Papa, no more running."

"*Va bene*, that's good." Joe leaned over and opened the passenger door. "Go upstairs. I come in a minute."

****

The realization that Day was once again back in Belmont threatened an onrush of tears. She sucked them back and watched her father barge inside Enchanted Gardens trying to catch Luis playing video games. Six years ago, Luis had walked over from Taft High School looking for a job sweeping up. Now, to Joe's good-natured chagrin, the boy had become his right-hand man. Luis had computerized the restaurant's books, increased revenue with two-fers and walk-in traffic by installing video games. Best of all, he learned to speak Italian. "*Luis fa piu che la figlia*," the old-timers said. "Luis is better than the daughter."

Day waved at Luis through the window and walked

7

around the back of the restaurant and up a flight of steps. Joe owned the entire brownstone, and Day had been born in the apartment on the second floor. Enchanted Gardens occupied the first floor and nobody lived on three. Keeping her mind deliberately blank, Day used the key she'd had ever since sixth grade and entered the living room, what Joe called the front room. A window fan whirred softly and despite an early June heat wave, the living room was cool, dark, and smelled of cigarette smoke and wax from the votive candle flickering in front of a statue of Mary Magdeline. *La Magdalena,* a free-spirited siren-turned-saint, fell in love with Jesus, and according to Maria Danese, Day's mother, married him. Maria died young and her daughter didn't remember much of her, but Joe was fond of claiming that Maria had been a wild rose who'd left a life of adventure in Italy to be his wife. Day often wondered if she'd inherited Maria's restlessness, but what did that matter now? She was back home and determined to stay put.

The place looked neat, but from the dusty furniture and dingy curtains, Day knew it wasn't clean. There was a bathroom off the kitchen and two bedrooms at the end of a small hallway. Her bedroom hadn't changed at all. The single bed was covered with a lacy spread crocheted by her mother's aunt, a rag-and-ribbon area rug lay on the floor, its lurid colors only slightly faded, and a roll-top desk still bore gouges from the point of a compass. The one closet was hung with navy blue Mt. Carmen High School uniforms and drip-dry blouses in pastel shades. Sweaters were folded in plastic bags on the top shelf.

Day studied two gilt-framed photographs on the

dresser, Papa standing proudly in front of Enchanted Gardens the day he bought the building, and Mama sitting with toddler Day in a plastic kiddy pool in the backyard. Papa claimed Day looked like Maria, although she couldn't see it. Mama had been small and plump with a kewpie doll face while Day's height, long, narrow eyes, and prow of a nose favored the Danese side of the family.

"You mama she love you so much, Deanna," Papa was fond of saying "To tell the true, when you born, I was a little jealous."

As she always did, Day searched Mama's young face for a resemblance. Her mother's mouth had been pouty, eyes gray, hair wispy and pale, whereas Day was dark, with thick curly hair and a wide mouth bracketed, even when she frowned, with tiny laugh lines. Mother and daughter looked nothing alike, except for a dreamy, unfocused gaze, a kind of yearning expectation for…what? Day peered at the snapshot. Something was hiding behind Maria's pursed smile, some vaguely disappointed hunger that a new country, new husband, and new baby hadn't entirely satisfied. Maybe that's what Papa meant when he talked about a resemblance. Both women possessed a striving aura, the aching residue of unfulfilled dreams. But Day would never know; Maria was barely a memory, less substantial than the softly whirring table fan lifting a corner of the bedroom curtain. Mama's smell and feel were gone; no lullaby trilled in Day's ears and no home-baked amaretto cookie triggered an onrush of Proustian recollections. All that remained was what Papa said about Maria, and as the years passed, he said less and less.

For Day, growing up had been all about her father, Enchanted Gardens, and cousin and best friend, Beanie Bonito, now Beanie Siragusa. Day had relatives in Queens that braved the badass Bronx once or twice a year, but that was pretty much it for blood. However, half the population of Belmont felt like family, even Officer Hank, the local beat cop, who spent more time cadging pastries in Mrs. Navona's bakery than enforcing the law. Carmine Carciofalo, President of the Belmont Neighborhood Association, did that.

Joe Danese was Day's star. When she was six and wanted to cook, he let her mess up the kitchen by making pizza from leftover dough, marshmallows, and strawberry jelly. As a teenager, Day was allowed to redecorate the house, picking out a blond wood hutch with a secret pull-out bar and flowered wallpaper for every room. She was permitted to hang out at nearby Orchard Beach, go to the movies with Beanie on Saturday afternoons, and drink watered wine at dinner. A car was the only pleasure Joe denied his beloved child, confessing later that he feared she'd drive away and never look back.

Despite Joe's loving largesse, Day grew into maturity feeling deprived. All the other kids at Our Lady of Mount Carmel Elementary School had mommies who baked cupcakes for the Overseas Mission Fund, not a daddy who donated ten pizzas with the works. In high school, her classmates called their mothers, *She,* grousing "*She* won't let me watch Basketball Wives, *she* says blush is slutty, *she* hates my friends." But Day had no *she* to complain about, just a permissive father who let her be free as long as it was safe.

Day fell back onto her old bed and stared at the ceiling. The water stain that looked like Sicily was still there, and spider webs hung from the molding in greasy threads. Her head ached and she padded to the bathroom to swallow three out-of-date Bufferin, sucking water from the tap. Her face in the mirror was ghastly; the endless quest for romance, excitement, and adventure had aged her. Einstein was right when he said stupidity was doing the same thing over and over expecting different results. Ordinary ladies from the Bronx didn't have adventures, the perfect Paragon man didn't exist, and there was no glass skyscraper, tropical island, or misty mountain range that made up for a hollow soul.

Day was eighteen when she began escaping her childhood of books and daydreams. She hadn't gone gently and certainly not successfully into that good night of the unknown, and had returned every time disconsolate and discouraged. Life had become a hula hoop, spinning like crazy until it lost steam and collapsed. But she was ready to explore more meaningful avenues of validation now. A career? Dedication to the less fortunate? Erudition? Forget that last one. It had taken thirteen years and practically as many schools in as many cities to finish college. As for a job, all Day had ever done was sling pizza at Enchanted Gardens. She needed to feel whole, not the appendage of another man or Joe Danese's nutty kid who kept running off with a full tank of hope and returning on empty.

The door slammed and Day heard Papa making noises in the kitchen. "Deanna!" he called. "*Dove sei?* Where are you?"

Maria Paoletta Gil

She splashed her face with water, plastered on a smile, and joined Joe at the kitchen table set with a steaming Styrofoam coffee cup and a hero sandwich wrapped in greasy paper.

"You breakfast, Bellissima," Joe sad. "*Mangia.*"

Reluctantly, stomach rebelling, Day took a sip of the thick, sweet *cafelatte*. "It's good, Papa. You make good coffee."

"Of course is good. Everything I make is good. I make you and you good." He pushed the sandwich closer. "Peppers and egg, not too much garlic."

Day unwrapped the sandwich and took a bite. It was delicious. Papa was a wonderful cook. "I'm sorry I blew it again, Papa," she confessed.

Joe tapped his forehead. "Don't think about that now. Think about this." He took a velvet box from his pocket. "Happy Birthday."

"Happy Birthday?" Day said, puzzled. "It's not my birthday."

"*Si, si,* not today but it's this month so we celebrate early. Nothing wrong with that."

The Bufferin had to be ten years old. Day's head was pounding, and her stomach gurgled. She wanted a cool shower and a long sleep, but Papa's eyes were bright and eager. She replastered the smile, opened the box, and gazed in bewilderment at a garish, heart-shaped locket the size of an Oreo cookie. It was ringed by a filigreed border, studded with glittering multi-colored stones, and opened into two recessed ovals for pictures, locks of hair, or possibly two halves of a pepper and egg sandwich.

"You like?" Joe asked.

Day favored slim, silver bangles and hoop earrings

delicate as tinsel, and she never wore necklaces of any kind.

"It's very nice, Papa."

He fastened the chain and stood back beaming. "Diamonds, rubies, emeralds, and eighteen-carat gold," he said proudly. "One ninety-nine ninety-five at *Affuso's*, down from two-twenty."

Day lifted the locket off her chest, resisting the urge to grunt. "It's heavy."

"You betcha." Joe kissed his daughter on both cheeks. "I have to go back downstairs, make sure Luis no put jalapenos in the tomato sauce. You rest. *Andratutto bene.*" All will be well.

****

The next morning, Day found a jar of petrified Sanka in a back cupboard and chipped off enough to make a mug of coffee. She jotted down a to-do list: *clean, buy groceries, get a job, look for a place to live,* mentally adding, *but not for a man.* Gathering courage, she asked to borrow the Buick, although she hated driving it as much as Papa hated lending it. The relic-on-wheels was long and wide as an ocean liner, rattled like a hay wagon, and resisted parking. Day was a freshman in high school when Papa had docked it in the loading zone in front of Enchanted Gardens and accepted congratulations from the crowd. The nuns from Mt. Carmel School tossed a few coins into the back seat for luck. Officer Hank fished them out later.

Day parked in Joe's favorite spot at the shopping center, last row, a mile from other cars but a bull's eye shot for the security cameras. She bought cleaning supplies, a new bedspread, and a couple of gallons of antique white and mint bisque paint to cover up all the faded pink rosettes. She intended to hurry back knowing Papa would worry, but the traffic was murderous. Day's eyes pivoted from the car's unpredictable temperature gauge to the international vista that made up the environs of Belmont. The Bronx Zoo and the Botanical Gardens looked the same. Salsa, rap, and reggae still blared from the Concourse, along with swoony Bollywood and Korean love songs. Turbans and headscarves vied with Yankee caps and the air smelled of ginger and pork fried rice.

The old First Bronx Federal Savings and Loan that used to be Banco Hispanico was now a dollar store or maybe a church that sold furniture. Day couldn't be sure as the sign above its double doors was in Arabic. The few pizza places weren't busy. Everybody knew the real deal was a short walk away in Belmont.

Day's immediate neighborhood resembled a walled Renaissance town, but that was deceptive. Many former residents, mostly Italians, had moved to the suburbs, although some still occupied the side-street row houses with concrete front porches and back gardens planted with zucchini and tomatoes. Kids played stickball in the street and elderly women, Italian, Albanian, Spanish, Middle Eastern, it was hard to tell, frowned at passers-by, even at Day until they recognized her, and then they frowned even more.

She stopped for a light and watched Officer Hank select a peach from the display in front of the fruit market then step into Navona's Bakery for his free cannoli. Belmont never changed; same thing all the time. Day never changed either, she thought ruefully, ricocheting home after every adventure with the same untamed hair, tortoise shell reading glasses, broad hips, and broader expectations, more mixed up despite the brave facade. Countless cities and countless men, well three or four of them, hadn't left her content, only confused. Day had never been the discerning type, never looked before leaping, but you'd think she'd have learned a thing or two.

She stopped at a light on Arthur Avenue wondering briefly what the rents were in Chicago, one of the few cities she'd never seen, then cursed her *opera buffa* life. She had to stop leaping into the abyss; the future was a crapshoot if all you did was shoot craps.

The light changed and Day mashed the gas, the only way to get the Buick to move, barely missing a pregnant woman crossing against the light. The woman raised a fist, yelling "What the fuck, bitch," and dragged a baby stroller closer to Day. Her magenta hair spiked in irate clumps, purple sandals laced up to her knees, and an outie belly button peeked below an acid green crop top that said *Doesn't Play Well With Others*.

Day stuck her head out the window and shouted, "Hey, Beanie. It's me!"

"Holy shit, cuz," Beanie exclaimed. "You're back. What the fuck happened this time?"

Chapter 3

Day pulled over to the curb, climbed out of the car, and rifled Beanie's magenta spikes. Albina Siragusa was her second cousin and best friend. They'd attended Our Lady of Mount Carmel School from kindergarten through eighth grade and spent three years together at the high school until Beanie dropped out to marry Vinny.

"Love the do," Day said. She cocked her head at the little boy fidgeting in the stroller. "This can't be Michael."

"Him? Nah," Beanie answered. "Mikey and Vinny Junior are in school. That's Anthony." Beanie patted her stomach and made a face. "And if this next one ain't a girl, I'm sewing it up. So spill. You hooked up with another rat bastard who was gay or married or just a rat bastard?"

Day looked around the crowded street. The words *Belmont* and *privacy* were complete opposites. She decided to avoid, for the moment, filling in Beanie on the details.

"How's Vinny?"

"Okay," Beanie said. "Works with sanitation now. We bought a house by the hospital. If you're not doing nothing, come on over and we'll talk."

Day loaded Beanie, Anthony, and the stroller into the car, and minutes later, was walking past the statue of St. Francis of Assisi in Beanie's front yard that was so befouled with pigeon droppings, his face was invisible.

"Vinny's mom gave that to us when Anthony was born," Beanie remarked. "I wanted one of those jockeys that looks like Kanye but the bitch gave me fucking Jesus."

"That's St. Francis," Day pointed out.

"Oh yeah? Well, it don't matter. I ain't wiping bird no shit offa no statue's ass."

Beanie lifted Anthony from the stroller and led Day up concrete steps to a covered porch, through a set of ornately carved double doors, and down a hallway lined with gold-veined mirrors.

"Beer?" Beanie asked, popping a can of Bud in the narrow kitchen.

"No thanks." Day eyed Beanie's stomach. "Are you allowed to drink in your condition?"

Beanie took a long swallow. "Nah. I'm quitting. What'll you have? I got grape juice, Juicy Juice, iced tea, Kool-Aid, Gatorade, lemonade, soda, Snapple."

"Coke is fine," Day said

"Coke? Did you hear me say Coke?"

"You said soda. How about a Pepsi?"

Beanie rummaged. "Fuck, Junior must have drank the last one. Take a Bud."

"I don't like beer."

"World traveler and ain't learned a damn thing," Beanie scoffed.

"I've never been out of the country, Beanie."

"And I ain't never been out of the Bronx," Beanie retorted."But I can still read you like a tweet." Anthony began to whimper. "Let me put mommy's sissy pants down. Then we can sit on the porch and dish."

While Beanie was gone, Day roamed through the messy kitchen to the equally messy living room/dining room combination. Clothes were piled everywhere but they were folded, the dining table was stacked with books and papers, and an interrupted Parcheesi game, but there were no plates in the sink or coffee cups floating with cigarette butts. Beanie's house was a trainwreck but a clean one. The pots were scoured, the rugs vacuumed, and the knick-knacks free of dust. Fondly, Day remembered trying to hide the stains on her Ralph Lauren rip-off while Beanie's gypsy-layered stripes and prints and hi-top sneakers were always immaculate.

She peeked out the sliding glass door at a swing set and picnic table in the fenced yard. Potted geraniums ringed the deck and a huge urn sprouted one tomato plant and two of basil, a purple and a green. A pair of tiny red sneakers hung from the back of a chair and she rubbed them against her cheek. *This is nice. I should have this.*

In school, Beanie was the hellion who smoked in the lavatory and made fun of the nuns, especially the one with whiskers who taught gym in size twelve nun-boat sneakers. Beanie never got a higher grade than C-minus, and begged Day to do her homework so she could play hooky with Vinny. Neighbors called Beanie a shameless hussy who would surely end up in jail or worse, but she fooled them all. Got a job at Allstate, married Vinny, albeit three months pregnant, and settled into a conventional life.

"My Shangri-la," Beanie said, coming up behind Day and surveying the yard. She'd traded cut-offs for a sort of billowy romper that tied at each thigh and above her breasts. Despite a mildly ballooning middle, Beanie looked small and fragile. A tiny fretwork of blue veins etched her eyelids and her pale skin seemed almost translucent.

"Vinny built the barbeque and put up the fence. He wanted a tool shed, a grape arbor, a gazebo, and a pool with a water slide. Go for it, I said. And while you're at it, how about a motocross track, and a baseball diamond, and a fucking dance pavilion?" Her eyes twinkled. "I guess for a guy who grew up with five brothers in a two-bedroom apartment, a backyard must feel like Yellowstone." She grabbed a bag of Cheezy-Chips and took Day's arm. "Let's talk on the porch so I can hear Anthony from the window."

Sitting beside Day on the porch swing, Beanie lit a cigarette and inhaled greedily.

"Should you be smoking?" Day asked.

"Nah." Beanie breathed a voluptuous exhale. "I'm quitting." She leaned close. "Now spill, kiddo. I want to know all your secrets."

"No secrets," Day responded glumly and launched into the sorry saga of the married professor.

"That's pretty bad." Beanie nodded sympathetically. "But you ain't no kid. Pretty soon they're all going to be married. Why don't you cut your losses and stick around? Belmont ain't so bad."

"I'm thinking about the Bronx but not here, not Belmont."

Beanie looked affronted. "What's wrong with Belmont? It ain't exactly a craphouse." She flicked ashes over the wrought iron railing. "Yeah, okay, it is, but it's your home no matter how many Italians jump ship."

"My father will be happy," Day said.

"You shitting me? Papa Joe would drive his precious Buick into the Long Island Sound if it would keep you here."

"Yeah, well. I'm exploring options."

Beanie studied her cousin. "You been doing that exploring bullshit for as long as I can remember and ain't come up with nothing. Am I right? And you're what, forty?"

Day gave her a look.

"Yeah, okay, so we're both thirty-four." She dug for another smoke. "Not for nothing, Day, but what have you got to show for all the running around? Did you at least get your degree in, what was it, selling newspapers?"

"Journalism, and yes, I did," Day answered, not at all proud of her answer. "I took some online courses and I can pick up my diploma downtown."

"Well, big whoop," Beanie remarked dryly. "Look, I'm not saying my way or highway. I know Vinny don't got Elon Muskrat's money or Henry Cavill's ass, but you got to dive in and start swimming. Shit, Day, you ain't even dipped a toe."

"That's not true. I fall in love and want to get married, just like you."

"Not like me, Day. You pick losers. Guys you know won't deliver. And you do it on purpose. Don't give me that look. You do it because you're commitment-shy."

"That's not true either."

"Give me a break."Beanie folded her arms. "That Cuban guy with the bou-tique-ho-tel?" She pronounced the four syllables distastefully. "I knew from the git-go he was swish."

"You never even met him," Day retorted.

"Didn't have to. I saw the pictures. Only Italian guys can get away with hair like that and still be straight. And what about all that crap in the hotel, peacock feathers and bleak lavabos, for crying out loud? What the fuck's a bleak lavabo?"

"Beleek," Day mumbled. "It's rare pottery and lavabos are little fountains you hang in a garden so that–"

"Spare me." Beanie plowed on. "What about Mr. Atlanta District Attorney? Did you really think he'd get down on one knee and propose?"

"Why not?" Day answered. "He certainly wasn't gay."

"He was gorgeous," Beanie allowed. "And very generous, picking up the tab for my cab and dinner when he was in New York. But for one thing, the guy was ambitious, and for another, Earth to Day, he was a Protestant." She didn't give Day a chance to react. "Yeah, yeah, god is god and all that, but where were your brains? You're from Belmont, for crap's sake. Italians stick with Italians." She blew a perfect smoke ring. "Lex Luthor would have never proposed anyway."

Day shifted uncomfortably. "Martin Luther. And how do you know? What did you see that I didn't?"

Beanie shook her head."You *saw*, kiddo. You saw and you knew but you packed up your shit and went south." She bent close. "The guy wanted to be mayor, or senator, somebody Rachel Meadow interviews on, what's that boring station you watch, CNN?

"Maddow and MSNBC isn't boring."

21

"Whatever, but there was nothing you could do for him, a nice Italian girl who combs her hair with her fingers? It was just a matter of time before he went back to his secretary. Now her name I remember, Cialis."

"Amaryllis," Day said numbly.

"Yeah. All the dick drugs sound the same. Anyway, she was the daughter of a judge, for crying out loud," Beanie fairly shouted. "You never had a chance."

Anthony's whimper floated through the open window. Beanie jumped up and took the stairs two at a time.

Day stared out at the traffic. Two EMT workers were leaning against their truck eating pizza. Idly, she wondered if it had come from Enchanted Gardens. Day too had speculated about the hotel owner. He'd been an athlete in bed but a little too inventive, insisting on a playlist of pre-coital scenarios, patient-nurse, prisoner-jailer, and so on. Day had gone along because she'd been crazy about Miami and her private lanai on the hotel grounds. She'd been crazy about Atlanta, too, and Seattle and Los Angeles. Day sighed. It was always the cities more than the guys.

Beanie returned with Anthony who'd drifted back to sleep. "Get us a couple of beers, will ya?" Beanie said.

Day obliged, opening the cans and handing one over. "I suppose I set myself up," she admitted."If I went through all the guys I dated in the last twelve years, none of them would have panned out."

Beanie brushed her lips across the top of Anthony's head and glanced at Day through lowered lashes. "Bobby Leone would have."

Day thought briefly about her one and only Italian boyfriend. Bobby Leone was handsome in a cherubic way, not very tall but well-muscled from hours working out at the gym, steady and predictable with no enchanting edges, no frisson of danger, and no mystery. Just a regular guy from the Bronx. Bobby hadn't proposed exactly but claimed to want a wife and kids and if Day just waited until he finished college and found a job, they could tie the knot and live in a nice semi-detached like Beanie's. Day sipped beer, and considered life as Mrs. Bobby Leone. It might get monotonous, but Bobby would never leave her for a political career or to chase after a hunky driver with a truckful of Beleek lavabos. She sighed noisily. Bobby was good and steady and dependable as bread, but who wants bread in a world full of cheesecake?

Beanie broke into Day's reverie. "What's with the groan?"

"The Bobby Leone file is trashed, cuz," Day answered, rising. "Thanks for the beer. I have to get back and clean the apartment."

"Yeah, okay," Beanie said matter-of-factly. "But have you searched Bobby online lately?"

"Why would I do that?

"No reason."Beanie shifted Anthony to her shoulder. "Come over for dinner tomorrow night. Vinny's barbequing."

"I can't. I promised Papa I'd waitress."

Beanie patted her stomach. "Just like old times, me preg, you working with Papa Joe. Guess some things never change."

The smile on Day's lips didn't reach her eyes. "Guess you're right."

Chapter 4

Waitressing was easy. Day had helped in the restaurant since she was small, wiping the tables, bringing the bread, standing on a stool and stirring pots of sauce. When she was old enough to serve, Day remembered orders without writing them down and promptly refilled coffee cups. The guys from the precinct and firehouse teased her and left big tips. She liked the work, the noise, and good smells, the camaraderie, and cigarette haze that lingered thickest above the *No Smoking* sign. In memory, these things were pleasant, yet Day fled them over and over. Beanie called her an odd duck and kept reminding her that men do what they do without much thought and most of them will drop you for another woman no matter how snaggle-toothed she is. According to Beanie, the trick was finding a good one like Bobby Leone that Day already was too dense to grab when she had the chance.

On the afternoon of Day's thirty-fifth birthday, Beanie took her shopping. Day modeled a filmy summer top that gathered under the breasts and fell in soft folds.

"Tits like yours and still alone," Beanie remarked dreamily. "You ought to have your own page in Guinness: *Hottest Chick in the World Without a Man.* Guys are so dumb."

"Not your Vinny," Day said.

Maria Paoletta Gil

"I grabbed Vinny when he was young enough to train. But don't kid yourself, cuz. Even the better ones sometimes ain't shit." Beanie wagged a finger."Stop trying to please guys. They don't know what they want any goddamn way. Long as you do, the rest comes easy."

Day shrugged back into her T-shirt. "Sounds okay, but what if I don't know? What if the man for me doesn't exist?"

"Go with the odds. Pick the one who comes closest, like you-know-who."

Day groaned. "Bobby Leone's a spoiled mama's boy."

"Nobody's perfect."

Beanie paid for the top and a pair of white jeans that Day wore to her birthday dinner at Enchanted Gardens. All the Siragusas were there along with Luis and his wife and baby daughter. Mrs. Navona sent over a white chocolate cheesecake and Officer Hank stopped by for leftovers. Surrounded by love, Day ate too much and laughed until her jaw hurt. Papa beamed but Beanie kept shooting evil looks.

"You're itchy, cuz, "Beanie said, having a smoke out on the sidewalk after everything had been cleared away.

"What do you mean?" Day didn't need to ask that question. There was no fooling Beanie the Witch.

"I see it in your eyes," Beanie responded, lighting up a second cigarette. "You're getting ready to run."

"No, I'm not. It's just, it's just—"

Beanie stared her down and Day gave up trying to explain.

"What's wrong with me?" she cried. "Why am I

like this? Belmont is my home. I care about everybody here tonight; they're my friends and family. And don't make that face, Beanie. This time it's not about a man. There is no man."

"Uh-huh," Beanie remarked.

"I swear it, Beanie. A relationship is the last thing I want right now. Like you said, I have to figure myself out first."

Day was a tiny bit witchy, too. There was something behind Beanie's probing scrutiny. Her cousin was scheming, planning some kind of surprise and that was never good.

****

Enchanted Gardens was open on July Fourth but Day left early to attend the Siragusa's annual backyard bash. She promised Papa to help close out at the end of the day, but Joe insisted he and Luis had it covered.

"Stay, stay as late as you want," Joe said with a magnanimous wave, almost pushing Day out the door. "You work too hard. Have a good time."

His eyes held the same calculating look as Beanie's had after the birthday party. Day suspected they were up to something.

"Looks like you want to get rid of me, Papa," she said.

Joe shrugged. "Who me?"

"You been talking to Beanie?"

"Why I do that? I no do that. Now go, but change you pants first. You got tomato sauce on the pocket."

Day showered, covered the tomato sauce stain with a clean T-shirt, and her humidity-hair with a New York Yankees baseball cap. By the time she arrived at the Siragusas, the sun was down and most of the guests had gone to watch fireworks at Orchard Beach. Vinny dozed on the porch swing but when he saw Day, he jumped up and said, "He's not here yet."

"Who's not here?"

Beanie ran out and shushed him. "Jesus fucking Christ, will you zip it, Vinny."

"Who's not here?" Day repeated.

"Nobody. Go make a pot of coffee, big mouth," Beanie ordered her husband. Vinny winked at Day and left them on the swing.

"Why did he wink? What are you and Papa up to?"

Beanie ignored the question. "Glad you made it. The restaurant must be busy. I'm always telling Papa Joe to ease up."

Despite Beanie's racy reputation in high school, Joe was her biggest fan, maintaining Beanie was *simpatica* and took good care of her widowed mother. Joe frequently asked Beanie's advice about his wayward daughter's many failings, usually when Day was standing right there listening.

"You didn't say anything to make Papa worry, did you?" Day asked.

"Never," Beanie swore, eyes and hand to God.

Vinny came out with two cups. "Cream and sugar, right, Day?"

Day never got to answer. Her attention was caught by a vintage, candy apple red Pontiac Firebird rumbling into the floodlit driveway. A man in mirrored glasses rolled down the window. He hit the horn and the first five notes of *O Sole Mio* rang out. *Ba-ba-ba-baaa-ba.*

"What in the world?" Day's jaw dropped.

The man emerging from the car's tinted depths raised a thickly muscled forearm and waved. Day froze.

His wedge-shaped body, thatch of butterscotch curls and tight Gold's Gym T-shirt instantly sent her gut up her throat and back down again. She punched Beanie's arm.

"Ow!" Beanie yelped. "What'd you do that for?"

"I knew you and Papa couldn't be trusted," Day accused.

Beanie rubbed her arm. "Lighten up. It's only Bobby."

"I'm not ready for this," Day hissed. "It's late, I'm tired, and I look like hell."

"You look fine," Beanie said loyally. She snatched the cap from Day's head, grimaced, and stuck it back on again.

Bobby Leone swaggered through the front gate and climbed to the porch. At the top step, he whipped off his glasses and fixed long-lashed honey-colored eyes on Day.

"Dayglo. Long time no see."

"Hey, Bobby," she answered. "How's it going?"

Just like everybody else who never left Belmont, Bobby Leone had hardly changed. He was handsome, toned, and as the pampered youngest child and only son in a family of daughters, totally self-absorbed.

"Beans told me you were back," he said.

Bobby had pet names for everyone. Beanie was Beans, Vinny, Vincenzo, and Day, from her heated teenage blushes, Dayglo.

"Couldn't stay away from Leo the Lion, am I right?" Bobby struck a muscleman's stance. He'd also nicknamed himself.

Day tugged awkwardly at her T-shirt. Bobby gave her the once-over.

"Scared of me?"

"Go on inside, Bobby," Beanie said. "Me and Day will be right there."

"I will not be right there," Day whispered, glancing at Bobby's retreating back. "I'm going home."

"Relax, will you." Beanie reached for Day's cap again. "You got a scrunchie or something?"

"No." Day pulled the cap lower on her unruly curls. "Better?"

"Not much." Beanie squinted. "You wearing make-up? Never mind." She looked at Day's feet. "Where'd you get those gondolas?"

"They're my sneakers." Day slid her feet under the chair.

"Don't buy them in the dollar store no more. And listen, Bobby's a great guy. He's rich, owns two of the biggest cleaning franchises in the Bronx. You could do worse. As a matter of fact, you *have* done worse. All's I'm saying," Beanie coaxed, "is have a cup of coffee and catch up. What could it hurt?" She stood and extended a hand. "Come on. Be nice."

"Give me a minute, okay?" Day said. "I'll be right there."

Day rocked the swing with size nine feet. Bobby was an old friend. They'd spent one long-ago summer of bad movies, beach parties, and backseat necking, then gone off to different colleges. Period. End of story. Day had dropped out and started her twelve-year odyssey in search of nirvana, and Bobby, who moved his lips when he read, persevered to graduate and become a business owner. Bobby Leone was a success while Deanna Danese had amounted to nothing unless you count dreamer, dilettante, and dumbo. But that didn't mean she was desperate enough to backtrack and start over with an old boyfriend. Day was going forward even if that meant saying bye-bye Belmont. For now however, and for Beanie, she'd join the others in the living room, but only for a minute.

Day dug for a scrunchie and attempted to gather her hair into a smooth knot. A mirror and some blush might be helpful, maybe a dab of cologne. But why bother? She took a deep breath and headed inside to say hello and goodbye to Bobby, zipping back at the last minute to toe off her sneakers.

Chapter 5

It wasn't as bad as she thought. Bobby turned out to be a good listener. Day hadn't remembered that. And he made her laugh, which she did remember. Over coffee and anise biscuits, Bobby told her he purchased his first *On the Go* cleaners five years ago and now operated two of them in the Bronx with plans for expansion into Westchester. He still lived at home with his mother, no surprise there, but in the basement apartment he had completely renovated with a state-of-the-art security system, 46-inch flat screen TV, pool table, nine-foot sectional sofa, and shag rug.

"It's purple," he said. "The color of love and imported from some head-rag country that ends in istan."

Bobby asked politely about the various cities Day had lived in but confessed he'd never leave New York. When Day said it looked like she wouldn't either, Bobby seemed pleased. Vinny yawned; Beanie and the kids went up to bed. Bobby apologized for the late hour and offered to drive Day three blocks to Enchanted Gardens. When she declined, he took her arm and walked her home. The restaurant was closed but the lights were on and a green Subaru was parked in the loading zone, a huge, red bow affixed to the windshield.

"Smokin' wheels," Bobby exclaimed. "Yours?"

Day shrugged. Papa always bought American, and

never a compact.

Joe ran out from the alley. "Roberto," he cried, shaking Bobby's hand. "Nice to see you."

"You selling the Buick, Papa?" Day asked.

He looked affronted. "You crazy? The little car is for you. They make Subaru in Indiana now. That's United States."

Bobby helped a stunned Day into the driver's seat and waved as she and Joe took off for a cruise down Pelham Parkway. The night was fresh and warm; a salty tide scented the air.

"It's a beautiful car, Papa," Day said. "Thank you."

"You deserve the best, Deanna. You Mama, she always look for the best, for the, how you say, *felicita perfetto*."

"Perfect happiness, Papa," Day answered with a catch in her voice.

The Parkway was deserted. Stoplights flickered in lockstep, all green, all yellow, all red. Day coasted to a stop at a red light and drank in the quiet summer night.

Joe's eyes appraised her. "Maria, you mama, after she wash the dishes and you sleep inna crib, she take off the apron and look out the window. Giuseppe, she say, look how big *il universo*. So much in the world to see and to do. You, me, and Deanna, we going to have everything. We going to pitch a wagon up inna stars."

Day's throat tightened. She was so right to assume that aiming for something more, something better, was part of her DNA, the inherited gene of hope.

"Maria she die too young," Papa continued softly. "Before I have time to give her what she want, before I can fix the pain in her heart." He pulled out a handkerchief and blew his nose.

"What do you mean, Papa? What pain?"

"Maria, she my wife but I no understand, Deanna. I ask all the time, *cosace?* What's wrong? But you mama, she say don't worry, Giusieppe, is nothing." Joe pointed to his heart. "Maria have *un grande malinconia*, great sadness deep inside that I no can fix. Please, Deanna. No you be sad. Give me a chance to fix for you."

Day gripped the wheel. "I'm not sad, Papa. I just get a little mixed up, that's all." A car pulled behind them, tooted, then pulled around and sped on. "I want you to be proud of me, Papa," Day continued. "I want to be proud of myself."

"I am proud of you, Deanna. I see how hard you try. *Certo*, you make mistakes. Everybody do. But you no give up for nothing. You heart is full of love and you want to share love with everybody, make everybody happy." Another car tooted. "*Dai,*" Joe said, frowning. "Let's go before somebody smash up your pretty new car."

Day shifted into first and hit the gas. Joe gazed out the window. "*Ho s'bagliato con tua madre,*" he murmured softly. "*Non voglios s'bagliare con te.*"

The soft summer air blew away his words but their meaning hit Day dead center.

I failed with your mother. I don't want to fail you.

Chapter 6

The following week, Day drove into the city she had left in shame two months earlier. Her diploma was waiting downtown at New York University's bursar's office, a degree of sorts cobbled together from random courses taken at half a dozen colleges in as many cities. Crazy way to graduate maybe but the sheet of embossed paper in a leatherette sleeve symbolized the first step toward the new and improved Deanna Danese. The next step was a job. Day had sent resumes to the Morgan Library, the Ethical Culture Society, and the Museum of Natural History with no response except the auto-generated, *Yeah, we have it. Don't hold your breath.*

The July morning was stunningly hot. She cranked up the air conditioner and shifted into fifth, gliding down the West Side Drive as smoothly as the sailboats on the Hudson River. Grant's Tomb, obsidian-eyed co-ops, the endless ribbon of gray water. At midtown, she took a left off the highway and meandered the rest of the way down Fifth Avenue, grinding gears only once when she lost concentration at the dazzling sight of the arch in Washington Square Park.

Manhattan! Lovely, impersonal Manhattan. She parked on West Fourth and bought a Sno-Cone. The hoopsters were a little sluggish in the heat, but the ring of spectators didn't seem to mind. Day watched for a minute, assailed by the smell of car exhaust and sweat, along with another big city smell unique to New York, her favorite city. Day couldn't put her finger on just what it was about the Manhattan air.

Miami's air was techno-tropical and you wheeled around Venice Beach in a soup of Bain de Soleil. Atlanta was as dry and crisp as ironed dollar bills and Seattle's low clouds dripped coffee. New York City wasn't like any of them. Its essence was feral, not jungle feral but funky-feral, like a post-cataclysmic wasteland where everything has been broken down and reconstituted into something new yet achingly familiar. Downtown sojourners welcomed your shame, glory, absurdity, whatever banner you carried or tried to hide, and walked on by.

Day found a parking spot off Sixth, picked up her diploma but was dismayed to find the placement office closed. Post-its on the door announced summer jobs, au pairs, and house sitters mostly. She pulled off a few but wasn't hopeful. Back on Sixth, Day found a parking ticket on the windshield and left it there while she ducked into Carrera's for a drink. The bar was dark and welcoming, and she nursed her Stoli rocks twist peacefully until a strange man smiled and tipped his glass. He was handsome in a corporate way, suit, tie, and styled hair; not remotely her type but maybe a tiger lurked beneath the gloss. Day smiled back then wished she hadn't when he walked over and hiked onto the next stool. The hand he offered was smooth and be-ringed, the fingernails painted with colorless polish. His breath smelled not of the Scotch he carried but of a hasty spritz of mint freshener. She refused his offer of another drink and fled to the anonymity of the street.

****

"A moment of weakness," Day told Beanie. "Being in the city again went to my head. No more men. And don't bring up Bobby Leone."

"You're an idiot," Beanie responded. "The guy's rich. He'll show you a good time. And it's not like you're busy or nothing."

They were on Beanie's front porch again. It seemed to Day that she wore a rut on the sidewalk between the restaurant and Beanie's. There was no place else to go, nothing to do.

"Quit pushing me, Beanie," Day complained watching Vinny Junior and Mikey shoot hoops in the driveway while little Anthony dozed in his mother's lap.

"I ain't pushing, cuz. Just giving you, what you call it, options."

"I like Bobby," Day admitted. "He's different now, more easy-going."

"Different, hell. He's rich is what he is."

"How rich can Bobby Leone be if he's still living in Belmont?"

Beanie made a sour face. "Rich enough that he ain't no snob like some people."

Instantly contrite, Day apologized and tried to explain. "I messed up and I'm trying to do right this time, but I still get those feelings, you know. Like there's something more or better or different in another place and I want it."

Beanie gave Day a quick, one-armed hug. "I'm sorry too, cuz. You ain't been home that long. It's going to take time." She grinned impishly. "Don't they say when you fall off a horse, get right back on? Now I know Bobby likes to think he's the one, true Italian Stallion, but he's just a guy. Give him a chance."

****

July melted into a hot, sunless August, the sky blindingly white all day, blank and oppressive all night. Day sank into low-level despondency, helping sling pies at the restaurant, bending Beanie's ear until the wee hours, then falling exhausted but sleepless into bed. Beanie was patient.

"AI, that's my advice," Beanie said.

"Huh?"

"It don't mean no artificial intelligence like that creepy computer thing that does Junior's homework. AI stands for *Act as If*. See, Cuz, if you smile like you mean it, stick out your chest and put up a good front, your brain will go, hold on, this bitch been striking out but now she's batting three hundred. Better pay attention. That's the first tennis of my philosophy."

"Tenet."

"Shut up. When you run into somebody who wants to bring you down, don't cry, don't even give him the finger. Just smile at the fool and keep moving. Poor guy will scratch his head and go, 'Shit, this fucking bitch don't break.' Get it?"

"Yeah, Beanie, yeah. I get it," Day retorted, up to her ears in well-intentioned lobs.

Beanie made a face. "Don't rough me off, okay? You ain't trying hard enough. Look in the mirror; you're hot, well, you will be with decent clothes, makeup, and a haircut. And for crying out loud, get rid of those goddamn sneakers!"

Chapter 7

Cooler weather cleared Day's head and blew in some common sense. She didn't have to marry Bobby but a night out with an old friend who was lively and full of compliments couldn't be bad. She phoned him. Bobby answered immediately and asked Day out for dinner. No recriminations, no hesitations, just, "Hey, Dayglo. Glad you called. There's this great French restaurant in New Rochelle. Hombre's. I'll make a reservation."

"French?" Day said doubtfully. "Hombre is a Spanish word."

"I'm telling you, it's French and it's right up your alley, classy as hell. Sure you don't want me to pick you up?"

Day vividly remembered being alone in a car with Bobby. "It's okay. I'll meet you there."

Hombre's turned out to be Ombre, a dark bistro with shadowy tables on a patio overlooking the Long Island Sound. Day, wearing white jeans and a black cotton top, spotted Bobby at the bar. He was immaculate in a crisp gray suit and pearl tie. She walked over feeling underdressed.

"You look terrific," Bobby said, kissing her cheek.

He led her to a table and consulted knowledgeably with the wine steward. Day was hopeful, but when the wine arrived, it was sweet, pink, and smelled heavily of…pumpkin? Papa would have gagged.

"Here's to you," Bobby toasted.

Day sipped. Pumpkin all right, laced with, oh Jesus, licorice? Fennel? Bobby ordered without consulting her, but that at least turned out all right; scallops in a cream sauce, asparagus, fingerling potatoes, and cassis sorbet for dessert. It was quite a feat for a man who used to roll his slice of pizza around an order of fries. Throughout the meal, Bobby asked questions without probing and didn't interrupt Day's answers. He told her he'd just closed the deal for another *On the Go* cleaning store on Laconia Avenue and planned to branch out upstate next.

"That's where the money is," he said. "I'm not smart like you, Dayglo, but I can smell a dollar behind a brick wall."

Bobby suggested a walk on the beach after coffee but gave in without fuss when Day said maybe another time. He escorted her to the Subaru and helped her inside.

"This was fun," Bobby said, leaning in the window and giving Day a soft kiss on the lips. "Thank you."

"Thank *you*," she replied, meaning it.

Driving home, Day reflected on the evening. Bobby had been the perfect gentleman, holding out chairs and opening doors, and he looked amazing with his movie star face and tailored suit. Next time she'd wear a dress, bigger earrings, and maybe even heels; Bobby hadn't seemed all that short. *Next time?* Where had that come from? Her first date with Bobby was barely over and here she was planning an outfit for the next one. Beanie's AI had been right on the money. Make like a happy person and ergo, you *are* a happy person. The few hours Day had spent with Bobby Leone were like a cooling rain shower in the desert.

She pulled into the loading zone and parked behind the Buick. Time to scale down her dreams, make them less sweeping, less grandiose but still positive. There *was* a decent job out there, a good man, and a nice apartment close to home but far enough away from her father to feel like an adult.

The lights were still on in Enchanted Gardens, but all the other windows in the building were dark except for the votive candle flickering in Papa's living room window.

"I wish you were here, Mama," Day breathed. "I wish you could show me how to have everything without giving up anything."

She heard the whine of the restaurant security gate and watched Luis close up for the night. He was short like Bobby, muscular but leaner and more graceful. Luis rolled when he walked, keeping time to an inner beat; Bobby lumbered as if his muscles were a heavy add-on that cost extra. "I like Bobby, Mama," Day confessed. "But he doesn't consume me, know what I mean? The others were like air in my lungs. At least that's what I thought until I found out that the book didn't match the cover. There has to be a man out there with a brain, soul, and heart in a body that makes mine sing." The curtain in the front room fluttered. "What are you trying to say, Mama? That you understand and I should be patient? Or do you agree with Albina that I'd better wipe, flush, and get off the pot before the stink gets worse?"

"Hey, *Flaca!*" Luis snapped the grate's padlock and walked over to Day. "How'd it go with Leo the

Lion?"

She shrugged. "My father inside?"

"In the back, still working. You know Papa Joe. I tell him, get a cot, move in."

Day walked around the alley to the rear door. The heat lingering from the ovens spilled into the yard and wouldn't dissipate until it was almost time to fire them up again. Joe sat in one of the booths, hunched over the guts of the wall air conditioner spread on the table. The fake leather banquette was torn and mended with tape and cemetery moths flittered around the rusting wall sconces. No matter how hard Joe tried to keep the place clean, grease coated the walls.

"Hey, Papa," Day said. "Tough night?"

He looked up and the weariness left his eyes. "Deanna! You have a good time? That Roberto, he's a nice boy, eh?"

"It was okay." Day answered. "Air conditioner break down again?"

"No, no. She fine. Just old like me."

Joe's face was gaunt and fleshy at the same time; pouchy eyes, frown lines. He looked exhausted. Day slid into the opposite bench.

"I've been doing a little research," she began, worried. "Central air conditioning is very cost-effective."

"That mean cheap?"

"Not cheap, but in the long run it pays for itself." Joe nodded. Day took the gesture as encouragement. "So would a little update," she continued. "It wouldn't be a bad idea to fix up the restaurant starting with this room."Since returning, Day had decorated with miniature jack-o-lanterns at every table and had ordered

42

turkey and Santa Clause candles for the holidays. She longed to do more.

"Enchanted Gardens needs a facelift, Papa."

Joe looked skeptical. "How much?"

"Not a lot. We could start by replacing the booths with tables and covering them with checkered tablecloths."

"You going to wash and iron?"

"They have pretty ones now that look like fabric. You throw them away after every customer."

He looked aghast.

"They're not that expensive, Papa. The whole thing, tables, paint, new flooring, won't cost that much. Besides, you can apply for a small business loan."

"No, Deanna," Joe said after a moment. "*Senza lavoro non si fa l'amore.*"

The phrase translated into, *No love without work,* which to Italians meant, *Don't play if you can't pay.* Day smelled defeat.

Joe gave her a long, speculative look. "I got a little in the bank for *cose speciali*, new things? Understand?"

"Like the top floor?" Day asked. "You sneak up there at night and start banging things. What's going on?"

Joe slid from the booth. "We talk about upstairs. Come."

Day followed him out the back door, through the alley, and up to the apartment. He poured two glasses of seltzer, added a splash of brandy to his, and held out the bottle.

"No thanks, Papa," Day declined. "I had wine tonight."

"Ah, *vino d'amore.*" Joe kissed his fingers.

"It's not like that with Bobby. We just had a friendly dinner."

"Give the boy time. He's Italian, no?"

"You were going to tell me about the top floor," Day reminded with a smile.

Joe belched lightly, frowned, then patted his heart.

"You okay, Papa?"

"It's nothing. A little gas."

But he continued to rub, frowning. Day felt a prickle of alarm.

"When was the last time you saw the doctor?"

"I'm okay, Deanna, just old. My parts no work so good no more."

"Call the doctor tomorrow," Day insisted.

"Tomorrow his day off."

"Then call him at home. You two have been friends for years."

Joe went to his desk, unlocked a drawer, and removed a wad of papers tied with rubber bands. Luis had computerized Enchanted Gardens' books and printed out a report every week, but Joe only trusted the bank's mailed monthly statements. Day scanned several of them.

"How much the bank say I got?" Joe asked.

"Not as much as you used to, Papa. You've made quite a few big withdrawals lately. There's plenty left but the amount is going down steadily."

"But she still good, no?" Joe said proudly. "I got a MRI too."

"IRA."

"*Si, si*, MRA. Is enough you think to fix up the restaurant?" He added another splash of brandy to his glass.

"Plenty," Day replied, cautiously hopeful.

"*Va bene.* Then you do. Why I pay somebody fix up Enchanted Gardens when I got a college graduate in the family? But no go crazy. I want to recognize my restaurant."

Day didn't have to think twice. If she wasn't too ambitious, the dingy back room could be made into a cozy, bistro-style dining room. It would be fun and, as Beanie reminded her often enough, it wasn't as if she was busy or nothing.

"I'd love to do it, Papa," Day said. "But only if you call the doctor tomorrow. Deal?"

Joe shook hands. "Deal."

"Now," Day pressed, "give me a shot of brandy and tell me what you're doing on the top floor."

Joe tossed back his drink, scraped his chair, and yawned. "No tonight. Maybe another time."

Chapter 8

By All Soul's Day, November second, the coldest on record, Enchanted Gardens was centrally air-conditioned. In addition, Day had nearly completed renovating the back room. She had reupholstered the booths that Joe adamantly refused to trash, and added a few cafe tables set with disposable checked tablecloths and napkins big as bath towels. Teardrop chandeliers replaced the grimy wall sconces, and several mirrors hung where the stained *Viva Italia*! and *FIFA* posters used to be. The room seemed larger and more intimate at the same time. Bobby knew a guy who knew a guy who built a backyard deck for summer dining and covered the floor with bronze tiles approximating travertine. Joe said no to the sound system Day had her heart set on and put his foot down to a new Sierra Volare Double Rotator Pizza Oven. The old fire-breathing dinosaur was the first thing Maria had ordered for Enchanted Gardens, and as far as Joe was concerned, they could bury him in it.

The best new addition wasn't to Enchanted Gardens, however, but to the Siragusas. Beanie's baby, Lorenzo Marcantonio, Renzo for short, was born. Day fell instantly in love with her chubby godson and visited him often. Beanie looked unwell. She was pale, had lost her baby weight and then some, but insisted she was fine.

Joe kept up his end of the bargain and went for a medical checkup. He reported that he was in reasonably good health for a man of his years and, "For the love of God, Deanna, leave me alone." Day suggested a trip to Italy, insisting that she and Luis could run the restaurant. That got Joe so riled up, he hid out on the top floor banging and stomping around like a wild horse.

"What's Papa doing up in there?" Day asked Luis.

"Making an apartment."

"To rent?"

Luis shrugged. "Maybe Papa Joe has girlfriend."

Officer Hank, who had stopped in for his free chicken cutlet hero, said, "Don't be silly. He's past all that."

"He's sixty, Dude," Luis retorted. "Not dead."

Day looked up from reading *The Belmont Bee.* A delivery truck was pulling into the loading zone. "I think the girlfriend might be from Home Depot," she said.

A man with a clipboard walked into the restaurant. "Mr. Joseph Danese?"

"Papa's upstairs. Can I help you?" Day answered.

"Somebody has to sign for this stuff." The man handed Day the clipboard. "I could use help unloading."

Day scanned the manifest: sheetrock, nails, peel and stick tiles. Papa was indeed transforming the third floor into an apartment. She made a mental note to ask Luis for this week's financial statement.

Joe barreled in from the backyard, snatched the clipboard, and rifled the pages. "*Finalmente.*" He nodded with satisfaction. "I wait all day."

He directed Luis and Hank to carry everything to the attic. Hank cited a bad back, but Luis hopped to.

"What's going on, Papa?" Day asked.

Joe put a finger to his lips. "Shhh. Is a surprise."

"I can go see for myself, you know," she said.

Joe was obviously eager to brag about the surprise. "Okay, nosy-nose. Is you Christmas present, big one. No expect nothing else under the tree this year."

Day had a sinking feeling.

Joe took her hands and smiled proudly. "You always say my apartment she too dark, you no like the furniture, the bathroom is mousy."

"Musty."

"*Si,* mousty. So I made a nice apartment just for you; lotsa sun, big living room, bedroom, kitchen with real fake marble countertop, no Formica, and," he added with a flourish as Luis and the delivery man unloaded the very item from the truck, "a Jacuzzi bathtub."

Day felt as if a hive of wasps had lodged inside her stomach. She wanted her own place, that was true, her next priority after a job. But she didn't want to live in Belmont, and certainly not one floor away from Papa. Day stared fixedly at Joe until his grin slipped and his fingers crept to his chest.

"You no like?" he asked shakily. "You want I move up and fix downstairs for you?"

No, Papa, no.

Luis and the delivery man began to haul the Jacuzzi up the stairs. Joe asked them to wait a minute. "Is no trouble for me to move, Deanna," he went on, his hazel eyes so like Day's, speculative. "I go up, you stay down. Simple."

"It's not that, Papa."

"Then what it is?"

"Uh, guys," Luis grunted. "This shit weighs a ton."

Day felt trapped but didn't want to hurt her father's feelings. A job wasn't a fool's dream anymore. She'd had a nibble from the Museum of Natural History. If they hired her, she had hoped to find her own place and move out. But she could also save money living on the top floor for a year or so, and move later.

"It's fine, Papa," Day conceded. "The attic is fine, perfect. I'm sure I'll love it."

Day followed the Jacuzzi upstairs. The new home-in-progress was bright and roomy with a separate kitchen big enough for a table. Remembering Beanie's AI, Day enthused about everything and lingered after the men had gone, mentally selecting colors and placing furniture. By the time Day decided where to hang the television, she was really excited.

****

"Shut up! Get out!" Beanie exclaimed that evening when Day phoned with the news. "So you're staying in Belmont for real? No more disappearing acts?"

Day cleared up any misunderstanding. "I'm staying for now. Papa's happy and I guess I am too."

"Don't guess, be happy, you'll adjust. What am I saying? You won't have to adjust. You're home." An infant's wail, eerie and disembodied as a cat in the night, threaded through the phone line. "I gotto go," Beanie said. "You made the right decision, cuz. Belmont's the place for you. Nothing bad can happen here. It's almost six months and you ain't died or nothing." The baby wailed louder. "Shit! Always when I'm on the phone," Beanie griped. "Vinny, for crying out loud. Don't you hear your son? God forbid you should get off your ass and—Oh, never mind." Back on the phone, Beanie rasped in a tired tone, "Sorry about that. Give Bobby a play, will you please? Poor guy keeps asking me why you're blowing him off."

"I'm not," Day replied. "It's just that I have to do things in proper order. Now that I have a place to live, I'll get a job and then I can start dating. I want to see Bobby again. I told him so."

"That was in September, cuz," Beanie corrected on a windy exhale. "It's almost Thanksgiving now. Bobby texted me that your phone's turned off. Well, it's on now. Fucking call him." Beanie muffled the phone with her hand and Day was barely able to make out her next few words which sounded like your father's an asshole, Renzo.

Day hung up and considered Beanie's strong suggestion. Papa wouldn't have the apartment ready until Christmas. The museum job was promising but she didn't have that either. Ergo, priorities one and two were pending but remained unrealized. If she started seeing Bobby, her whole carefully thought-out schedule would be out of sync and Day wanted to do things right, in proper order like a normal person. But she wasn't normal, which is why a system, a blueprint, made her feel protected against going off half-cocked. Determined as Day was, the threat of flight lingered.

****

Day's Belmont three-room apartment was slowly morphing from cluttered workspace to an airy gem. For the first time since she was in her twenties, Day wouldn't be bunking with a Paragon man who suddenly turned his back and stopped making eye contact. Now she could hang all the pictures she wanted, buy furniture, cook food in her own pots, and eat it with her own knife and fork out of her own dishes. Papa and Beanie were happy, and darling Renzo was only a few blocks away. It looked like Day was back in Belmont.

The one-eighty didn't really sink in, however, until Bobby called.

"Hey, Dayglo," he said. "Ready for a repeat at Hombre's?"

He certainly got right to the point. No, How you been? or, Why haven't you returned any of my five thousand messages?

"Let's just get together and talk, okay?" Day suggested. "We don't have to do anything special."

Bobby liked that and invited Day over to his place.

"When?" she asked.

"Anything wrong with now?"

Chapter 9

When Day rang Bobby's doorbell, the swoony notes of "*O Sole Mio*" filled the vestibule. He yanked open the door bare-chested, wearing what he always wore at home, tan cargo shorts and a St. Christopher medal the size of a hubcap. Day followed Bobby to an enclosed rear porch, not sure what to think about his depilated chest glowing with the scientific sheen of a tanning salon, dark blond curls, and a body as honed as Michelangelo's David if David frequented the Renaissance version of Gold's Gym.

Bobby's thick-lashed fawn's eyes regarded Day with a covetous challenge. "Beer? Coffee?" He hauled a pile of clothes from a wicker loveseat. "I have a kitchen down here, not that I ever use it. My mother cooks for me."

"Nothing for me, thanks," Day said.

Bobby picked a dirty sock off the floor and stuck it in the pocket of his shorts. "My mother usually cleans too," he explained sheepishly. "The old gal must be busy today."

"How is your mother?" Day asked for want of anything else to say.

"Ma? Great. Let me show you the rest of place. I redid it myself." Bobby walked Day through several rooms, pausing and pointing like a docent. "That's the media room, there's the game room, my home gym with state-of-the-art equipment, bedroom's over there. The living room is small since I spend most of my time on the heated porch. I put in double-glazed windows. Sure you don't want a beer?"

Day sat on the wicker loveseat. "I'm fine."

Bobby squatted in front of her and smoothed her calf. "You sure are. Always had the prettiest legs in Belmont. I used to wonder what they'd feel like wrapped around my–"

Day jumped up. "I think I will have that beer. I'll get it."

"That's my good girl," Bobby said. "Everything's better with brew. Get me one too."

Day felt him watching as she crossed to the kitchen and reached inside the fridge. "Your apartment is so interesting."

"Isn't it? Beans calls it my man cave. Vincenzo's jealous." Bobby accepted a beer and patted the loveseat. "You said you wanted to talk. Sit next to me. I'm listening."

Bobby didn't protest when Day returned to the wicker chair. He was still sure of himself but less cocky than he used to be in high school. Really, she had no reason to feel uncomfortable and rethinking, decided to sit beside him on the loveseat.

"Ombre was great," she said, popping the tab on the can.

"What?"

"Hom-bre's," Day pronounced like in a John Wayne movie. "I had a good time but we talked about other people. Maybe tonight we can talk about ourselves, about us."

Bobby's pale eyes fixated on hers. "Okay, Dayglo.

Shoot."

She cocked and pointed. "Over the past twelve years, I thought I was in love with a lot of guys. I moved in with them and tried to make a life for us as a couple." Bobby's face hardened. Day paled. Maybe mentioning a checkered past wasn't the best way to open a dialog. She changed course and started again. "I've decided to stay in Belmont. I'm going to get a job and settle down."

Bobby tipped back, swallowed, and emitted a small belch. "Sorry. Go on."

"That's it. I'm staying put. No more Road Runner."

He crushed the beer can, tossed it toward the trash and missed. The can joined several of its mates on the floor.

"I'm glad you've changed," Bobby said. "But see, Day, I haven't. I still weigh the same, still five seven and a half, still got all my hair, all my teeth." He winked. "Still in love with you."

The can sweat in Day's hands. "Bobby," she began.

"Shhh," he said, a finger to his lips. "Hear me out. I must have told you a hundred times that I loved you. You blew me off, made jokes, ran like a rabbit in the crosshairs. So I said to myself, be patient, Dayglo will come around—she's no dummy. And now, here we are, back where it all started twelve years ago, same old Bobby, but if you're telling me the truth, different Day."

"You can't have been waiting twelve years for me," Day said incredulously.

"Why not? Love is love."

"But I don't know if I love you, Bobby. I wonder

sometimes if I can love anybody. Beanie and Papa of course, that goes without saying. And Renzo has my heart. But to love a man, *really* love him not just what I imagine he should be." Day shook her head.

"You were always flaky," Bobby answered. "Hiding behind all the damn books in your room, pretending to be a queen or something in an ivory castle. Folks around here thought too much reading gave you crazy ideas, made you different. But I knew, still know, it made you better. You're the best and that's what I want."

Day sighed. "You got it wrong, Bobby. I'm not the best; I'm not even good. I'm—" She hesitated. "I'm irresolute, fly-by-night. You can't depend on me, and worse, I don't fit in. I look around and see all these happy people on one side of a big wall, and me on the other wondering how they figured it out."

"So ask," Bobby said, shrugging. "Or climb over and join the crowd."

"It's not that easy. I don't know where to start. What if they don't want me?"

He put his arm around her. "I want you. Start with me."

Bobby made it clear that he was interested in a serious relationship, not a hook-up, no fooling around and moving on. He was over thirty and ready to give himself to one girl, to "share the wealth" was how he put it, preferably with Day. But there were "other fish in the sea", he continued. He was a guy and guys "had needs".

"I waited twelve years for you to see the light, Dayglo, and I'm not going to wait twelve more. The ball is in your court."

Despite the clichés, the argument was logical and Day was lonely for a man's touch. She recalled Bobby's early attempts at lovemaking. No matter how many times he had failed to remove her bra, he remained cheerfully indefatigable. But they weren't kids anymore and he may have reached his limit.

Day agreed to a second date at Ombre.

****

Over the next several weeks, Bobby and Day ate at Ombre, watched action films in darkened triplexes, took fall foliage rides to the country, and drank beer in his apartment. By Belmont standards, they were a couple, although aside from brief hello and goodbye kisses, Bobby seemed to have morphed into monk mode. He would rest his hand on the small of Day's back, hold her arm when they walked, but nothing more. Day was on tenterhooks. For a man in love, Bobby's behavior defied reason. But then she remembered he was also a man with a plan.

Weeks became months as Day paced her room in frustration. What had happened to Bobby's "needs"? Hers were surely rearing their ugly heads. Maybe she should find another Paragon, somebody less focused on a future. She knew all about that kind of man. But she had made up her mind to forget Brigadoon; it was magical but disappeared. Day was back in Belmont, playing Bobby's game by Bobby's rules.

Chapter 10

One frosty November night, the little bell above Enchanted Gardens' door tinkled constantly as customers churned in and out carrying boxed pizzas, white paper bags dripping with sauce, and aluminum plates of baked ziti.

"I'm sick of that bell," Day said to Luis, who was putting on his coat.

"What bell? Oh, that. I don't hear it anymore."

"Delivery?"

"Nah. Papa Joe gave me the night off. It's my daughter's birthday and the wife made *sancocho*." Luis checked his watch. "Oh shit. I better bounce."

Day worked alongside her father until nearly eleven. The place was busy, and Papa looked exhausted, hoisting the peel without the usual graceful zest, frequently wiping the back of his neck with a napkin. She deftly sliced the last order into eight even triangles and pushed him out the side door with the cash box. By one a.m., she had swabbed the counters, mopped the floors, and put out the trash. The ovens were less hot but still fiery as she made her way upstairs dripping perspiration.

Papa was snoring in front of the television, glasses on the end of his nose, palm resting on his heart. He looked ill. Day decided to call the doctor even though it was late. He was an old family friend and might tell her more about her father's condition. All the doctor said, however, was to make sure Joe takes his meds and keeps appointments.

Snow was predicted over Thanksgiving weekend. Enchanted Gardens was open for business but Joe said it would be slow. He promised her he'd take it easy and urged her to accept Beanie's invitation for turkey and lasagna.

Beanie canceled at the last minute. "I don't got my old steam back yet," she said. "So I'm sending the kids to Vinny's mother's and we're going to that Polynesian place on the Square. Please come so it don't feel like a goddamn date."

"Make it a romantic dinner for two," Day advised.

"Fuck romance. I wish Vinny would join the kids so you and I can get hammered on those pineapple coconut things with the little umbrellas. Pick you up at six."

Day spent the afternoon painting the hallway of her new apartment. The bathroom was done, the bedroom and living room walls were primed and ready. All that remained was the kitchen and Papa promised it would be completed for Christmas. By five o'clock, she was showered, dressed, and watching from the window for Vinny's minivan. Belmont looked like a cinematographer's idea of a town in Siberia. Most of the shops were shuttered and the buildings above them dark and lowering. Passing automobiles splattered arcs of slush, and sleet glittered on the sidewalks. At five-thirty, a car pulled up beside the loading zone where the Subaru and Buick hulked under blankets of snow. Vinny? Day wiped the windowpane with her palm and took a closer look. The door of Bobby's Firebird opened and Bobby stuck out a loafer-shod foot. Seconds later, he drew it back in and phoned Day.

"I'm downstairs, Dayglo. Wear your boots."

"You're coming with us?" she asked.

"Hurry up. I'm sticking out a mile here. Some *cafone* is going to skid right into me."

Day bundled up and grabbed her bag. So it was going to be a couple's night after all. Way to go, Beanie.

****

The Polynesian Pu-Pu was crowded. The Siragusa party of four waited at the Baka Bakeke Bar. Day and Beanie got looped on huge, sugary concoctions heavily laced with rum and Triple Sec that were served in a Hawaiian war canoe big enough for Renzo's bath. The men drank beer and looked on indulgently.

"Another one of those, Dayglo, and I'll have to carry you home," Bobby teased.

"Not hardly. I outweigh you."

"Oh yeah?"

He slid from his stool, hoisted Day above his head, swung her around, and deposited her back down with a kiss. Onlookers clapped. Bobby struck a pose. Day felt herself blushing. When they were shown to their table, Bobby ordered the most expensive meal on the menu, King Kamehameha's Banquet, insisting the night was on him. Everybody talked at once, said, "Oops. Sorry," then nobody said anything for a few seconds until somebody giggled and Beanie nearly spit her Fiji Fritters into Vinny's Sasapalassa Shrimp. Day couldn't remember when she'd had a better time.

The windows were covered with heavy drapes made to resemble grass skirts but Vinny kept peeking outside and checking his phone for road conditions. He announced that it was bad and they'd better settle up before they had to spend the night. Vinny and Bobby argued about the bill while the women escaped to the Lililuokalani Lounge.

"So?" Beanie said. "What I tell you? He's terrific, ain't he?"

"Vinny?" Day said evenly. "A real doll."

Beanie flicked a few drops of water in Day's direction. "Be serious. Do you like Bobby?"

"Of course I do."

"You going to keep dating him?"

Day studied herself in the mirror. The bathroom lighting was cruel. Every laugh and worry line accused her. She studied her temples—no gray yet, but Papa had started graying in his forties so that wasn't far off. Day admitted that she'd always been fond of Bobby; he was her first steady. It was about time to give an ordinary Belmont guy a shot.

Day glanced at Beanie, who was piling on the blush. The cakey pink color only emphasized her sickly pallor and gaunt cheeks.

"You doing okay, cuz?" she asked.

"I'm great," Beanie answered. "What about you? Ready to make it official with Bobby?"

Day dropped her paper towel into the trash. "No. Maybe. I don't know. Stop asking me that question."

She left a puzzled-looking Beanie and walked out, past the Mahalo Aloha Coat Check, and into the parking lot.

Muttering, "Bitch. No wonder you ain't got no friends," Beanie followed.

****

Bobby's Firebird skidded all the way back to Belmont, but he managed to maneuver it into a *No Parking Here to Corner* spot a few doors down from Enchanted Gardens. He had warned Day to wear boots but his own footwear was a handsome pair of butter leather Palm Beach Gucci's. He set the brake and didn't move.

"Shall I get out?" Day asked

He opened the door a crack. "Plow's been through and made things worse."

"Guess I'll have to carry *you* this time," Day quipped.

Bobby turned to her, all smiles. "Does that mean I can come up?"

"Sure. I'll make coffee if you don't mind sharing it with Papa."

"Hell no. Thanks, Dayglo."

Day walked ahead of Bobby, essentially opening a path for his mincing steps. At her door, he wiped off his shoes with the ends of an Armani scarf and propped them against the heat register. Joe gave him a pair of slippers and they talked business while Day fiddled with the espresso machine.

"How's the new store?" Joe asked Bobby. "You get much traffic?"

"Not yet, Papa Joe. We just opened a few weeks ago."

"Wait until the new development on the boulevard opens," Joe said. "You going to have a line."

"That's the idea."

"Roberto know his stuff," Joe whispered to Day before turning on the eleven o'clock news. Within minutes, he was snoring.

Over coffee in the kitchen, Day whispered, "Tonight was fun, Bobby."

"We always have fun together."

She added sugar and stirred. "I wasted so much time."

Bobby's eyes held hers. "It doesn't matter. Anyway, I got used to it. You were here and then you were gone." He shrugged. "But you've always been my horse, my money win. I knew you'd see the light someday. See," he continued, "I want regular stuff, nice house, nice car, couple of kids and enough dough to take care of my family. Deep down, you want that too, Dayglo."

Day held his earnest gaze. "Beanie says you're already rich."

Bobby bent close. "I do all right." Day wanted to tell him about her confusion and loneliness, but the words died in her throat. Bobby got up and took her into his arms. "I can do better if you let me."

"Papa's a light sleeper," Day whispered

"He knows the score," Bobby said. "Let's go to your new apartment."

"There's no furniture."

"Not a requirement."

"No, Bobby, not tonight."

A glint of annoyance flashed in his eyes. Bobby quickly masked it with a laugh but it troubled Day. She didn't want to argue and wake up Papa who'd for sure put in his two cents, so she took Bobby's hand and led him upstairs. He knew what to do and didn't take his time. The sex was over in a heartbeat, before Day had actually begun. But she let it go. After all, Bobby did say he'd do better.

Chapter 11

The Museum of Natural History called Day for an interview the following Friday. She jumped for joy a few minutes, then trimmed her nails, gave herself a facial, and decided what to wear. Day had planned to take the subway but, too nervous to sleep the night before, she woke up late Friday morning and decided to take the car. Big mistake. Traffic inched along the Cross Bronx Expressway and the West Side Drive was no better. To make matters worse, there were no spaces in the museum's employee parking lot. She had to scout up and down packed sidestreets before locating a spot blocks away on Amsterdam Avenue. Sprinting, boots crunching snow, hair and shoulder bag bouncing, she arrived at the main entrance with no time to spare.

The job interview was for an assistant editor of *Natural History Magazine*, a venerable glossy Day hadn't realized came right out of the New York Museum. She'd borrowed a few copies from the Belmont Library and was impressed. Working for *NHM* had the cachet she needed to begin a new life. Unfortunately, when Day asked the guard for the magazine office, he looked blank until she gave him the interviewer's name, Grace Nakamura, Editor-in-Chief.

"Oh, you want the newsletter," he said. "That's in the basement. Back outside and around to the Seventy-Seventh Street entrance. Take the stairs and keep going.

When you think you've reached the bottom, there's one more floor and a long corridor. The newsletter office is all the way at the end, last door, only door; can't miss it."

Day wended her way two blocks west and another south, then negotiated through rows of parked cars in the museum lot to a stairway that narrowed and darkened the deeper it descended. At the cavernous bowels of the building, just like the guard had warned, a narrow corridor in the Ninth Circle of Hell led to a door marked *Newsletter*. Fortunately, it opened into a brightly lit carpeted space crammed with file cabinets and two metal desks, the larger of which was occupied by a pretty blonde woman who looked up.

"Can I help you?" she said.

"I'm Deanna Danese," Day said, out of breath from rushing. "I'm supposed to–"

"Oh, thank God you made it," the woman cried. "I thought the boss was going to explode. Go, go, go! Forget your coat and get in there. She's furious."

Day tried to explain about snow and traffic and that she was only three minutes late, but the agitated woman pushed her down a short hallway to a door marked *Grace Nakamura, Editor-in-Chief,* and gave her a shove.

"Good luck. See you when it's over."

Day took a breath and knocked.

"Come!" The single syllable sounded like a gunshot.

Shaking a little, she stepped into a frigid, windowless cubicle. The small woman sitting stiffly behind a desk shot her a hard look. She could have been anywhere between twenty and sixty and had smooth, alabaster skin and round, pale eyes.

"Miss Denise," she said, mispronouncing Day's name. "You are late."

"I'm so sorry, Miss Nakamura. I misjudged the traffic. And this freakish weather–"

Abruptly, the woman stood. Her dark suit was impeccable, and her pageboy bob was smooth and shiny as licorice.

"Excuses are a waste of time, Miss Denise," she admonished with a glare. "And it's *Mrs*. Nakamura, not Miss." She turned away and picked up the phone. "Get me Loco. I must speak to him immediately."

Stiff as a column, face red, Day didn't know what to do. She hadn't been offered a seat or even a greeting.

Nakamura shooed her off. "We're done here, Miss Denise. Out you go."

Wrong foot, wrong foot, Day thought grimly, backing away. "I'm sorry to have kept you waiting, Mrs. Nakamura," she apologized miserably. "Please give me a chance. I'm a good worker and–"

But Nakamura wasn't listening. A light on the phone blinked and she snatched it greedily. "Loco, you bad boy," she cooed. "Have you been avoiding me?"

In the outer office, Day buttoned her coat and waited to say goodbye to the pretty woman at the computer. When she finished typing and clicked the mouse, Day stuck out her hand.

"Thank you, Miss...I'm sorry, I didn't get your name."

"I'm Marti Sloane." The woman shook hands. "Where are you going? Welcome aboard."

Day gulped. "Welcome aboard? I thought...I haven't been interviewed yet."

"Oh, that." Marti opened a file on her screen. "Let's see. Here's your resume, the application, a recommendation letter; oh, you wrote copy for the *Miami Herald*."

"Captions," Day muttered. "I wrote photo captions in the Out & About section."

"That's still journalism," Marti said, scrolling. She smiled. "Everything's in order. If you want the job, you're hired."

Day's mouth dropped open.

"You know the salary, right?" Marti went on, laughing. "It's the best we can do. To be honest, most of the other applicants were kids and Nakamura hates anybody younger than she is. So," Marti added cheerily, "you want coffee, tea, this job?"

"I'd love a cup of coffee," Day replied gratefully. "I was going to stop on my way but the traffic, and this snow."

"Can you believe it? Going to be a rough winter." Marti slipped a pod into the coffee machine and closed the lid. "All we have left is Breakfast Blend. That okay? Take off your coat. Have a seat. That's your desk." She handed Day a stack of four-page fold-over pamphlets. "These are hard copies of our newsletter. It's mostly online now but Nakamura wants paper too. Cream and sugar?"

Day declined. She needed something strong.

"You'll enjoy the work," Marti said. "We cover departmental news, fundraising campaigns, send out regular stats; donors want to know where the money goes. Our picture archives are the best. You maintain them, by the way, the archives. The boss prefers Loco's photos, of course, so use those first."

"Loco?"

"He's a nature photographer; does free-lance for the Explorers Club, National Geographic, the Smithsonian; travels all over the world. Nakamura wishes we could keep him here exclusively. She's nuts about the guy."Marti cupped her palm over her mouth. "Oops! Shouldn't gossip. Not professional. Forget I said that."

Day instantly liked Marti. "Tell me more about the newsletter."

"It's a big deal to the higher-ups, brings in cash. You'll write most of the articles and edit the ones contributed by museum members before Nakamura sees them. She's picky about reprints so stay away from those unless she specifically asks for one. You maintain membership stats and contributor lists, answer e-mail, help with layout, and maybe design a new masthead. Nakamura wants to upgrade. But don't sit at your desk all day. When the boss is out of the office, visit the other departments. Make friends with the staff and try to get hold of their databases so you can use them to target marketing. It's an invasion of privacy but Nakamura doesn't care. She knows where all the bodies are buried anyway, and isn't above digging them up to increase circulation. Nobody likes her so you'll have to use your charm. And get familiar with the archives. They'll be a big help with your articles. Use Loco's pix a lot; they're amazing." Marti grinned and flashed a diamond. "You'll probably be doing my job too in a couple of months. I'm leaving to get married."

"Congratulations," Day said. "I miss you already."

Marti chuckled. "My work's mostly secretarial. That and keeping Nakamura happy. Might as well tell you upfront, she's a hardass and a stickler for punctuality. Lunch is twelve to one, but you better be back here by five to. And," she added, glancing at Day's wool slacks, "she prefers skirts to pants, although that's not in the Employee Regulations Handbook."

"Which she doesn't care about either," Day quipped.

"I can see you're going to fit right in," Marti said. "But just so you know. It makes it easier if you play by the boss's rules. Make Grace happy and you'll be happy. And don't call her Grace."

"What does she do?" Day asked.

"Not much until deadline. Her ex-husband was head of acquisitions. I think she got the job here as part of the divorce settlement. She kept his last name but she's not Japanese; don't know where she's from, doesn't talk unless it's about work." Marti raised a finger. "Just remember nothing goes out without her imprimatur. She's the last word on the newsletter and treats it like a work of art, which, in Grace's hands, it usually is. She's good at this job and respects excellence. That's why Loco gets away with murder." Marti stirred Equal into her coffee. "Well, that and because she has a major crush."

"I didn't hear that," Day said.

"Just remember," Marti added. "If the newsletter looks good, Grace looks good. And there's nothing more important to her than looking good."

"Got it. When do I start?"

Marti indicated the second desk. "Right now."

****

Day spent the morning reading back issues of the newsletter and getting comfortable with the computer.

At eleven fifty-five, Nakamura appeared wrapped in a full-length fur coat that definitely wasn't faux, and checked her watch.

"Five minutes to reach the cafeteria, Miss Denise. Miss Sloane, I'm going out."

"Cafeteria?" Day asked when Nakamura had slammed the door behind her.

"Best part of working here. We get free lunch. Come on before all the good stuff is gone."

In the pleasant, brightly-lit employee cafeteria, Day took the chow mien. Marti made do with yogurt and Diet Coke.

"Got to fit into my wedding dress," she said.

"Does Mrs. Nakamura ever eat in here?" Day asked around a mouthful of gluey rice.

"She usually brings something from home and eats it at her desk. When Loco's in town, they go out to lunch."

"So they're like, an item?"

Marti chuckled. "Hardly. Loco's just a gentleman. Grace is the one with the letch."

Day swallowed. "Is Loco good-looking?"

Marti thought a moment. "Hard to describe but he's, I don't know, the kind of man that makes you want to throw your thong at him. Except, Loco's not a thong-catcher. He keeps pretty much to himself."

Day scraped her plate clean and considered seconds. "I can't wait to meet the man. He must really be something."

Chapter 12

Day found that she liked the cachet of working at one of the world's premier landmark institutions and with a cohort of quirky intellectuals which all the employees of the Natural History Museum seemed to be. She liked having her own desk despite the office's glacial temperature. Grace Nakamura's temp was another story.

"We get two weeks' vacation and six personal days a year," Marti explained. "But," she added in a cautionary tone, "take them at your own risk."

"Even vacation?"

"Theoretical vacation, you mean," Marti answered with a shrug. "You may not be able to take your two weeks together, or at all. It depends on the workload. The best thing is to tell Grace you'll work from home. She'll still count it as vacation though."

On the way home after her first day at work, Day was chilled to the bone, the thermostat at the Newsletter office being set at sixty degrees as per the Ice Queen. Cranking the Subaru's heater all the way didn't dispel the shivers and Day hoped she wasn't catching a cold. Along with everything else, Nakamura frowned on sick days too.

Traffic uptown was worse than in the morning. Day didn't make it to the Bronx until almost seven, and dragged up the stairs.

"*Ue!* I put in the new windows," Papa shouted down from the top floor landing where he was working. "How the interview go? You take a long time. I make minestrone. Is on the stove. Oh, and Roberto call me looking for you."

Mrs. Nakamura forbade personal calls during working hours and Day had turned off her phone. It started ringing the minute she left work and kept ringing all the way home. It was Bobby but she didn't feel like answering. He was against her working, insisting that since they were going to get married one day, she should learn to depend on him. So far, Day had been able to deflect all wedding talk but Bobby was getting adamant. She didn't know what was worse, avoiding the engagement ring or inciting Bobby's temper.

"I got the job, Papa," she called up to Joe. "They started me right away."

"That's good. You like?"

"Yes. I'll tell you about it later. Thanks for the soup."

Day turned on the gas under the minestrone, showered, and pulled on warm, comfortable sweats. She played her messages. One from Beanie asked about the job and dozens of querulous ones from Bobby wondering where the hell she was. Day texted Beanie a TTYL but didn't return Bobby's calls. He'd be pissed and impossible to talk to and she didn't feel like calming him down with excuses about overtime and traffic. He'd want to come over too, and handling Bobby Leone tonight was just too much work. All she wanted was to find the grated cheese, eat soup, and go to bed. Work began at nine tomorrow. *Work.* What a wonderfully, self-affirming prospect.

Day was picking out an outfit for her second day at the Newsletter when the notes of *O Sole Mio* drifted up from the street. *Shit.* Minutes later, Bobby's signature knock, three rapid taps, a pause, then two more, sounded at the door. *Shit, shit, shit*. Day had forgotten to lock it and Bobby hated that. She braced herself when he barreled in scowling.

"How many times have I told you to lock your door? Anybody can walk in."

There was no way to get into the building without first entering the restaurant, going through the back room, and out the alley door, which Papa and Luis kept locked. How many times had she told Bobby *that*?

"Sorry," Day said. "It's been a hectic day."

"No excuse," Bobby growled. His jaw was tight, eyes cold.

"I have minestrone. Want some?" she offered, placating.

He let out a breath. "Papa Joe's minestrone?"

"Uh-huh."

Bobby pulled out a chair and shook the tension from his shoulders. "Sorry I snapped, Dayglo. I'm an asshole."

He finished the leftover soup, helped Day wash the dishes, then perched on the edge of the coffee table and punched the remote. The TV flared to life on a basketball game. With a contented sigh, Bobby stretched out and closed his eyes. Day let him sleep while she got ready for bed.

A few minutes later, she woke him. "I'm tired, Bobby. I have to get up early tomorrow." She didn't add, *for work.*

"Oh, right." He sat up. "You don't need a job, you know. I can take care of you."

"I like it," she replied tentatively. "The museum is an interesting place." Again, she swallowed *with interesting people*. You never knew what Bobby might misinterpret.

"Don't get used to it, okay?" he said. "We could have had a nice night but you're in pajamas already with cream on your face. What kind of crap is that?" He turned off the television and threw down the remote. "All right. Forget it. Lock the door behind me and keep it that way."

"I will, Bobby. Goodnight."

He hesitated, then winked and patted her behind. "That's my girl."

Bobby Leone blew hot and cold, always had. Day remembered him sharing his toys but also throwing them. He was easily angered, even as a child, and in college, Bobby Leone was famous for taking his friends clubbing and then getting into brawls.

At Ombre once, Day had complained mildly that she wasn't a fan of fennel and would he please stop putting slices of it on her plate. The casual request annoyed him so much that he slammed down his napkin and left. After a few similar incidents, Day watched what she said and how she acted. She learned to *prepare* for dates with him, shore up her defenses, be agreeable, and pretend. Day pretended to enjoy sitting ringside at boxing matches, car and gun shows, and hours of watching ESPN. What she liked, street fairs, long walks, classical music, exploring new places, bored him. Their dates began at Ombre and ended with a quick roll in the hay at his apartment. Out of respect for his mother, Bobby always drove Day home afterward, always apologized if he'd been peevish, and never stopped saying he loved her.

Bobby's dual personality drove Day crazy but she was as unassertive with him as with all men. She'd fall for a guy, follow him around like a puppy, adopt a new hometown, and assume a new lifestyle. It was fun while it lasted and to be honest, she learned a few things, like trimming sails from the pilot, and frying conch from the attorney. There was nothing to learn from Bobby; he was all Bronx all the time, which sure wasn't news to her. Unlike the others, however, who got that glazed look all too soon, Bobby's love endured. He wore everything on his sleeve and Day could depend on grudges, peeves, kisses, and compliments. Bobby wasn't a paragon, but he wanted to get married, which fit right in with her plan for a stable, mature life. On her own, she kept striking out; Bobby was a home run.

****

One afternoon at work, Marti showed Day a photograph of her fiancé and asked about Bobby.

"He's Italian," Day said.

"Cute?"

"Very. Curly blond hair, light brown eyes. He pumps so his chest and arms are…" She made a muscle.

"Sounds like a winner," Marti observed.

"He's shorter than me. I don't wear heels, but he wouldn't mind if I did. He always tells me I'm beautiful but…" Day let the statement trail.

"But what?" Marti prompted.

Day thought a while. There were so many things she could tell Marti, but it was complicated. Why get into her feelings about Bobby with someone who was madly in love with her own man and couldn't wait to be with him?

"There is no but," Day said. "I really like Bobby. I do. We have fun. Everything's going great. My life is going great."

Chapter 13

Despite having a disagreeable boss, Day loved her job. In three short months, she'd gotten to know most of the staff from Exhibits to Security, Administration to Maintenance, and many of them joined her and Marti in the cafeteria for lunch. Editor-in-Chief, Grace Nakamura, never left the office unless the mysterious Loco, whom Day had yet to meet, was in town. Every afternoon, at precisely eleven fifty-five, Nakamura telephoned Marti, even though she was hardly five steps away, and ordered her and Day to take lunch. The boss carried her own lunch in a small, insulated bag and made tea in an electric kettle, an odiferous concoction that smelled like sewage.

"What's in that tea?" Day asked Marti in the cafeteria one afternoon, digging into butter chicken over rice. "It stinks."

"Don't know. Youth serum, I'm guessing. She's close to fifty, you know."

Day had to put down her fork. "You're kidding. Her skin's like marble and she wears those tight little suits and spike heels. I thought Nakamura was in her twenties."

"Nobody knows anything about her," Marti said. "Except that she's divorced from the acquisitions guy. I heard Grace got everything, the house, two cars, this job. I can't imagine why she wants to work, especially here where everybody liked her ex so much and nobody likes her. Grace treats people like idiots, except for Loco."

"Nakamura sure doesn't like me."

"Don't try to figure out the boss." Marti sighed. "It'll only get you in trouble. Your articles rock, you've got an eye for layout, and I wasn't supposed to tell you this, but the boss likes your design for the new masthead. She's going to start using it, maybe for the fall issue but definitely next year."

"Really?"

Marti nodded. "Grace'll take the credit, of course, but she knows whose idea it was. When it's time for you to move up, she won't stand in your way. It makes Grace happy when somebody she's trained gets noticed. And by now you ought to have it burned in your brain that when Grace Nakamura is happy—"

They finished the sentence together. "Everybody's happy."

Marti glanced at the clock above the door. "We better hurry if we want to make a pit stop."

Day wasn't one to check herself out in every shiny surface and storefront window but on any given day, a bathroom mirror gave a good indication of what was what. Now, side by side at the sink with Marti, Day compared their faces. Marti was a looker, no doubt about it; regular features, naturally blonde, round blue eyes, and a perfectly formed mouth. Day's mouth was a little wide, hazel eyes long and tilted at the corners, and a small nose slightly beaky. But her jaw was strong, her cheekbones broad, and on the whole, she liked what she saw. Her newly minted, new-found self was better than okay and she supposed Bobby was the one to thank for it.

"I'm going to steal some of Nakamura's fountain of youth tea," Day said, tapping under her chin. "This neck won't stay firm forever."

Marti scrutinized Day's reflection. "I think you're beautiful but in an unconventional way, exotic like a gypsy but wholesome."

"I'm the gypsy-next-door," Day quipped.

They laughed, shouldered their bags, and began descending many running feet into the subterranean depths of the newsletter office.

"And you already have your cute, curly-headed guy," Marti added. halfway down. "Grace needs all the tea she can drink to snare Loco."

Marti talked a lot about Loco. Day imagined the man a small-boned Castilian dandy tangoing petite Nakamura across the dance floor, his elevator shoes gliding, her teeth clamped on the stem of a rose.

****

On Valentine's Day, Bobby took Day to Ombre. Over coffee, he placed a small, velvet box on the table, grinning like the Cheshire Cat.

"What's this?" she asked.

"A Valentine's gift. Open it."

Day picked up the box. "You already sent me flowers."

"Go on, open it. I can never do enough for my girl."

The box held a ring, delicately wrought in onyx and silver and set with a tiny diamond chip. Bobby slipped it on Day's little finger.

"You like it?" he asked eagerly.

The ring shimmered in the candlelight. "It's

beautiful," she said. "I love it. Thank you."

"I picked out a cabochon ruby the size my grandmother's goiter, but Beans said you'd rather have something small and elegant to show we're engaged."

Day froze. "Engaged?"

"Don't make that face, Dayglo. I won't press you to set the date but I'm not marrying anybody else and neither are you. So what's the harm?

Bobby made sense, Day had to admit. And Beanie kept preaching. "He loves you. You want kids before your eggs hard boil. Jump on that stick, bitch."

Day sighed. It was time to jettison act as if, to stop acting at all and just *be*.

Bobby paid the bill, left his usual generous tip, and kissed her at the door of her apartment.

"Want to come in?" she asked.

"You mean like for coffee or something?" he gulped, obviously taken by surprise.

"We already had coffee," she said, pushing him into the living room. She opened her arms wide, he got the message, and from then on it was smooth sailing. Bobby seemed to sense that he and Day were at last on the same page and he visibly relaxed. No more snits, demand for attention, or stalking off affronted when he didn't get it quick enough. For her part, Day started to think about wedding venues, a chaplet or a veil with a train, and cake flavors.

****

April brought balmy weather. Since another birthday was just around the corner, Day decided to eschew the usual Museum cafeteria lunch and go shopping. In a small designer boutique on Broadway, she tried on a plum-colored dress in a clingy, bias-cut fabric. It fit every curve and hollow of her body and cost the equivalent of a week's salary. But it made Day feel slim and voluptuous at the same time. In the dressing room, she stuffed the old skirt and blouse into the boutique's fancy shopping bag and smoothed on a little blush. Not bad except for the loafers. She needed spike heels, slutty Blahnicks or Miu Mius. Unfortunately, Day couldn't walk in the ones she tried on at Shoegasm and settled for a pair of dusky pink, comfortable size nine wedges with thin straps that crossed over her instep and around her ankle. Feeling like Cleopatra on the Nile barge, Day sailed back to the museum. But when she pushed open the door to the office, her sails luffed and she stopped, dead in the water, unable to move. It was, as she remembered it later, a moment captured in time, crystal and luminous as dew.

"Day," Marti said, indicating a tall, muscular man in black jeans. "Come meet Loco.

Chapter 14

A heart-stopping man was half sitting on Marti's desk. He leaned forward to offer his hand.

"Lakota Campbell. Marti's been telling me about you."

Loco? The photog? Nakamura's squeeze? This compelling hunk was no wiry Spaniard with spit-shine shoes and a bolo tie. This was a devastatingly hot paragon with a sexy name and dark as the night; black jeans, black tee shirt, sun-browned skin and ebony hair that hung in a single braid down his back. Day tore her gaze from his chiseled face to the silver belt buckle low on Lakota's hips. She swallowed, hunting for a witty remark.

"Great belt." *Dumb. She was an idiot, a schoolgirl. Press rewind and start over.*

Lakota's eyes flashed with amusement. "Thanks. It's a squash blossom."

"I know that. Navajo, right?" Day tittered. How was it Navajo? She didn't have a clue. *Dumb clueless idiot.*

"Could be," Lakota said, a grin creasing his mouth. "I bought it in Poughkeepsie."

"Oh, Poughkeepsie. I've been there. On the mall, right? A lot of trendy ethnic shops on the mall." *Shut up. Shut up. Shut up!*

Marti saved her. "Loco might be with us for a

while," she said. "Grace wants to shoot some footage around Hecate County."

"Hecate County?" Day took a deep breath and busied herself stowing bags under her desk. "Never heard of it."

"It's in upstate New York," Lakota explained. "Very small, shaped like a witch's hat." He made a pyramid with his fingers, long, brown, broad-knuckled fingers. "I live in the peak, in a place called Campbell Mountain."

"You own the mountain?" Day asked. That was a legitimate question, not too dumb.

He nodded. Day realized she was staring; couldn't help herself. The man was riveting; his presence overpowered her; they were the only two people in the world, in the universe. *God, what was wrong with her?*

"The mountain belongs to my father," Lakota said. "He deeded sections to me and my brother when we were young. I have about sixty acres."

"Developers are breathing down his neck," Marti noted.

Day had forgotten that Marti was still in the room, so focused was she on Lakota Campbell, on taking in the whole of him, lean height, scuffed boots, corded arms, and rugged face. But something more drew her— a feeling that she and this mesmerizing man shared a secret.

"You won't sell your land, will you? Not for anything," she said softly.

The look in Lakota's eyes, deep and warm as pitch, slowly changed from polite interest to frank appraisal. He regarded Day intently from her fluffed-up hair to her unpainted toes to her face, now flushed and soft with wonder.

"Some things are worth more than money," he said.

The scrutiny unnerved her. She was about to parachute back to Earth and start babbling about the beauty of nature despoiled by man's gluttonous greed, when all of a sudden, Grace Nakamura burst down the hall and breezed over on her size four heels—her size four, goddamn expensive designer spike heels.

"Loco!" Nakamura cried girlishly. "Two hours late but worth the wait!"

Marti shot Day a *What did I tell you* look.

"Did you see that?" Marti said after Lakota had escorted Nakamura to a delayed lunch. "Boss lady practically threw herself at Loco's feet. Come in late, leave early, and take all your personal days while he's here. Grace won't notice."

"How long will Lakota stay?" Day asked, hoping the question sounded casual. She was certain something had passed them, something exciting and promising.

Marti shrugged. "Who knows? A week, a month. Loco could stick around all summer or disappear tomorrow."

Day crossed her fingers behind her back. "He's something, isn't he?" she said. "Native American?"

"Part," Marti answered. "Mother was Sioux, I think. She's dead. Dad's Scots. He has a half-brother, Mal. Very cute, tall like Loco but skinny and sandy."

"Why do you call him by that ridiculous nickname?" Day asked irritably. "I thought he was Mexican or something."

Marti stared at her for a moment like a cat with cream on her lips. "I don't know. Ask him."

Day made a show of settling in her chair and positioning the screen. She swirled the mouse, hit the keys, and continued writing an article about Africa's shrinking savannah, all the while gratified that a dowdy skirt and blouse were folded in the shopping bag and she'd met the most devastating man in the world wearing a new, kickass dress.

****

For the next two weeks, Lakota Campbell breezed in and out of Nakamura's office. He stopped to chat with Day and Marti but never for very long, obviously aware the boss was waiting. Day was enthralled by his graceful, powerful body, startling looks and quiet manner. She went online and searched Rainwalker Ridge, the town in upstate New York where he'd mentioned he'd been raised. It was nestled deep in the mountains of Hecate County and looked like nothing— a rutted main street flanked by farmland and rolling hills. Campbell Mountain, however, was imposing. Day longed to be alone with Lakota in the endless, panoramic swath of green, but the empty cafeteria would do, or a corner of one of the museum galleries. She wanted to ask Lakota about some of the things Marti had told her, about his heritage, travels, and love of nature. But the desire went unfulfilled and there was little she could do about it.

Frustrated, she took to looking for Lakota's black Jeep Renegade in the parking lot and listening for his steps coming down the hall. If only she could catch a few minutes with him before Nakamura showed up. Day didn't want to jeopardize her job, especially now she'd been favored with a few grudging compliments and thrown a meaty bone. When Marti left to get married and Day took over her desk, there might be a raise and a new title in the offing.

****

May in Belmont was dominoes time. The old regulars faced off on rickety tables in the back of Enchanted Gardens, smoking and slapping tiles from noon until sunset. On Memorial Day, Joe Danese took a break from the ovens to inform the players that Deanna and Roberto Leone were *inamorati*. Day wished he hadn't, but supposed it was true. She and Bobby saw each other every Saturday night. Bobby drank an espresso in the restaurant and then ran upstairs to announce whatever he had planned, usually dinner at Ombre, and a movie. Afterward, back in Belmont, he'd drive around the block a few minutes searching for a corner parking space, and when his Firebird was perfectly aligned, he'd accompany Day to her apartment, stick out his hand for her keys and ostentatiously praise her for locking the door.

In the living room, Bobby would scroll the remote while Day changed her clothes and joined him. They'd watch his shows for an hour or so, saying little until he reached for her. As a lover, Bobby was swift and almost clinical, a few seconds of foreplay, the straddle, the up-and-down, and the sighing roll-off. He fell asleep immediately but always awoke after a few minutes, ready to go home. Relieved, Day would kiss him goodbye and get back in bed to spend the rest of the night wondering what it would be like if Lakota Campbell was lying beside her.

Day's dating routine varied only if Bobby got angry, like if she looked bored or noticed another man.

"I see what you're doing," he once badgered at the

stock car races. "You like that guy? You like him? You sorry you're with me and not him, is that it?"

"I was looking at the car," Day declared.

No amount of protestation calmed Bobby's ire or soothed his bruised ego. Jealousy shut down his reason and he would carry on relentlessly. "You want to go home? I'll take you home."

Occasionally, Day might offer gentle remonstrance, something like, "Please, Bobby. You're attracting attention. People are staring."

If she walked away, Bobby might suck in and apologize. But that was rare. Day generally suffered insults quietly and out of fear since Bobby Leone was a loose cannon with a hair-trigger temper.

Every Sunday morning, he took Day for breakfast, the only meal his mother didn't prepare. Day didn't eat breakfast; food in the morning nauseated her. But to keep the peace, she'd pick listlessly at the eggs, bacon, home fries, fruit, coffee and toast he'd ordered for her, or move things around on her plate. This annoyed Bobby as much as eye cheating.

"Who doesn't eat breakfast," he complained more than once.

"Most Italians have coffee and maybe a tiny sweet roll," she once volunteered mildly then realized too late it was the wrong thing to say.

"You trying to start something?" Bobby shouted in the crowded diner. "You want me to go so you and the waiter can get it on?"

He was the one who walked out that time, sticking Day with the bill.

Day began to see her week as a diagram, two parallel lines, one representing a volatile boss and twitchy lover, and the other Papa and Beanie. The former plummeted raggedly while the latter sailed upward off the chart. Day knew why she put up with Grace Nakamura—the job meant everything. But Bobby? What stopped her from sending that lit fuse packing? Maybe his generosity, omnipresence and commitment, or that every time she longed for a baby like Renzo, marrying Bobby was the quickest way to get one. Day believed it when Bobby said he loved her. He was honest, held nothing back, and despite doubts, she hoped to leverage that into a satisfying relationship. Plus, Bobby made her feel grounded. Well, no, not really. If Day was the honest one, she'd have to admit it was apathy and an unavailing past that kept her in the relationship. Challenges, radical change, chasing adventure with her heart on her sleeve had proven dangerous as fireworks.

Lakota Campbell was fireworks.

Chapter 15

Day was a list-maker, or rather thought a woman as scattered as she was should write down and prioritize. *Make Grace Nakamura Happy* was the first item on her life goals chart. Marti was teaching her the ropes and she hadn't called out or been late again. Nakamura hinted at a small raise and even offered mild praise for Day's improvements to the newsletter. Her copy was always flawless and she'd introduced photo captions, the occasional cartoon, and one-click translations to the on-line edition. Things were swimming along until one serendipitous, or possibly calamitous, morning when Day and Lakota reached the parking lot at the same time and it all went to hell.

Lakota parked in the row in front of hers and Day watched him open the Renegade door, unfold his long legs and stretch.

Oh my.

Tall, lean, wide shoulders and narrow waist, big hands raking through long, black hair. How could one man be so, so…there were no words. Okay, yes, *major crush* were two of them. She constantly daydreamed about Lakota Campbell, but it was silly. The man was quicksilver and she was engaged to be married. When Lakota began walking toward the museum entrance, however, Day checked her face in the visor mirror and barrelled out of her car.

"Lakota, hi," she called out.

He stopped and smiled. Day slowed down when she realized she was running. "You're early this morning," she said breathlessly.

His smile broadened; Day's threatened to become goofy. Alone with the paragon of her dreams and nowhere near Grace Nakamura's domain, she stared entranced.

"I'm going across the street for coffee," Lakota said. "That stuff in the office tastes like water. Want to join me?"

Day did. Oh, how she did. But it would make her late and mar a perfect record. And what if Grace saw them arrive together, arrive *late* together, carrying paper cups of coffee no less, both from the same place? Bad idea. She had better not. It would mean disaster; total disaster.

"Sounds good."

Lakota bought two coffees to go, his black, Day's cream and sugar, and carried their cups to the Central Park entrance.

"It's too nice to sit inside," he said, lowering his long body down to the steps. "You mind if we sit here?"

How could she not want to drink coffee with a glorious man on a glorious May morning? There was one window in the boss's office, high and narrow and facing Seventy-Ninth Street. Even on tippy-toe, Nakamura wouldn't be able to see her and Lakota. And if anybody saw them, why would they tell? One museum employee was merely drinking coffee with another, and anyway, nobody talked to Nakamura. Nevertheless, Day was nervous sitting so close to the man of her dreams. Her hand quivered peeling back the plastic tab on her coffee cup. It had been a while since anything, or anybody had made her quiver like that.

"This coffee is so much better," Day said. "Thanks."

Lakota nodded, his attention on the parade of horse carriages trotting into Central Park.

"How's Hecate County?" she asked.

He grinned. *Oh my god, that mouth.*

"It's nice to see my family once in a while. I miss them."

Lakota lapsed into silence, sipping, contemplating the street. This man was easy in his skin and didn't need small talk. Day followed suit but she was jittery. Employees climbing the steps greeted them. Had Grace already arrived? She was usually the first one at her desk, and if for some reason she was late, she wouldn't use the front entrance, would she?

"How'd you get the name Loco?" Day asked. Chatter relaxed her.

"My baby brother, Mal," Lakota answered. "He couldn't pronounce Lakota. Everybody calls me that now." He turned from the street to look at her. "Except you."

Day blushed. Almost forty, a battle-scarred veteran of the romance wars, silly Deanna Maria Danese was blushing like a teenager.

"I like your name," she said. "It's beautiful."

He turned back to the street. "My mother gave it to me."

"Marti said you were born in South Dakota."

"Smack in the middle of the Badlands."

She was framing a response when Lakota drained

his cup and stood. "Want to take a walk with me? I'll show you my favorite place in the museum."

It had to be after nine by now but the most appealing man Day had ever met was offering his hand. She let Lakota pull her up and they walked to the Hall of Africa together.

Soft, hypnotic sounds, the primeval melodies of hillock and plain, thrummed as they meandered past showcases of elaborate headdresses, ceremonial wear, and beaded masks. Lakota paused at a display of primitive musical instruments and named each one, *djembe, sese, kalangu.*

"The music of Africa reminds me of my childhood," he said, his voice low and close. "Not the Scots side. Bagpipes are an acquired taste, but the music of the diaspora. Dispossessed people sing the land."

"You're part Sioux, aren't you?" she asked. The warm dark oceans of Lakota's eyes cascaded over Day like a blessing.

"Oglala," he said. "My mother named me to honor my nation. Black Elk, Red Cloud, and Crazy Horse were great Lakota chiefs, but the French pushed us out, said it was relocation, and called us Sioux after the Mississauga rattlesnake."

She felt her cheeks color. "Oh, I'm sorry. I didn't know."

"Native Americans don't understand the word. For us, to relocate is to disappear. I suppose you could say I disappeared after my mother died."

Lakota's voice was grave, his face sad. Day yearned to understand.

"You didn't grow up in South Dakota?" she asked.

"I was a baby when my father took me east. As soon as I was old enough I went back home."

"But your father was home too. You're half Scots."

Lakota chuckled softly. "I like that about you, Day. No pretense. You say what you mean, and everything shows on your face."

She knew she lacked wiles. Beanie was always trying to train a little subtlety into her, coaxing her to flirt and tease, maybe shake a little booty. But Day never got the hang of it. Now here was this wonderful man actually applauding her lack of cool. A rush of pleasure warmed her face and neck.

Lakota pointed a finger. "You're glowing. Something's made you very happy."

Embarrassed, Day pressed both palms to her cheeks in a vain attempt to cool the raging heat Lakota had ignited.

It's you, she wanted to say. *You make me happy.*

****

Day was half an hour late getting to her desk. Marti gave her a thumb's down sign and jerked her head toward Nakamura's office. Half defiant, half nervous, Day walked down the short hallway wishing it were longer. The boss's door was open.

"Twice late," Nakamura harangued before Day even stepped inside. "Not acceptable, Miss Denise. I set standards of excellence here. My department is known all over this institution for efficiency and precision. I will not tolerate—"

The finger-wagging invective went on and on. Nakamura's voice took on the oboe-like drone of adults in a Peanuts movie. Day zoned out and pictured Lakota's brown hand holding the coffee cup and soft lips mouthing the words *djembe, sese, kalangu.* Fortunately, Marti put through a call from Lakota. The boss snatched up the receiver and forgot all about Day.

At lunchtime, Lakota showed up in the newsletter office, winked at Day, and headed straight for dragon lady's door. Day wondered grimly where he'd been since they'd parted almost three hours ago. Surprisingly, he strolled into the museum cafeteria moments later, alone, spotted Day and Marti, and walked over. Day's heart pounded in her chest like a Senegalese war drum.

"Eating in today, Loco?" Marti asked.

"Grace is busy. Mind if I join you two?"

There was a tiny coffee stain on Day's white tank top and the humidity had caused her hair to puff into a halo of tangles. She wondered if a piece of spinach from the veggie wrap she had hastily gulped was lodged in her teeth and if her bra strap was showing.

Day rose to make quick repairs. "Excuse me. I'll be right back."

"I'll miss you," Lakota said.

"I'm only going to the bathroom," Day replied, flustered.

Marti laughed. "He means me, silly. I'm leaving in a week."

Day hurried off, her cheeks blazing. The stain came out but her hair fought back. She gave up and ran back to the table. Lakota was gone.

"Grace dispatched the bloodhounds," Marti explained dryly.

"Nakamura has it bad, doesn't she?" Day responded, annoyed with herself for leaving.

"The boss is in lust, but nothing's happening there.

Loco likes them big and mush-hearted, like you."

"Mush-headed, you mean," Day said. "But I like him too."

She heard the tremor in her voice. So did Marti, who pretended to peek under the table.

"Getting ready to throw your thong?"

Day sighed and faced reality. "Bobby's serious about marriage and, you know." She waffled a hand in the air. "Lakota comes and goes."

"You're right about that," Marti said. "Grace is annoyed because Loco postponed a fall shoot in Hecate County to take an assignment in the Marianas. He'll be gone all summer."

So Lakota wasn't going to be around for picnics and strolls in the woods, Day thought, for moonlight swims and dances under the stars, not that he'd ever ask her to do those things with him. She stuffed her disappointment where it wouldn't show, gathered up her trash, and went back to work. Lakota Campbell was pie in the sky, castles in the air, and impossible dreams.

Chapter 16

Beanie and Vinny spent Memorial Day weekend in the Poconos. They took the three older boys but left baby Renzo with Day.

"We'll be at Poco-Mo-Wac Lodge," Beanie explained. "It's like two, three hours away. Call if anything but you'll be fine." She handed over Renzo, who was too excited to nap. "Give him a bottle and put him down. He'll fall right out. You'll be fine too."

Day stood in her living room amidst a canvas bag of baby things big as Bobby's beer fridge; diapers, wipes, assorted toys, formula in bottles, two pacifiers, and jars and jars of baby food, spinach, banana, sweet potato, beef stew, chicken and rice, apple sauce, all in unappetizing shades of garden soil.

"You eat this sludge, Renzo?" Day asked. He screamed. She changed diapers, struggled with footie jammies, warmed bottles. Renzo kept screaming and refused to drink. She walked back and forth from the living room to the bedroom at least a hundred times while Renzo cried, rocking, humming and almost crying herself.

"Auntie Day is here," she soothed. "You know me. You know this house. Please stop crying and go to sleep."

Day's back hurt. Renzo was heavy and she was exhausted, having worked late to get the newsletter out before the holiday weekend and then taken Marti for a good luck drink. It was still early and she wanted to wash up, have a glass of wine and watch a documentary about the Marianas. None of that was possible, however, until Renzo went to sleep. Finally, Day turned out the lights and climbed into bed with him. Renzo took the bottle and drifted off.

It was nice lying there with a baby in her arms thinking about Lakota and the few minutes they'd spent alone together. Day was certain she wasn't imagining that there was something more than visceral between them. Lakota wasn't a casual man; the way he looked at her, held her hand and spoke about earth longing. She had seen him charming strangers with interesting conversation, but Lakota rarely talked about himself other than in the most general way. Yet in the Hall of Africa, he'd been trying to explain something personal about his heritage and deadly Massasauga rattlesnakes. If they'd only had more time she would have told him that she too grew up without a mother and how she loved Papa and adventure, and faraway places.

With Renzo tucked into his porto-crib, Day fixed a dinner tray and found a Marianas documentary on Netflix. It had just begun when the bell rang with the insistent staccato she knew well. Renzo started up again; Day ran for the door, holding him in her arms.

"Dammit, Bobby," she cried, yanking open the door. "You woke the baby."

He took Renzo from her. "What'd you do to the poor kid? He never cries with me. Aww, Lorenzo the Magnificent," he crooned. "This bad lady making you cry? Come to Uncle Bobby."

The phone rang. Cursing, Day answered it.

"What?"

"Not going too good, huh?" Beanie asked.

"Dammit, cuz," Day snapped. "Did you tell Bobby to come over? You damn well did, didn't you?"

"It's Mommy, Lorenzo," Bobby sang in Renzo's ear. He snapped his fingers at Day. "Gimme the phone. Let him hear Beans's voice."

Day turned her back on the pair. "Everything was fine until Bobby rang the bell and woke up Renzo," she said.

"Sorry," Beanie apologized, sounding anything but sorry. "I thought you might need a little help. Put Bobby on. Vinny wants to talk to him."

Day handed over the phone and went back to the couch. The documentary was rolling and looked interesting.

"Lorenzo's out like a light. What are you eating?" Bobby asked, looking askance at Day's plate.

"My dinner."

"That's not dinner. Let me make you something."

She wasn't hungry but Bobby went to the kitchen, opened the refrigerator, and started sniffing plastic containers. "What's this, lentil soup?" he called. "You make it or Papa Joe? Ooh, chickpeas. Where's your olive oil and garlic? I'll put on some pasta and make us a sauce that's out of this world."

"Us?" Day said, dripping sarcasm. "I asked you not to come over this weekend because of the baby."

Ignoring her, Bobby searched for ingredients. "Where you keep the olive oil?"

"No, Bobby," Day said in a tired voice. "I want to finish what I'm already eating and go to bed."

"This all the onion you have? I'll get some from

97

Papa Joe. Get in here and drain the beans. I'll be right back."

"I said no."

At the command in her voice, Bobby approached. His fists were balled at his sides and his face was a tight mask. Fear shot through Day.

"I'm tired of your shit," he growled.

"What shit?" Day said, the words dry in her mouth. She held her breath. "I'm beat and just want to go to bed."

Like his ears had suddenly popped, Bobby shook his head and blinked. "Can we talk?" he asked, sitting next to her. "Please?" he added in a totally different tone.

Day hesitated.

"Please?"

Bobby's eyes were no longer frozen barriers but liquid and shining. Bad Bobby had gone and Good Bobby was in the room. Day slid to the farthest end of the couch and waited.

"I'm sorry," he began, staring at the floor. His mouth worked; his Adam's apple bobbed. He fell silent, clearly unable to continue.

"What just happened," Day asked. "I thought you were going to hit me."

His head shot up. "Hit you? Ah, no, babe, I get angry sometimes, but I'd never lay a hand on you. You're my horse, my filly. I love you."

He rose and began to pace, slapping a fist into his palm. "Aw, Christ," he muttered. "Jesus fucking Christ."

"Why did you get mad just now?" Day asked.

"I shouldn't have come over," Bobby said

nervously. "I blew off my mother's dinner. She makes me shrimps on Fridays and she kept saying," he parodied Mrs. Leone's scratchy voice, "I cleaned all those shrimps for you, all those shrimps. But I wanted, I thought—" He barked an awkward laugh, a single harsh note. "She cursed me out. I got mad and took it out on you. Sorry." He rose, heaved a sigh, and crossed to the kitchen. "Got anything to drink?"

Day followed him. "I didn't expect you, Bobby. I had my hands full and all I wanted to do was eat something light and go to bed. But you barge in and start ordering me around. You do that a lot, don't listen then get mad when it's not my fault. That's not right."

He poured a generous glass of wine, sipped, and grimaced. "You have to cork this stuff, babe. It goes bad."

"Bobby."

He regained his seat on the couch. "Yeah, I know. I know. You're right. All that crap about making you dinner was grandstanding." He winked. "I'm a lousy cook."

Day kept her face blank.

"I was hoping if I showed up tonight while you had Renzo and if we cooked and ate dinner together, chilled on the couch with the baby like a real couple, you'd see how great it could be."

She shook her head. "We are a real couple, Bobby."

"No, we're not," he replied. "We've known each other all our lives. We're, you know, intimate, and I tell you every day that I love you, but you never said it back, not once. I've asked you a dozen times to marry me and your answer is everything but yes."

The marriage issue. She should have known. Bobby proposed every week and like the refrain of an old song, she repeatedly equivocated.

"I don't say no either."

"Maybe you should, Dayglo," Bobby replied. "I've been waiting forever. I'm all crapped out and it hurts."

She knew that feeling. Boy, did she ever. She had been on the receiving end countless times and now she was dishing it out, causing Bobby pain. But how to make it right short of becoming Bobby's wife? She didn't love him, at least not according to her definition of love as an all-consuming passion that blocked reason. For Day, love was the near worship of someone imposing as an icon, a man so different he complemented her totally, filled in all the blank spaces and made her a better person. Bobby was nothing like that. No, that wasn't fair. Papa often said that love didn't mean gazing at each other but at looking in the same direction. She and Bobby wanted similar things, their roots sprung from the same soil. They had grown up together just like she and Beanie had. Yet while Beanie was as necessary as water, Day wouldn't die of thirst without Bobby. He knew that and was telling her as clearly as he could to cut him loose if she didn't want him.

Day put a hand on Bobby's knee and said kindly, "I haven't meant to string you along. I know you want to get married and have kids. I want that too."

"But not with me. Is that it?"

Shamefaced, she replied, "I don't know."

Bobby drained his wine. "So there we are, on opposite sides of the tracks. I'll get a couple of slices from Papa Joe. Lock the door behind me."

Day watched Bobby slowly descend to Enchanted Gardens. He looked so sad. She should try harder to love him, but love shouldn't be something you have to work at. Love was crazy, unrealistic, obsessive to the point of farce and impossible to shake. That's why she was still unmarried, unmoored, and past her prime. She had started out right this time, following Beanie's act as if to the letter, dating Bobby, sleeping with him. Why sabotage her plan and make problems? She was his horse; the only way to win was to stay on the track.

Ashamed of herself, she checked on Renzo. He was uncovered, diapered rump in the air. She took him into her bed and considered her dilemma. The next logical step with Bobby, the 'til death do us part one, wouldn't fall naturally into place unless she removed the single obstacle that kept rearing its ugly head, no, its beautiful head. She had to sidestep, go around it, forget Lakota Campbell or end up a lonely old maid. Day checked her phone; no calls, certainly not from Lakota, who didn't know her number. Bobby did and would read her text as soon as he received it. *Give me one week then propose again,* she typed. *I promise to have an answer.*

Chapter 17

Day organized Renzo's things. Since he crawled everywhere, she baby-proofed according to Beanie's instructions, and when she was satisfied, resurrected the chickpeas from the fridge and made a salad, washing it down with wine. Day watched the Marianas film from the beginning with Renzo and learned that the islands formed a sub-tropical archipelago in the Pacific Ocean and were both volcanic and lush. All well and good, but which one was Lakota on, and did it have phone service? She could call him, this man she wasn't going to think about. And say what? I want to see you again? I want to crawl up into you and curl myself around your heart? All day, she tried to think about Bobby's marriage proposal. And all night she dreamed of dancing to marimbas on the Marianas with Lakota Campbell.

The weekend with Renzo flew by. He settled in, awoke laughing, and never stopped. They went to the park and played on the swings, rolled in the new grass, and picked flowers. He turned up his nose at savory beef with quinoa, but demolished a cereal bowl of *pastina* with mashed chickpeas, and napped peacefully while Day swept up cookie crumbs and washed bibs and onesies. Papa came upstairs for breakfast, played peek-a-boo, How Big is Renzo? and the Italian version of This Little Piggy. When Luis called him back down to the restaurant, Joe reluctantly handed back *il piccolo* reminding his daughter how much he wanted a grandchild.

Beanie returned on Monday, too soon according to Day, who could have spent weeks, months, her entire life with a baby like Renzo. She hated to let her godchild go, especially since Beanie looked terrible, worse than before the vacation, and certainly not like somebody who'd spent three days at a resort hotel.

"I think I ate a bad clam," Beanie said when Day expressed concern.

Her cousin was all cheekbones and eye sockets, and her hair, now dyed jet black instead of cranberry red, hung sparse and limp. Beanie gathered her baby and danced him around, Renzo's plump, robust pinkness exaggerating his mother's pallor and birdlike limbs.

"You should go to the doctor," Day advised. "Maybe you need a tonic or something."

"What I need is my stinky pants," Beanie said, nuzzling Renzo. "That all his stuff?" She indicated the unopened baby food jars. "What'd you feed him? Pepperoni pizza?"

"Renzo was an angel," Day said fondly. "I'm going to miss him."

"Have one of your own."

Downstairs in the restaurant, Joe took one look at Beanie and insisted she have something to eat.

"You the only person I know take vacation and lose weight," he said.

"It's the cigarettes," Beanie responded. "I got to stop."

"Me too," Joe agreed, lighting up and offering

Beanie one.

Luis put a large pie in the oven for Vinny and the boys, and made Beanie a sandwich. She nibbled disconsolately.

"You no like?" Joe asked.

"It's great, Papa Joe," Beanie answered apologetically. "I'm just not hungry." She glanced over at Day, who was feeding Renzo bits of mozzarella. "Must be that damn clam."

"Go to your doctor when the kids are in school tomorrow," Day repeated. "Papa can watch Renzo, right, Papa?"

"You betcha. I put him to work."

"I'm changing the subject, okay?" Beanie said. "Did Bobby propose again on Friday night?"

"Yes," Day said. "Why?"

"And you said yes, right?"

Day gave her a curious look. "Who told you that?"

"Bobby was waiting in the driveway when we got back. He wants me to go with him to Affuso's tomorrow to look at rings. Wait a sec." Beanie frowned. "Why ain't we screaming and jumping up and down? You did say yes, didn't you?"

Day sighed. "I told Bobby I'd give him my answer in a week, no more stalling."

Beanie blew smoke out the side of her mouth away from Renzo. Then she screwed up her face and stubbed out the cigarette. "These things taste like cow flop. So, cuz, you didn't say yes and you didn't say no. You must have been smiling when you didn't say no because Bobby sure as shit is. He thinks it's a done deal. You ain't going to let the guy down, are you?"

"Probably not," Day replied flatly.

Beanie was silent, measuring. Then she reached for Renzo. "I don't get it. Things were going great. What happened?"

"Nothing happened. I'm just not sure is all."

"Why?"

Without the baby close to her chest, Renzo's bottom warm on her lap, Day felt cold. She hugged herself, suddenly miserably aware that Beanie was studying her skeptically. Beanie read Day like she read the gossip sites, unimpressed with the façade, probing behind the toothy smiles and designer gowns for truth. Right now, Beanie was giving Day the head cocked what-you-hiding-from-me-bitch? squint.

Day decided to spill. "Here's the thing, cuz," she began, averting her eyes from Beanie's basilisk glare. "It's nothing, nothing at all, but there's this guy at work."

Beanie had been leaning forward, all ears for the spill. At Day's confession, she jerked back hard, nearly falling over.

"Oh shit."

Chapter 18

At precisely five to twelve on Wednesday, the red button on Day's office phone blinked. She picked it up immediately.

"Yes, Mrs. Nakamura. I know it's lunchtime. I'm on my way to the cafeteria."

"Not today, Miss Denise. Come to my office."

Day was hungry and on Wednesday they always had a killer moussaka and Greek salad.

"Yes, Mrs. Nakamura. Right away."

Day made certain her blouse was neatly tucked and headed down the tiny hallway into the lion's den. The boss's little round table was set with napkins and two plastic containers. Laid across one was a set of chopsticks, on the other, a plastic fork. Nakamura directed Day to the place setting with the fork, poured hot water from an electric kettle into a China teapot, stirred and affixed the lid. The steam rising from the spout smelled like decomposing garbage.

"I hope you're hungry, Miss Denise. I made a lot," Nakamura said.

Day swallowed bile. She'd been ravenous two minutes ago but the tea stink was nauseating. Following Nakamura's example, Day removed the cover from her plastic container. Inside was a bed of seaweed. Day had eaten seaweed salad before and liked its briny, salty bite. But this seaweed was somehow different, more brown than green for one, there were no flecks of sesame, and it didn't appear to have been dressed with oil and that delicious rice wine vinegar. Moreover, the brownish mess was topped with strips of a yellowish substance that resembled nothing so much as greasy rubber bands.

"It looks delicious, Mrs. Nakamura. What is it?"

"Just vegetable and chicken skin," Nakamura answered. "I boil them together to blend the flavors. This way no condiments are needed." She bared her teeth in a rictus of a smile, thankfully gone as soon as it was attempted. "*Itadakimasu,* as my good-for-nothing-husband used to say."

Day forked a tiny mouthful. Thankfully, the concoction had no taste. What it did have was feel. Sweet Jesus, did it ever have feel. A worm of chicken skin curled on Day's tongue, slimy and viscous. She longed for a Coke to wash away the ickiness, but here came the tea, fetid, lukewarm, and to Day's astonishment, thick as syrup.

"That's gravel root tea," Nakamura announced proudly. "But I mix in valerian, durian pulp, and a whole cup of turbinado sugar. It's good for the bladder."

Day placed the cup as far away from her nose as possible and pushed her food around, pretend-eating like they do in the movies, forking infinitesimal morsels that never truly touched her lips.

Nakamura ate about a quarter of the rubber chicken skin and recovered the container. "You go ahead and finish, Miss Denise," she said. "I'll save mine for later."

Day breathed a silent prayer of thanks. "What a good idea, Mrs. Nakamura. I'll take some home too, if I

Looking pleased, Nakamura went to her desk, wrote on a piece of paper, and slid it face down to Day.

"Don't look yet," she cautioned, holding up a warning finger. "I'm willing to increase your salary for satisfactory work and for assuming Miss Sloane's duties. The amount I have written is not open for discussion, of course, but I hope you agree with it."

Why wouldn't I?

Nakamura answered the unspoken question. "If you do not agree, then I'll be forced to look elsewhere for an assistant editor. I would rather not as you are competent and innovative."

Assistant Editor. Whoo-hoo! Give me that paper.

"Thank you, Mrs. Nakamura," Day said. "I shall do my best."

She signed and Nakamura nodded. "See that you do. Now, I shall be replacing the old masthead. I want you to add seasonal touches like flying bats for Halloween, a snow scene for winter, and so on. Your Hecate County article will open the fall issue. Loco will do the photographs."

Day had been listening more to the rumbling in her gut than to the boss's directions, but at the mention of Lakota's name, everything flew out of her head like Nakamura's bats.

"I thought Lakota was away," she said.

"He owes me," Nakamura replied with a satisfied expression. "I'll drive up there with him to scout location shots. We often do shoots together."

Day rose and walked toward Nakamura's door. "Thank you for lunch, Mrs. Nakamura. For everything."

"Miss Deniece," Nakamura called sharply. "You forgot the leftovers and you didn't turn over the paper. Don't you want to know your salary?"

Day returned to the table, picked up the container, and looked at the numbers Nakamura had written. She couldn't focus and didn't care what the hell they were. Lakota was back.

Her elation lasted until the commute home. Stuck in traffic, she switched stations to listen to African tribal music and focused on her dilemma. Bobby expected an answer on Saturday night. A delay would piss him off more than a rejection. Tomorrow was Thursday, which gave her a little over forty-eight hours to chase after a dream or settle down with reality. She'd had the entire week to decide but every time she listed the pros and cons, her brain crashed after writing *Bobby/Belmont* on one side of the page and *Lakota/the World* on the other. How could she compare becoming Mrs. Leone with riding the badlands behind a sexy, honey-skinned hunk, his powerful thighs gripping the horse's flanks while she gripped him? And besides, sustained analysis wasn't her forte.

Day pulled around a stalled vehicle. Forty-eight hours, soon to be forty-seven, forty-six, then no more hours until either lift off or dud. What to do? She didn't love Bobby in a romantic way; nor did she love Lakota. How could she when they'd only just met, been alone once, and once more in Marti's company? No, Lakota couldn't and shouldn't be a factor in any decision about Bobby. Day should throw out adventure and consider family. She knew Bobby's mother and sisters, the three witches of Macbeth, Papa liked him, and Bobby was Vinny's best friend. He proclaimed his love often enough and would do anything to make her happy. Day would have to endure a huge Italian wedding like Beanie's and live in Belmont, but Belmont was no longer the deterrent it used to be. Actually living in the Bronx as an adult had shown Day that adventure can be found everywhere.

Belmont's three-season street fairs were legendary—the Christmas shopping extravaganza attracted crowds from all over, and famous people ate in its restaurants. Manhattan was close, and Pelham Bay Park with its half-moon beach of fine white sand was practically in the backyard. And what about City Island? Where else could you walk from the projects to a quintessential nautical community every bit as authentic as Newport? Best of all, Renzo was in Belmont. If Day bailed on Bobby to traipse the globe with an unknown, long-haired commodity like Lakota Campbell, Renzo would grow up without her.

Day signaled and exited right. There was nothing wrong with Lakota in the abstract. It was enough that they occupied the same planet, and breathed the same air. She sailed onto the Cross Bronx Expressway picturing his low voice, long legs, and broad shoulders. Shamelessly, she had grilled Marti and discovered that he was close to forty, always on the road, and a magnet for women. Lakota was unattached; the road and whoever paid for his photographs were his only commitments. He slept in hotels, a sleeping bag, or a yurt at the edge of a precipice. Did he want children? Probably not. Did he want a nice house on a corner lot near the hospital? Day and Marti had both laughed at the question.

Day pressed the accelerator and breathed in.

Whatever was growing alongside the road tonight smelled heavenly, gardenias or honeysuckle mixed with something smoky. Lakota smelled heavenly too, not of Aramis like Bobby, but of clear winter skies, freshly mown hay, and marshmallows toasting on a stick. She had felt the warmth of his hand in hers and brushed his iron forearm once. What would it be like to lie against all of Lakota, chest to belly to thigh?

Just imagining awesome sex with Lakota Campbell made Day's body hum. She reached into her bag. Where was her phone? She should call him. Suddenly, she swerved and hit the brakes, scarily aware that she'd been topping eighty. *Down girl. You want to sleep with him and he probably wants to sleep with you. Why not stop driving yourself nuts and make it happen, no strings attached?* Because a few trips to Nirvana with Lakota would mean losing her job if Nakamura found out, losing Bobby, and most likely herself. One night with the sexy sixpack and she'd never be the same again.

Cruising at the speed limit, Day wondered where she was. Nothing looked right. Where had all the trees come from? This should be the Bronx and Bronx trees weren't dense and dark and whispery. She continued forward slowly until an exit sign for the Bear Mountain Bridge and the United States Military Academy appeared ahead. Wait. What? Bear Mountain? West Point? She had somehow overshot the city and driven onto an eerily empty rural road.

Day pulled over to the shoulder and regrouped. She must have veered left onto the George Washington Bridge when she should have kept going straight and now she was, Holy Mother of God, in New Jersey! For

Maria Paoletta Gil

the better part of an hour, Day had been careening like a
fool on the wrong side of the Hudson River mooning
over a goddamn Indian, oops, Native American hybrid
whose hot looks and manner had fried her brain cells.
Day hung her arms over the steering wheel and stared
straight ahead, lost in more ways than one.

Fuzzy bugs, like something shaken from a pillow,
swarmed in the headlight beams. A few vehicles
whizzed by. The woods buzzed with frogs or crickets or
hissing mass murderers for all Day knew. The sign for
the United States Military Academy was glaringly
visible and Day guessed she was on the Palisades
Interstate Parkway heading north. Exits on the PIP were
few and far between, her gas tank was below a quarter,
and she needed a bathroom.

"Mama," she muttered. "Your daughter is a fool."

Day dug into her briefcase for the pages she had
printed out about Rainwalker Ridge. One of them was a
map of the southern quadrant of New York State, which
included Orange County. West Point was in Orange
County; so was the Bear Mountain Bridge that led
south to a string of small towns and, eventually, hit
Yonkers, familiar territory and an easy hop home to the
Bronx. She was about to stow the map when she
spotted a triangle in an upper corner highlighted in
yellow. It was Hecate County, a lopsided witch's hat
crushed between Orange, Ulster, and Sullivan Counties.
Lakota was raised in Rainwalker Ridge a town in, ta-
dah! Hecate County. What the hell? She was so close.

"You trying to tell me something, Mama?" Day
asked, tracing the route with her fingers. If she stayed
on the Parkway and took Route Seventeen West, she'd
be skirting the brim of the witch's hat in no time. Why

not make a research stop for the fall issue? Call it fieldwork. With a full heart and a full bladder, Day merged back onto the highway and hit the gas.

Day hadn't been driving long when she crossed the border from Orange into Hecate County and spotted Rosalie's Luncheonette lit up like a regatta. Twinkling icicle lights, lopsided weather vane, hanging rain gutters. She took the exit and pulled into the parking lot that, at seven on a June evening, was crammed with pick-ups and SUVs.

I'm in God's country, she thought, hurrying inside and scanning for the bathroom. It was tiny and immaculate with wainscoted walls, a basket of printed paper towels, and liquid soap in a honey bear dispenser. In the dining room, Day walked past a counter full of booted men in John Deere caps, and thumbed through a copy of a local real estate magazine. It was full of vinyl-sided capes and cute ranches interspersed with a smattering of fancy double-wides, and adverts for burger joints and dollar stores. Hecate County could have passed for the Belmont of New York State. She was about to slip the magazine into her bag and find a table when something caught her eye, an advert for Campbell & Sons Construction. Lakota's last name was common enough but you never know. She looked for an address but there wasn't one, just a phone number and website. She was checking her phone when a woman with an armful of menus approached.

"One?"

"Yes. Just me."

The hostess seated Day at a corner table set with a rattan placemat, silverware rolled in a cloth napkin, and an impressive array of condiments better suited to a shelf at Trader Joe's. In addition to the usual ketchup and mustard, Day examined half a dozen bottles and jars containing mysterious relishes like Jamaican Pick-a-Peppa, Red Devil Hot, malt vinegar, chow-chow, piccalilli, and something called Rosalie's Rock 'n Roll Relish. She'd try that on whatever she ordered, which turned out to be, as usual, too much.

After polishing off an excellent slice of pecan pie, Day called for the bill. But instead of her waitress, a stout woman in a plaid shirt and Doc Marten high-tops approached.

"Excuse me," she said, extending a hand. "I'm Marge. How you doing? Mind if I sit?"

Marge was maybe sixty, with short gray hair and arresting blue eyes.

"Uh, sure," Day said, wondering if the fragile-looking chair would collapse under the woman's weight.

Marge offered a business card reading, *Hometown Realty, Jeremintha, New York. Marge Coots, Broker/Owner.* "I saw you with our book," she said. "You looking for property in Hecate?" She pronounced the county name, unlike Lakota, in three syllables, Heck-a-dee.

Day thought fast. She wasn't looking for property but what better way to get to know a place than with someone who sold pieces of it? And Marge Coots was sure to be acquainted with the locals and not averse to talking about them.

"Actually," Day said, "I'm researching an article about Hecate, uh, Heckadee County, for my job. I work at the Museum of Natural History in New York City."

"Folks around here say it both ways, Hecate,

Hecadee," Marge explained. "It's named after the goddess of the crossroads because we're like a bull's eye bang in the middle of three other counties. Of course, there are those who believe Hecate was the goddess of witchcraft and ghosts and all kinds of skullduggery. We play that up on Halloween; do a thing in the cemetery where Old Lady MacGruder dresses up and scares the heck out of the kids."

It seemed that Marge did like to talk, Day noted appreciatively. "My name's Deanna but everybody calls me Day. Can I buy you a cup of coffee, Miss Coots?"

"It's Marge, honey. And I get my coffee free here. Everything else, too. Rosalie's my sister."

Marge settled in and gave Day the official rundown. Hecate was the smallest county in the state, established in 1772, population around 85,000, some leftover dairy farms and light industry. There was a forest preserve and a natural glacier lake. Campbell Mountain was the highest point.

Day flipped through the real estate magazine until she came to the ad for Campbell Construction. "Would Campbell Mountain be the same Campbell as this?"

"Sure would," Marge answered. "Ewan Campbell bought up most of the land around Rainwalker Ridge when he came here in, let me see, early-oughts, with Loco, his half-breed boy. Ewan likes to build from scratch, but most folks want those cardboard boxes they cart over the Interstate on the back of a flatbed. Ewan and Mal, that's his other son, work on both. It puts food on the table." Marge took a toothpick from her shirt pocket and stuck it in her mouth. "You work for the History Museum in New York City, you say? Then you must know the older Campbell boy."

Day's cheeks flamed. "Yes. I met him once or twice."

Marge nodded. "Loco's a good lad, helped with the beauty they're putting up in Boggy Fells. Contemporary, all cedar and glass."

"Now? Lakota's here?" Day exclaimed.

"Don't think so," Marge replied with the same look on her face Marti wore whenever Day mentioned Lakota. "Loco hardly ever is. But I could show you the house."

"It's dark out and I'm really not in the market," Day mumbled disappointed, a brief flair of hope extinguished.

"How about tomorrow, then?" Marge pressed. "I've sold lots of houses to folks who weren't looking." She waved for the check and signed it. "This is on me. There's a Red Roof Inn next exit off the highway. Sleep on it and I'll show you around in the morning. You'll get good material for your article. What do you say?"

"I hadn't planned on an overnight," Day answered, knowing exactly what she was going to say. "I didn't bring anything with me."

"There's a department store same exit as the Red Roof," Marge offered winking. "A girl can always use another pair of pajamas."

Chapter 19

The next morning, Day's phone rang as she was struggling with the coffee pot in her room at the Red Roof Inn.

"You may have your day in the field, Miss Denise," Nakamura barked. "But next time, don't presume I'll approve your rashness. Field trips must be arranged in advance. That's the rule."

"Thank you, Mrs. Nakamura. I know the rule, but I found myself in the area and—"

"You have left me without an office manager," Nakamura's words snapped like teeth. "I will have today's calls routed to your phone. Voucher mileage, but accommodations and meals are on you since you embarked on this escapade without permission."

"Yes, Mrs. Nakamura."

"I want five thousand words in the morning. Goodbye."

Five-thousand words? "Shit!" Day cursed into empty air. She'd be answering calls all day and up all night writing. Shit, shit, shit! And she wasn't an office manager. She was the assistant editor who also happened to answer phones, make copies, order supplies, and...*Shit!*

By the time Day was on her way to meet Marge, she'd fielded calls from several newsletter subscribers, the Expeditions Department, Special Events,

Manuscript Collections and the Director of Accessibility who wanted a full-page write-up about the Immersive Experience in the Hall of Dinosaurs. She pulled into the luncheonette and set the ringer on vibrate. *Let them leave messages.*

The weathervane atop Rosalie's sparkled in the sunshine. It was going to be a glorious day; paint box blue sky, fragrant breezes, lilac, yellow and pink buds drifting everywhere. Day parked beside a red Jeep Renegade and felt a pang of anticipation. She was about to spend the day with a woman who knew Lakota, had probably watched him grow up. What could Lakota Campbell have been like as a child? In high school? Had he gone to college? When did he first start taking pictures? She certainly had a lot of questions about a man she wasn't going to think about.

"Hey there," Marge said, tapping on the car window. "Right on time. I only just got here myself. Had breakfast?"

"Coffee in the motel. I don't eat in the morning."

"City folk," Marge grumbled. "You're no toothpick so I'm guessing you eat lunch. We'll start out now and end up back here for my sister's chicken and waffles special."

"Sounds good. Your car or mine?"

Marge drove, zipping past tattoo parlors, American Legion halls, and mom-and-pop stores that appeared to sell everything from lottery tickets to tire irons. Every few miles, Day pointed out a storefront church, a gun shop, an adult bookstore, and so many Wal-Marts that she stopped counting. The sub-mediocrity of everything didn't compute with Lakota's cool, black-clad image and Day's bewilderment must have shown because

Marge's sales pitch suddenly amped.

"You haven't seen the real Hecate County yet," Marge said. "The woods, and fields and farms. Young folks want affordable ranches in a development but we have an older, richer population that goes for Ewan Campbell's masterpieces. Wait until you see the latest. I'll take you there. She pointed. "There's our first Burger King, used to be the Copper Kettle, and that there's the Hecate Herald, down to a four-page fold-over tabloid, sorry to say but it will fatten up again, just like Hecate County will if Campbell Construction has a say."

Day had been taking notes. She paused and lifted the pen. "So the county is growing?"

"Most certainly," Marge retorted heatedly. "Just look around you. New houses everywhere. They're cookie-cutter, I'll give you that. But we have some stunners, too. And some famous people. You heard of Dick Dorian LaFonde?"

"The actor?"

"Yep. Plays that detective with the talking dog. The Campbells are building a retreat for him and the third or fourth wife." She snorted. "Could be for both. Cedar and stone, big windows." Marge shifted gears as the road began to wind steeply up a hill. "Now we're getting into the thick of it. We're on Campbell Mountain, best view in the county from the top. You can see Jeremintha and Boggy Fells, the Tower of London on a clear day."

Day chuckled and put down her notebook. They had indeed driven through acres of lockstep condos and vinyl-sided ranch houses, but now all around were meadows and fields dotted with placidly grazing cows.

The air hummed with birdsong and smelled of flowers. This was more like Lakota, Day mused, open spaces and wildlife. Marge tooted at the attendant of a two-pump filling station and braked to let a turtle the size of a Volkswagen cross the road.

"We're coming into Rainwalker Ridge. Pretty little town. That big log house over there is Ewan and Faye Campbell's farm. To the left and a little below, over by that stand of copper beeches, that's the LaFonde place. Isn't she a pip?"

She was indeed, Day thought. Ultra-modern yet somehow natural in its bucolic surroundings. "Is that the house Lakota designed?"

"Well, the architect drew up the plans but Loco told him how it should be. Got a real eye for beauty, Loco." Marge winked. "Always dated the prettiest girls. You should know since you work with him."

"I know he's famous for his photographs," Day said evenly. "But I don't actually see Lakota that often."

Marge nodded. "Sounds about right. Never too long in one place, that boy. Took off the first time when he was about fourteen. Disappeared a whole month. Faye and Ewan went crazy. Turned out Loco was picking fruit with a bunch of Mexicans."

"Lakota told me he was born in North Dakota," Day said, wanting to hear more.

"Cutest thing Loco was when Ewan brought him home. Eight or nine and angry at the world. Never did fit in with the other kids. Didn't want to either. Kept his hair long and in summer, he turned black as a..." Marge slid a closed glance at Day. "As a person with a dark tan."

"Everybody at the Museum likes Lakota," Day offered.

"Oh, Loco can be a good ole boy when he wants to. People take to him and he's a Campbell, after all. But Loco keeps pretty much to himself." Marge grinned. "Except with the ladies. Don't know about now, but did they ever used to flock around. It's a miracle Loco managed to graduate high school, especially after what happened in senior year."

Day was all ears. "What? What happened?"

But Marge pulled into a small turn-around, cranked the hand brake, and got out. "We can't go any higher without breaking an axel. Come see the view."

Day plodded after Marge through dense underbrush still dressed for work.

"I've already seen the view of the valley," she called out, swiping at vines and tripping over hummocks and ridges.

"Not like the one from Loco's cabin," Marge called back. "His porch has a three-sixty."

Day quickened her pace. "Won't we be trespassing?"

"If anybody was here, Loco's Jeep would be down at the turn-off next to mine," Marge called back. "But you never know. He shows up when you least expect it."

They climbed for another minute and, all of a sudden, the way before them opened. A clearing bordered with young trees sloped gently upward to a small log cabin with a deep wrap-around porch. Smoke drifted from the chimney and an ATV was angled on the grass. Two dogs watched their approach. Day liked dogs but knew enough to freeze in the presence of strange ones.

"Those are just Loco's pooches," Marge said. "Hubshop and Bebop, or something like that. I can never remember their names. Hello, boys," she greeted the pair who trotted out to meet them. "Actually, this big one's a girl. I think they call her Mommy."

Day squatted down to rub ears and bellies and have her face resoundingly licked.

"Then Lakota's here?" Day said in a tone filled with wonder.

Marge gave Day another curious look and jerked her chin at the tall, rangy man loping toward them. "Nope. But Mal is."

The young man smiled Lakota's smile and called off the dogs. "Shappa, Makawee, leave the ladies alone." He gave Marge a quick hug. "What brings you all the way out here? Hope you don't think the place is for sale."

"This here's Deanna Danese," Marge said, perfectly pronouncing all six syllables of Day's name. "She knows your brother."

Mal stuck out a hand. "Malcolm Campbell. Mal for short."

"I'm Day," she replied. "I work at the Museum of Natural History in New York City. I met Lakota there."

Lakota's brother appeared to be half his age, fair and sandy-haired instead of dark, with blue eyes. Aside from his smile and easy walk, he looked nothing like Lakota yet Day's heart surged when she shook Mal's hand, so big and warm it stirred her memory. Mal invited her to the porch that circled the cabin and waited with Marge and the dogs while Day admired all four points of the view, each one more breathtaking than the last. The sky, a vast silver-white dome, curved over expanses that rolled down and away in swaths of jade, sage, and deepest viridian. Behind and all around, tall pines and broad, leafy oaks whispered in the light breeze. Day inhaled wood smoke and something else, something elemental like freshly turned earth, and stood motionless, overwhelmed by a reverential sense of isolation that was both majestic and intimate.

"It's-it's. I can't think of a word," Day stammered, taking a seat on a wooden bench.

"Loco built the place so the front faces west for the sunset," Mal explained. "There's only one room but it has everything you need. I'd give you the tour but..." He grinned, crookedly like Lakota, and Day's heart flipped. "...it's messy. Don't tell my brother."

"You staying here a while?" Marge asked.

"I'll be taking care of Shappa and Makawee probably through the winter," Mal answered. "Right now most of my stuff's dumped all over but you can come in."

Day's heart sank. Nakamura had said that Lakota would be back for the Hecate shoot in a matter of days. She mentioned this to Mal who shrugged.

"Who knows? Faye, that's our mother, wants Loco home for Christmas, but knows not to get her hopes up. See, my brother's part Teton Indian. His mom, my dad's first wife, was an Oglala Sioux. They have restless blood. Can't stay put." Mal fixed Day with that slow Lakota Campbell smile. "We're used to it but sometimes I wish—" He broke off. "Doesn't matter what I wish. Loco always comes back sooner or later, right, Marge?"

"So far."

Chapter 20

The trek back to Marge's car was less arduous. *I could get used to this,* Day thought, planting her feet on the wooded path with more assurance than earlier. Maybe not to the tacky towns and seedy strip malls, but marooned up here so close to heaven with just Lakota and the dogs? How wonderful would that be?

Marge spun dirt and gravel and backed onto the road. Day opted for a direct approach.

"You were telling me something happened to Lakota during senior year in high school," she asked. "What was it?"

Marge navigated the steep descent and shotgunned onto the macadam roadway. At the gas station in Rainwalker Ridge, the attendant waved again. Marge pulled in and exchanged a few words with him. Day waited impatiently.

"It was a big scandal round here, though I suppose you city folks wouldn't think so," Marge began, underway again. "Had to do with the ladies, of course, two this time, the Esposito gal Loco was practically engaged to, and Jeanmarie Renfrew." Abruptly, she veered from the subject. "That there's our community college. It's part of the state university system. Want to see our county seat? They're building a new municipal center near the courthouse"

Day nearly reached over and shook Marge.

"Maybe after lunch. Please, finish your story."

"Guess you're wrung out with nothing but coffee for breakfast," Marge observed. "Me and Rosalie always have a big meal in the morning, oatmeal, eggs, sausages. Our mother, may she rest in peace–" Marge didn't continue but slowed down. "Let me show you our cemetery. It has some headstones that date back two centuries."

Day thought she might have moaned. "Can we eat first? I'm starved and you can tell me all about the scandal."

Rosalie's Luncheonette was crowded but Marge strode confidently to an alcove in the rear where her doppelganger greeted her.

"Chicken and waffles all around, Ro," Marge said, taking a seat and motioning Day to do the same.

Day tried again. "So about Lakota and those two girls?"

"Oh yes, Kim Esposito and Jeanmarie Renfrew." Marge poured neither cream nor sugar into her coffee but nevertheless lifted her spoon and stirred. "It happened twenty years ago but I remember like it was yesterday." She nodded to other diners, mentioned a new listing, an upcoming closing.

Day drummed her fingers. She'd get the skinny out of this woman if she had to buy a house to do it. "You were saying, Marge?"

"Loco really liked Kim," Marge obliged. "She wasn't so fat then; big but shapely, know what I mean?" Day barely nodded. "Anyway, Ewan and Faye were expecting an engagement after graduation. Then Jeanmarie started with the accusations and everybody was talking about her and Loco. But he never said a word, just shut down, know what I mean? Moody as all heck, started getting into fights, lost his after-school job at the filling station."

Marge took a sip of coffee and stared at the ceiling. Day was on the edge of her seat.

"And then what?"

"Loco broke it off with Kim but Jeanmarie ran away, clear across the country she went, to Oregon. Ohio? No, Oregon. Nobody heard anything more until we read her obit in the Herald. She was sixteen, poor kid."

"She died?"

"Yep. We all expected Loco to do the right thing seeing as how he always talked about honor, know what I mean? About his people, his tribe and their respect for life." The expression on Marge's plain face was resigned. "But what can you do? The boy, well, I guess he had to be a man to get into a fix like that, wasn't what he seemed. Ewan and Faye must have been shocked as heck, disappointed too. But you know them, salt of the earth."

"I don't know them," Day said, frustrated. "What are you saying? I don't get it."

"Apparently, neither did Loco," Marge replied. "We all tried to talk some sense into him but, oh, here's the food!" Marge beamed at the dishes heaped with thick waffles and golden slabs of chicken, licked her lips, and hefted the pitcher of maple syrup. "Dig in!"

Evidently, Marge Coots was incapable of talking and eating at the same time. Day did as she was told, grateful that her companion was a fast eater. Fifteen minutes later, Rosalie refilled their coffee cups and pulled up a chair.

"Gossiping again, Marjorie?" Rosalie accused her twin.

"It isn't gossip if it's true," Marge protested. Rosalie fixed her with a *you got to be kidding* look and Marge laughed. "All right. It's old news, anyway, more than twenty years since it happened."

"The Loco business?" Rosalie asked.

"What else? Hottest thing around here."

Day bent eagerly toward Marge, but it was Rosalie who spoke.

"Loco was wild as a cougar and never close to anybody except Faye and his dad, but we all thought, after Jeanmarie died, he'd marry Kim. She'd have accepted the situation. Kim loved Loco something crazy."

What situation? Day was dying to know but chose not to interrupt the flow.

"Loco did nothing of the kind, didn't propose, didn't so much as talk to Kim," Marge said, picking up the narrative. "He just collected his high school diploma and disappeared."

"Where?" Day asked.

Rosalie shrugged. "Big mystery. One day he was walking by the diner in his dirty boots, and after that, nobody saw him again for years. Faye cried a ton, I can tell you."

"Kim, too, that poor gal, "Marge added. "I don't think she ever got over Loco, but eventually she married Lonnie Gottshalk, right, Ro? They have a bunch of kids now and she's wide as a rest stop on I-95."

The sisters shared a smile and Day pressed both palms to her cheeks. "I still don't get it," Day fairly groaned. "What happened to Lakota? Where did he disappear to?"

Two pairs of identical blue eyes gazed placidly at Day. Marge said, "I got this, Ro." And then answered the question in a stage whisper. "Don't spread this around; it's been a secret for years."

"Who she going to tell? She doesn't know anybody," Rosalie said.

"She knows Loco."

"Oh, yeah."

Day's toes curled but she trusted they were almost there. Marge nodded gravely.

"Loco went to get his son."

****

Things had a way of working themselves out, Day mused on the drive back to the Bronx. She had dared to imagine, all evidence to the contrary, a family life with Lakota, a home in a world-class city and a pair of tall, dark-haired children, a boy and a girl, Joseph Laughing Pony and Maria Sun Bear, or something ridiculous like that, as ridiculous as she was. Day chuckled a little sadly at the folly of her vision, but thank God, she'd found out just in time. Lakota had a wanderlust that wouldn't quit, and a son he'd never mentioned. Day wondered who had raised the boy and where he was now. In any case, it had nothing to do with her. Now she could stop spinning and face in one direction. She had crossed the Rubicon. No, wrong analogy. Something biblical was better, more profound, and in keeping with a life of maturity and decency. The scales had fallen from her eyes. Yes, that was better. The dream scales had fallen and Day was no longer blind.

Chapter 21

Day pulled in front of Enchanted Gardens and waved to Papa and Luis. Upstairs, she kicked off her shoes, booted the laptop, and began to transcribe the Hecate County notes. She hadn't seen Lakota and thank God. One look and she would have made a bigger fool of herself than she obviously was. Beanie called and without so much as a hello said, "I got your message and you'll want to congratulate me for not bothering you every two minutes. But now you're home, spill. Did you see Cochise?"

"Jesus, Beanie. His name's Lakota and he's out of the country. I didn't go there to see him. I was working on an assignment."

"And I'm freaking Taylor Swift." Day heard Beanie light a cigarette and continue talking through the exhale. "When you called to tell me you were spending the night in his hometown, I thought I'd shit my pants. Bobby's got the hall booked and the church reserved for Valentine's Day. What the fuck are you doing?"

"All I told Bobby was that I'd give him a straight answer if he asked me again," Day snapped.

"If he asked you again! For crying out loud, Day. The guy's on automatic rewind."

"I didn't promise to say yes. All I said was–"

"You had no right to–"

"No right?"

"Hanging out like wash and—"

"That I'd stop—"

Beanie let out a windy sigh. "Okay, okay. You're family and I ain't going to get nasty but, so help me, cuz, if you go running after Tonto and it don't work out, stay the hell away. Not from me, I can take it, but from Bobby."

"I won't," Day replied. "I mean I will. And no more ethnic jokes, please."

Beanie groaned. "This PC stuff is such a crock. My kids play Cowboys and Native Americans, now. That don't even sound right." Another exhale. "So, anyway, what are you saying? That you'll stay away from Bobby or you won't?"

"How can I stay away if I never go away?"

Silence on the other end. Then, "So wait, wait," Beanie cried. "You're marrying Bobby? You ain't bullshitting me with that how can I come back if I ain't left crap? You're serious?"

"Yes," Day said. "I'm serious."

"About Bobby?"

"Yes."

"Holy Mother of God," Beanie shouted. "Vinny, Vinny!"

Day gripped the phone. "Don't you dare tell Vinny until I've had a chance to talk to Bobby. Beanie! Beanie?"

But it was too late. Day heard Beanie's loud, excited announcement to Vinny and everyone else on the block. In minutes, it was going to be all over Belmont.

"You're incorrigible, Beanie," Day said and hung up. The phone rang again.

"You calling me a hot air balloon?" Beanie asked affronted.

"That's dirigible. Incorrigible means you're a pain in the ass."

"Oh, yeah," Beanie admitted cheerfully. "That's true. And I won't make fun no more of Indi...Native Americans or whatever they are, okay?" A pause. "How dark is the guy, anyway?"

Chapter 22

The diamond Bobby gave Day was pear-shaped and just short of ostentatious. Day claimed to love it but confessed to Beanie that it was so huge it made her feel a little silly.

"Wait until you see the wedding ring," Beanie responded. "You'll have to put your arm in a sling."

A Valentine's Day wedding was Bobby's preference. But the venue was Day's call. "Go as grand as you like for the reception," Bobby said. "I'll pay."

Day reminded him that the groom traditionally paid for the honeymoon, the bride for the wedding. Papa had money put aside and in any case, Day didn't want a bank-breaking blow-out; no horse-drawn Cinderella carriage or white doves pooping on everybody's heads. And forget Palacio Del Re where Beanie's reception had been held, with the hot and cold hors d'oeuvres, four-course meal, and twenty-foot long Viennese table. Day wanted simple; champagne and nibbles in the Mount Carmel Church hall was fine.

Bobby said okay, but Day worried. He kept adding to the guest list, making outlandish suggestions like hiring a cruise ship and transporting everybody to Hawaii. Her efforts to rein in Bobby sometimes met with good-natured success but more often with smoldering resentment. Bobby accused Day of being ashamed of him and of wanting to play down the wedding. "Why don't we just elope?" became a frequent, testy question. "Why are you marrying me at all?" another.

Day soothed Bobby. Gentle humor added to his sense of insult and retorts only fueled his fire. The best approach when Bobby's "mad came down", his phrase, was loving acceptance larded with fulsome praise. Day dared not touch him, but a few soft words chiding herself for lack of foresight, coupled with admiration for his abundant possession of same, usually worked wonders. Soon, watchful avoidance became Day's tiring constant as land mines exploded every week, every day, every hour. She hid her doubts from Papa, who was thrilled that Carissima Deanna was finally going to be a wife.

Joe threw a combination engagement and birthday party at Enchanted Gardens during which he talked to Bobby about transferring the restaurant to his name. Day didn't interrupt. Let Bobby handle the place. She already had too much responsibility handling him.

"Maybe it's time to retire, Papa," she said. "Take a vacation."

Joe, pale and thin, protested with a grin. "Me? I never no retire. Still young, strong."

Joe Danese had his own act as if. Italians called it *fare la faccia*, make the face, show one thing when you're feeling another. Joe smiled but Day saw the strain behind her father's eyes. Something was off.

"What's wrong, Papa?" Day began, helping him into the recliner. "Did Luis say or do anything to make you unhappy?"

Joe waved off the question. "Of course not. I love that *mascalzone* and I love Roberto, too. You no love so much but the love, she come in time."

"Then what is it, Papa? I can tell something's bothering you."

Joe rubbed his chest and looked away. The gesture had become characteristic, but Day asked anyway. "Are you feeling all right?"

"Why you all the time ask that?" Joe responded irritated. "A hundred times a day, you ask that. I'm fine, healthy as a mule." He pounded the arm of the chair. "*Fermati!* Stop! I no sick and I no scared. Nobody kill me!"

Joe stalked off and slammed the bedroom door. Day followed. *Nobody kill me? What the hell?* She knocked hard and when Joe didn't answer, barged in.

"I'm not leaving until you talk to me, Papa."

"Then look like you sleep on the floor tonight." He sighed. "Go to bed, Deanna. Is late."

Joe was perched on the edge of the bed, hands in his lap, head down. She sat beside him and began speaking softly in Italian.

"Che sucede, Papa? Cosa ha detto il dottore? Una cosa grave?"

Joe patted his daughter's knee. "No, Deanna. I swear. The doctor no say nothing bad. I have a little bump-bump in the heart, that's all. He give me medicine."

Day knew the doctor wouldn't breach patient privacy, but she vowed to call him in the morning.

"What else, Papa? Tell me."

Joe started to unbutton his shirt. "I tell you small thing, little thing. Then you go upstairs, okay? New supplier give me hard time. But I fix."

"What kind of hard time?"

Joe threw his hands in the air. "*Per la miseria,* Deanna? No make me mad. I fix, okay?"

For the moment, Day swallowed her fears but the next day, she buzzed Nakamura. "I'm slipping out to the loo for a minute."

The boss sighed extravagantly. "Must you, Miss Denise? It will be your lunch break shortly."

It was barely ten. Lunch was two hours away.

"I'm sorry, Mrs. Nakamura, but this can't wait. I'll be quick."

"I hope you're not getting ill. The fall issue–"

"I'm on it," Day interrupted.

Nakamura had been obsessing about the fall issue that would highlight Hecate County and feature scenes of its famed foliage. Lakota hadn't yet returned to New York to take the photos and Nakamura was venting her wrath on everybody within ten feet, which was mostly Day. She forbade Day to use other pictures from the archives and demanded dozens of revisions to the special holiday masthead.

In the ladies' room, Day phoned Bobby, whose usual gruff greeting ratcheted in her ear.

"Yeah. What is it?"

"Bobby, it's me."

"Dayglo! How's my racehorse? I was just thinking about you."

"I have to make this quick. I'm at work."

"I thought you weren't allowed personal calls. You told me never to call you at work. You shouldn't work, anyway. You told me–"

"Bobby," Day cut in. "Please, just listen. Something's up with Papa. It's been going on for a while now and I think it's about one of his suppliers.

135

He's worried, walks around in a daze. I think it's making him sick. You hear anything?"

"Yeah, I did," Bobby answered. "But it's over. I took care of it. Papa Joe owed the Farengas money and they sent the goon squad."

Day froze. "Goon squad? What does that mean? Did somebody hurt Papa?"

"As if I'd let that happen," Bobby scolded. "Papa Joe's fine. Nobody touched him."

Day checked the time. Five minutes gone. She had better hurry. "So it's all right?"

"Weren't you listening? You don't listen. I said I took care of it. The Farenga brothers got their money." Bobby's tone mellowed. "Want to get together tonight? I can't wait another day."

Day still had a lot of questions. Why was Papa having trouble paying bills? That never happened before. Farenga Brothers was the biggest wholesale distributor in New York. Papa had been doing business with them for years. Why would they all of a sudden resort to scare tactics? She told Bobby she'd see him at home and, hearing Nakamura's annoyed summons, hung up.

Chapter 23

After an hour of wall-to-wall traffic, Day pulled into the loading zone, tense and limp at the same time. Bobby was in Enchanted Gardens biting into a thick Sicilian slice. Customers were three deep, a good sign, and Papa had a napkin tied around his forehead to catch the sweat. Day waved, indicating Bobby should go out the back way and meet her upstairs. She had a pounding headache, no, two headaches, one between the eyes and one at the back of her neck, and was swallowing Advil when Bobby sauntered in. Day had left the door open for him, wondered for a moment if she should run back and lock it, then decided, *Hell, it's my door to my apartment. He'd better not say Boo.* When Bobby walked in scowling, she hurried over with a beer before things got ugly.

Bobby studied the can. "That's not my brand."

"Sorry. I usually pick up the kind you like on Friday since we see each other on Saturday."

He made a face. Day microwaved leftover mushroom noodles and sat at the table.

"Want some of this?" she asked.

Bobby opened the refrigerator. "I'll have ginger ale." He pulled out a bag from the Chinese restaurant. "What's this? I told you not to eat this shit. And don't put bags in the fridge. They pick up odors." He popped a can. "Your goddamn ice trays are empty. I wish you'd listen to me when I talk and keep ice on hand."

Day wished he'd goddamn shut up. "Sorry. I don't like ice." That was the second time she'd apologized.

Bobby shoved the soda back onto the shelf and slammed the door. "Well, I do."

Day was in no mood for his mood. Struggling to dislodge the angry retort simmering in her throat, she took a deep breath and said it again, for the last time. "Sorry. I'll run downstairs to Papa's and get a bag of ice, shall I?"

Bobby narrowed his eyes, gauging the depth of Day's sincerity. Obviously deciding it was genuine, he sat at the table and indicated the mushroom noodles. "How can you eat that slop? You better not heat up shit after we're married." Big, long-suffering sigh. "All right. I'm here. What do you want to know?"

Choosing not to remind Bobby he'd invited himself, Day put down her fork. "How's Papa's balance sheet? Luis does the books but said nothing about any shortfalls."

"Hell with Luis. He's out of the picture," Bobby said. "I do the books now." He leaned back and crossed his arms. "I'm not supposed to tell you and don't let on to Papa Joe I said anything, but here's how it went down."

The tale Bobby told was shocking and not a little scary. Joe was overextended and had been for some time. Like most restaurant owners, Joe Danese purchased on credit and paid out of proceeds. But for the past several months, he'd been in the red and paying suppliers, mainly Farenga, not in thirty, not in sixty, not in ninety days; in fact, not since last July. A lot of the smaller companies let Joe float. They knew his reputation. But the Farenga brothers also had a reputation; for good prices, a huge inventory, and stone balls.

"With those guys, it's cash or consequences," Bobby said.

Day shuddered. "Can they do that?"

"Farengas can do what they want. They harassed your father with collection agencies, then with lawyers, and then,"—Bobby made two fists—"with Carmine Carciofolo."

"Oh my God!" Day exclaimed. "Carmine the Cobra? He's Mafia."

Bobby shrugged. "Who knows? Maybe he is and maybe he isn't. Point is, Farengas got Carmine's henchmen on payroll."

Day pushed aside her plate, suddenly disgusted by the gummy strands of pasta swimming in a brown-flecked cream sauce. "What about the police? Can't Officer Hank do anything?"

"Papa Joe doesn't want the cops to know about his, ah…" Bobby waved a hand. "About his dealings, shall we say? And Hank? Come on, babe. You know better than that. Forget the law. The best thing Papa Joe did was call me."

Bobby said that he'd paid the Farengas, and Papa Joe promised to make good when his head was above water.

"But you know, babe," he assured Day. "I wouldn't take a cent from my future father-in-law. Matter of fact, since Papa Joe is skinned, I'm covering the cost of our wedding, too." Bobby waved magnanimously. "No more penny-pinching. Go for broke, not that I'll ever be."

The last thing on Day's mind was the wedding. "How can Papa have a cash flow problem? Enchanted Gardens is busy."

"It just looks that way because the place is so small," Bobby answered. "Don't get me wrong, you did a great job with the back room, but nobody goes there. That was poor planning like Luis' soda fridge and the damn video games. These days kids play on their phones. See, babe, I know you hate to hear this but Flaming Vesuvius went franchise a year ago. They charge twenty bucks for a medium with wings and even throw in a bag of garlic knots. Papa Joe can't compete with that."

"Their pizza tastes like sheet rock," Day noted.

"Granted. But there are a gazillion pizza joints in the neighborhood now, most of them franchises and that fancy new sit-down up the hill."

"They're all crap," Day insisted.

Bobby picked up Day's discarded fork and began poking at the cold noodles. "When Enchanted Gardens is mine," he said as Day's back stiffened, "I'll bring in my swat team, amp up the PR, possibly partner with another brand establishment or Papa John's if the numbers are right, and get rid of Luis."

"Fire Luis?" Day asked in a rising tone.

"In business, everybody's expendable. See, the tourists from upstate want a slice of Italy but not the same slice they can get at the joints in their neighborhoods. They'll go to Bella Roma and the kids and locals to Flaming Vesuvius because it's cheap. Papa Joe's regulars, sorry to say, they're kicking the bucket faster than the Carciofolo boys can make a point. Unless Enchanted Gardens changes, it won't last another year."

Day tried to make sense of Bobby's explanation but all she heard was that her father and Enchanted Gardens, the two staples of her life, were in trouble and she'd never had a clue. The tons of cash Papa had given her over the years, a new car, a new apartment, and all the while he was broke. Day wondered what else he was protecting her from.

A thought struck. "I know," Day piped. "I'll give up my apartment and we can rent it out. That should help."

"No, it won't," Bobby said flatly.

"Why not?"

"Papa Joe doesn't own the building."

Day's stomach heaved. "You're wrong. He paid off the mortgage a long time ago."

"I'm never wrong, Day. Not when it comes to business. Papa Joe refinanced the place so many times, there was no equity left."

"But that can't be. I'm certain. I know that—"

"Just listen, will you?" Bobby cut off her bluster. "The bank offered your father a variable rate with a huge balloon payment due like in ten seconds. The bums knew he couldn't manage it and in less than a year, Enchanted Gardens was theirs." Day's jaw went slack, but Bobby chuckled. "Cheer up, babe. I may not own a restaurant but all businesses are the same." He tapped his forehead. "Soon as I like the price, I'll buy back the restaurant and maybe turn it into a dry cleaners." He grinned, licked his lips, and scraped his chair. "Will you look at that? All this money talk made me hard. Let's go into the bedroom for a quickie."

Day didn't, couldn't answer, and Bobby, to her

relief, shrugged and punched his phone.

"Ma? Yeah, a little late. Day's eating some glop in a can. What you got? Good. On my way."

He kissed her, slipping his tongue in her mouth and cupping her buttocks. "You sure now?" he leered. "I can call Ma back."

She pushed Bobby gently through the door and leaned against it for a long time, deep in thought. Bobby had come to the rescue this time but how was she going to keep her father safe from the Carciofolo boys, and Enchanted Gardens from turning into another cleaners? Approaching Papa without getting him annoyed was tricky but necessary. This was as serious as a heart attack, and while people come back from heart attacks, Carmine the Cobra played for keeps.

Belmont was full of big-time and small-time hoodlums and Capo Carmine Carciofolo was the latter, but his tactics, what he termed "corrective precedures", evoked terror. Day had seen smashed storefronts, questionable fires, and the occasional beloved pet left beheaded on a doorstep, and she started spending her free time in Enchanted Gardens. She woke at dawn to help with the prep work, waited tables on weekends, and sometimes even mid-week when the firehouse or precinct held a meeting in the back room. In essence, Day worked two jobs, loved them both, but felt like a hamster in a wheel, moving fast, going nowhere.

****

Day was about to cover her desk computer and zip uptown to put on her Enchanted Gardens apron when the phone rang. It was probably Beanie, who had taken to harassing her for working so hard, and Day almost didn't answer. But then she remembered that Beanie hadn't been herself lately, forgetting things, and losing her train of thought in the middle of a conversation. Feeling guilty for neglecting Beanie, Day answered.

"Don't start, cuz. I've been busy. I'll stop by on my way home."

"Day?"

Her name but in a man's voice, deep and familiar with that raspy edge that made her knees weak.

"Lakota?"

"I hope you don't mind my calling. How are you?"

"Oh, don't worry about it, call any time. I'm good, fine, great, okay."

Day bit the inside of her cheek to stop the blithering. Why did this man always reduce her to idiocy?

"I'm sure it's after five there," Lakota said. "I figured you'd left the office."

"I'm just on my way. Mrs. Nakamura's already gone," she added dutifully. Lakota must want to talk to the boss. There was no possible reason for him to call her directly unless… Day bit her cheek again. Don't be an ass, he's probably in a helicopter over the South China Sea and doesn't have Nakamura's cell number with him. But then why…

"I don't want Grace," Lakota said. "I called you."

Day's palm began to sweat. She wanted to transfer the phone to her other hand but was afraid she'd drop it and lose the connection.

"Me?" Day said. "You want me?" That didn't come out right. "I mean, how can I help you?"

She heard whooshing noises in the background like Lakota was in a wind tunnel or under a waterfall. The man could be calling from anywhere, calling *her* from anywhere.

"Where are you?" she asked. "I hear strange noises." And then, before Lakota had a chance to answer, Day added hopefully, "Are you nearby?"

"Not yet," he answered. "But I'm flying in for a couple of days next month to do the Hecate County shoot."

Day's heart thrummed in her ears and conflicting emotions gripped her—joy because she'd see him again, disappointment at the brevity of the visit, annoyance at her lack of spine. Hadn't she decided not too long ago that Lakota Campbell was a cowardly flake?

"I'll inform Mrs. Nakamura of your return," Day said. "She's been waiting to hear from you and she'll want to–"

"Don't do that," Lakota interrupted. "Grace likes to assist me on local assignments but the only time I can make is the week of her annual shareholders' conference. If Grace knows I'm in town, she'll bypass it for the shoot." He hesitated. "And anyway, it gets complicated with her looking over my shoulder while I'm trying to work. Can you come instead? I'll need help with the setups and note taking and, ah–"

For the first time since Day had known him, Lakota sounded hesitant, uncomfortable.

"I understand," she said. "I won't breathe a word, but when you submit the pictures, Mrs. Nakamura is going to find out you went with somebody else." Day's brain buzzed and her heart leapt. *With me!*

"I'll deal with Grace later," Lakota replied. "You'll have to drive my Jeep while I get in and out and–" Another pause. "It's a stick. Your Forester's a stick so I know you drive a stick, and Mal can't make it, so-"

He trailed off. Lakota was having trouble completing sentences. He was, Day realized, nervous. So was she. A day with Lakota in the country was just what she needed, even though she had briefly, and stupidly, considered him a heartless quitter. Still, sneaking up to Hecate County without telling the boss was a foolish, reckless move. But she had survived being AWOL for Lakota once before, and this time it was by invitation. Would Papa understand? Would Beanie? Did she dare?

Lakota's breathing pinged off the satellite straight into Day's heart and she forced herself to think of a way to make it happen. Nakamura would be out of the office for two entire days at the shareholders' conference. The newsletter office was way down in the sub-basement; nobody came by so nobody would know she wasn't at her desk. And just in case, she could always hang a *Working in the Field* sign on the door and have calls transferred to her phone like Nakamura had done the last time.

"You still there, Day?" Lakota's voice sounded farther away.

"Yes, yes. I'm here. Don't hang up," Day cried. And then, in case she'd gotten it all wrong and Lakota wasn't asking her to join him, she added, "I'll be happy to go on the shoot with you if I can help. Next month, right? Friday the twentieth. Fridays are always light," she lied.

"Thank you." She heard the relief in Lakota's voice. "I'll make us dinner when we're finished."

"You cook?" she asked, nearly swooning.

"You kidding? I fried snapper for Princess Sophie

of Liechtenstein."

"She eat it?"

"All of it. Then she knighted me."

Day laughed. Oh, talking to Lakota like this was wonderful. "I'll have to call you Sir Lakota."

He was quiet for a second. Then, "You're the only one who doesn't call me Loco. I like that."

Chapter 24

Day was itching to tell Beanie about Lakota's invite but knew it was wiser to keep her mouth shut. When she stopped by on her way home, her cousin looked ghastly, chalky and thin, lank hair showing chestnut brown roots and the ink-black ends dry. The mood was somber too, Renzo being asleep in his room and the middle boys, Mikey and Anthony, away at their grandmother's. Beanie picked at the cheesecake Day had bought and Vinny tried to make jokes and teased his eldest, Vinny Junior. But the boy barely cracked a smile and excused himself to go to his room.

"Something's off," Day said gently when she and Beanie were alone. "What gives?"

"Well…" Beanie lit a cigarette. "The thing is, I ain't feeling so good. The doc says it's not the clam."

"What clam?"

"The one I ate in the Poconos, remember? I thought it had babies in my gut." She took a single drag and mashed the cigarette in the ashtray. "Can't wait until I enjoy drinking and smoking again. And eating. I can't eat for shit. That's the worst of it. Well, that and the pains."

Day said nothing, not wanting to inhibit the flow. She'd been trying to get Beanie to open up for weeks.

"My doctor wants me to have a few tests," Beanie went on matter-of-factly. "He says it could be lots of things. Problem is, I got to go to the freaking hospital for the tests, in case they, you know, find anything and have to cut it out."

"All right," Day said slowly, although her mind was reeling. "That seems pretty straightforward. I'm glad you're finally having it taken care of. I'll go with you."

"Not necessary," Beanie said. Then added brightly, the words tumbling out in a rush. "But can you watch Renzo this weekend and maybe for a few days after that? I know you work with Papa Joe and all but if I check into the hospital tomorrow and if everything's fine, I'll be home Sunday at the latest. My mother will keep Mikey and Anthony. Vinny Junior's in school and can stay by himself, but the baby—"

Day opened her mouth to speak but Beanie plowed on as if delivering a memorized speech. "The baby don't know my mother, see? She makes Renzo cry. Plus, she has arthritis bad so, if you can keep Renzo at your place this weekend and maybe a few days more, that'll be great. He loves you and Papa Joe and Luis and—" Beanie ran out of steam.

"It's fine. I love taking care of Renzo. He can stay with me as long as necessary. How about I bring him home with me tonight?"

Suddenly, Beanie deflated. She sank onto the couch and rested her legs on the coffee table. Her shorts ballooned around skinny thighs and a swollen blue vein snaked from knee to ankle.

Beanie squeezed Day's arm. "I'm glad that's over. I hate to impose on you what with you working all the time and the wedding coming up. How's that going, by the way? You and Bobby managing?"

Day shrugged. "I guess."

Beanie reached for another cigarette but held it between her fingers unlit. "You guess? What the hell's that mean? You're marrying the guy, for Christ's sake." Her eyes widened. "Wait a sec. You ain't broke up or nothing? Tell me you ain't broke up."

Day remained silent.

"Nah, you ain't," Beanie answered her own question. "You already measured me for that farty maid-of-honor dress ."

"It's a Ralph Lauren copy, elegant and understated," Day reminded her for the tenth time.

"You mean Ralph Lifshitz." Beanie made a face. "The dress you picked for the second greatest day of my life don't have a single ruffle, for Christ's sake. Anyway, stop distracting me. What's the deal with Bobby?"

Day widened her eyes with fake innocence. "No deal. Everything's great."

"Don't even, bitch. Bobby's pissed because you're working weekends, and I can't believe I'm saying these words, but you lost weight. What ain't you telling me?"

"Nothing, cuz. Let's go upstairs and get Renzo's things together."

Beanie put on an Evil Empire expression. Normally, the look was accompanied by a deep drag on her cigarette and a cone of smoke aimed like a death ray. Without the smoke, however, the effect was diluted. Beanie made up for it with four deadly words.

"You. Slept. With. Him."

"Who? Bobby?" Day exclaimed with false heartiness. "I sleep with Bobby every Saturday night, although, thanks to Renzo, I'll get a break tomorrow."

Beanie wouldn't be denied. "You know who I mean. That photographer you're all woke about. It don't make me no nevermind, but if it's like that with him, you two better do the nasty before you say your I dos."

"Why?"

Beanie shook a finger. "If you're hot to fuck the guy and don't, you'll regret it for the rest of your life."

Day knew when she was beaten. "I haven't slept with Lakota, but you're right, I want to. How can you tell?"

"It's all over you like stink on cheese," Beanie replied. "Trouble is, you ain't the old Day no more. I know it, Bobby knows it, but I'm afraid you don't know it yet. Not for nothing, cuz, but take my advice and get it on with Kokomo right away."

"Lakota," Day muttered

"Sorry. Why ain't his name Bill or something? Anyway, get it out of your system but don't start sticking feathers in your hair and doing a war dance– oops, sorry again, but you get me, right? Your traveling days are over, and from what you tell me, this Lakota guy's ain't never going to be over. Get it while you can, then let go when he goes."

Day wondered where Vinny had stashed the margarita mix. Hell, a straight shot of tequila was what she needed. "I'm going upstate on a shoot with Lakota," she said. "We'll be away all day, just the two of us. But what if he doesn't make a move?"

"You make it."

"What if he rejects me or thinks I'm too forward?"

Beanie rolled her eyes. "Jesus H. Christ, you got it bad. Okay, one at a time. First of all, what do you care what he thinks? You ain't never going to see him again after the sex, am I right? Second, he'll buddy up. Trust me, he wants it, they all do. And third, ain't you never got a good look at yourself? You're a winner, cuz, great face, nice ass, long legs, big boobs–"

"Big nose."

"Well, yeah." Beanie chuckled. "But you're hot. I'd do you myself if I was into pussy."

Vinny Jr. called down from upstairs. "Yo, you two. I can hear everything and I'm on Ma's side. Go for it, Aunt Day."

****

It was late when Beanie handed Renzo over to Day, along with three bulging bags of baby stuff, and one state-of-the-art car seat. She felt like a wraith in Day's arms when she hugged her to say goodbye.

"You're going to be fine, Beanie," she said.

"Yeah, course," Beanie replied. "And if I ain't, you get to keep Renzo."

Day gave Beanie a pretend punch in the arm. "I'll have my own little Renzo soon."

"Yeah, well, just let the Indian guy fuck your brains out then call it a day."

****

Bad things are like roaches; one in the soap dish means a million behind the medicine cabinet. Beanie's tests revealed an ovarian tumor. They'd done a biopsy and then a hysterectomy. Vinnie told Day that the cancer had spread but chemo and radiation would take care of it. He tried to smile when he said it but his face was ashen. Day's heart broke.

The new air conditioning system Papa had installed at Enchanted Gardens didn't work when the mercury topped ninety during a freak heat wave. The service man couldn't make it to the Bronx for a few days and sweltering customers went elsewhere. The owner of Flaming Vesuvius volunteered to host Hank the Cop's retirement party, originally planned for Enchanted Gardens. Day asked Hank to wait a couple of weeks so Papa could do it but he refused which ended his thirty-year friendship with Joe, such as it was. As a result, the Buick and Day's Forester collected a pile of parking tickets thick as a deck of cards and both vehicles were eventually towed. Joe found a paid lot adding to his already strapped finances and Day left her car in Beanie's driveway. Day and Luis put their heads together devising ways to attract customers to the restaurant. Day came up with Florentine Wraps, sautéed veggies in a pita, and Luis tried his hand at Caribbean Calzone, a Jamaican meat patty with ricotta and tomato sauce. Joe looked askance at these bizarre menu additions and business remained bad. One morning, Day turned on the tap and torrents of brown water gushed into the sink. Bobby sent his "guy" over immediately, but the restaurant had to close down during repairs and once they were made, Joe had to wait for the city's okay to reopen.

The bright spot through all of this was Beanie's recovery. Released from the hospital with a clean bill of health, she held court in her living room.

"Can you believe how fat I got?" Beanie asked Day, smiling brightly. "It's the freaking hospital tapioca. Never knew how much I liked that shit."

Day knew it wasn't fat but edema due to a laundry list of medications Beanie was taking, but said nothing. She stopped by the Siragusas every night after work sometimes bringing food from Enchanted Gardens and sometimes making dinner for the family herself. Day planned excursions to get Beanie out of the house, a movie, a drive in the country, the mall, until Beanie finally implored Day to get a life, and leave her the fuck alone. The hovering made her nervous and Day's cooking gave her gas.

Chapter 25

Between worry for Beanie and pseudo-porn dreams of Lakota, Day hardly slept. When the day of the shoot finally arrived, Lakota asked her to be at the cabin by six in the morning, and at five-thirty, she was parked on the gravel overlook where Marge Coots had first pulled over. Hardly aware of the underbrush and hanging vines, Day plowed to the cabin rewarded by the sight of Lakota in a pair of torn dungarees, shirtless, shoeless, flanked by the dogs. She had to stop to collect herself, swallow hard, and calm down. God, he was gorgeous! No man had a right to look so...so...what was the word? Handsome didn't cut it. Hot, appealing, sexy; those words were also lame.

Lakota didn't have a classic movie star face. His eyes were hooded, cheekbones broad, mouth wide, soft, tender and... Without thinking much about it, Day slipped off her engagement ring and zipped it into the pocket of her shorts. Lakota didn't have to know about Bobby; she wouldn't even mention the name. Why should she? Campbell Mountain was a different universe, a dimension of dreams and memories you leave behind when you wake up.

Shappa and Makawee caught wind of Day and descended.

"Hello, you two," she greeted them, walking toward Lakota's cabin and once again overwhelmed by an elemental sense of blissful unreality. Rainwalker Ridge sparkled in the valley below, cicadas hummed, and the air was heavy with honeysuckle, wood smoke, and the tang of pine tar. Day paused in reverential, isolated silence as Lakota walked over to meet her.

"Wait until you see it at night," he whispered, taking her bag and leading her onto the porch. "Mal says hello. Want some breakfast?"

"No thanks, but I could use a bathroom."

He pointed. "Around back, by the sweat lodge. You can't miss it." Lakota laughed at Day's look of dismay. "Never seen a sweat lodge? We'll go there after the shoot."

Day eased carefully into the tiny cedar outhouse wondering about Lakota's easy assumption that she would stick around for dinner after their work was done. She recalled his stumbling words over the phone, his nervousness as palpable as hers. What if he asked her to stay the night? Would she say yes? Despite Beanie's advice to "do the nasty", to get it over with and hurry home, Day wasn't sure. Sleeping with Lakota Campbell was bound to be a life-changing experience and Day had already changed her life three times from a young dreamer to Belmont dropout hungry for adventure, to a mature woman ready to shoulder reality. This was just a pit stop, she told herself, where she belonged at this moment, needed to be, and *should* be. There was something magical about Lakota just when it seemed all the magic had gone out of her life.

Day returned to the porch. Lakota was waiting for her in a kind of flack jacket, the pockets bulging with photographic paraphernalia, a camera around his neck. He eyed her shorts and tank top.

"I should have told you how to dress," he said. "Hold on."

Lakota went into the house and emerged with a mason jar of what looked like cooking oil. Pushing Day gently down onto the bottom step, he uncapped the jar, releasing a pungent aroma of citrus and camphor.

"What's that?"

Lakota hunkered down and poured some of the liquid into his cupped palm. "Bug balm. Old Injun remedy," he answered with a grin. "Good for chiggers, snakebite, and impotence."

He massaged the oil into her calf, smoothing the fragrant insect repellent over Day's legs, around her ankles, and under the straps of her sandals. His hands were rough on her bare skin, rough and stirring. She tensed and Lakota must have felt her muscles tighten because he stood abruptly.

"Rub it in thoroughly, just like I did," he said, holding out the jar. "Every place where your skin is exposed. The flies are fierce out here. I'll be in the Jeep."

Lakota strode off with Shappa and Makawee, leaving Day with an oddly charged feeling like she'd been plugged into something electric. She finished greasing, her hands no substitute for his, and moments later slid into the Renegade's driver's seat and started the engine.

Lakota directed Day through rugged hard pan, around dense copses, up verdant meadows, and down boulder-strewn fields dry as rusk. Occasionally, he'd tell her to stop while he selected a camera or changed a lens. He took several shots from the Jeep and occasionally climbed out and headed into the woods, the dogs yapping behind. Lakota studied angles, crouched, climbed trees, and spread flat on the ground, every movement smooth and graceful. Clouds of mosquitoes circled Day like pepper dust, never landing, and she was so transfixed she barely remembered to scribble on her pad the time, angle of the sun, and approximate location as he'd instructed. Sometimes Day made crude sketches and sometimes Lakota dictated combinations of letters, numbers, and technical names so rapidly she had to ask for a repeat. Then he'd grin, walk over to the Jeep, and do it himself, explaining what everything meant.

Lakota had brought along a skin of water but nothing else. By the time the sun was low in the western sky, Day's stomach was growling and a fine, uncomfortable layer of grit clung to her skin.

"Almost done?" she called.

Lakota hopped from a low branch and returned to the Jeep. "For now. But I want to show you something if you're not too tired—a special place."

Lakota was nothing if not cool but his face betrayed an unusual eagerness and Day happily followed him through dense woods, Lakota naming each tree they passed, spruce, ghost larch, sugar maple and pin oak, asking repeatedly if Day was all right. They emerged at a tranquil silver pond set in a mist-hung clearing. Filmy emanations floated like willow-the-wisps above the water and the air smelled damp and earthy. Lakota pulled Day against him and placed large, warm hands on her shoulders.

"Focus your eyes straight ahead and you'll see it," he said reverently.

Day trembled at the length of Lakota's long, hard

body pressed against her back and struggled to train her eyes on the mist. An eerie silence entombed her as the pond seemed to slowly rise above it, glowing pale and glossy as moonstone. A bird, its wings iridescent in the murky light, swooped down, skated across the surface, and fluttered off, leaving a gentle wake. The scene was magical, mythic. Pinned by the pressure of Lakota's hands and her own longing, Day felt connected to an ancient, primordial existence and eons of past and future lives. She sighed.

"What did I tell you?" Lakota breathed. "Isn't it something? I named it *Ohanzee Wahkan.* That means Sacred Shadow in Oglala. Only my father and Mal know about this place. And now, you."

"Thank you. It's beautiful."

"I knew you'd love it up here," Lakota said. "You have an ancient soul. You and I walked together in another life. I knew that the first time I saw you."

They stood for some time gazing into the hallowed shadows. Twilight stole the haze and filled the night with primal music; a lonely owl, fox kits crunching twigs, tree frogs. Enfolded in Lakota's arms, Day rested her head against his shoulder, her heart filled with stuporous longing even as her soul thrummed the inevitable clarity of truth.

This can't last; it isn't real.

It was dark when they returned to the cabin. Lakota prepared dinner and told Day that he had lived on the mountain with Ewan since he was a boy, just the two of them, roughing it in a lean-to. Then his father married Faye and they moved to a real house in the valley after Mal was born.

"You missed it up here on top of the world, didn't

you?" Day said.

"I did. I built this cabin in high school. Poor Faye used to trek up twice a week to pick up my laundry. When he got older, Mal stayed with me. My brother likes the quiet, too. We Campbell men are solitary."

Lakota lit candles and a kerosene lantern that hung from the rafters. He asked Day to shuck corn and set potatoes to boil on the two-burner propane stove.

"Your job takes you all over the world, doesn't it?" Day asked, relaxed and famished.

"For nine, ten months of the year, yes," Lakota replied. "I inherited wanderlust from my mother's people. But on the move or on the mountain, I like being alone." He winked at Day. "Unless the company's good."

"I spent most of my childhood reading in my room," Day confessed. "Papa and my cousin Albina are my best friends."

She recounted a little about Beanie's commonsense approach to life and her bravery in the face of illness. "I can't imagine a world without her. Beanie's my guiding star."

"You're lucky to have her," Lakota said. "I know people all over the world and I'm always happy to see them but they're not friends, not like you and Beanie. I never stick around in one place long enough."

They ate on the porch under the patient scrutiny of Makawee and Shappa. After dinner, Day rocked in a hammock while Lakota carried their plates to the kitchen. He blew out the lamps, settled in a chair next to her, and they talked late into the night about travel, the splendor of nature, and to Day's delight, pizza.

"This woman I know in Fiesole showed me how to

make *pizza capricciosa*," Lakota said. "I've never eaten anything so good. Do you cook, Day?"

"Not well but my father's a chef," she replied, wondering, *What woman*?

"I've eaten truffles in France, black rice in Spain, and foofoo in Ghana," Lakota mused. "This cabin is my home but so is the rest of the world."

Day chuckled. "I've never been out of the country."

Lakota held the hammock steady and smoothed a lock of hair from Day's forehead. "I'd love to take you with me on my next trip. We can eat our way across all seven continents."

"I'd be so fat," she said in a slightly shaky voice. Lakota's fingers smoothed her cheek and his hand cupped her chin.

"I'm due in Indonesia day after tomorrow," he said softly. "After that, who knows? Why don't you come with me?"

Come with you? Day moaned silently. *Oh Jesus, yes.*

Day's body felt light and drowsy with contentment. She closed her eyes and traveled with Lakota to Borobudur Temple in Indonesia, the Arc de Triomphe in Paris, icy fijords and burning deserts. It was wonderful; a wonderful and exciting pipe dream.

She smiled sheepishly and quipped, "Let's give each country a number, throw the dice, and go to the one it lands on." This was a game, wasn't it? They were just playing a game and soon it would be time to pick up her marbles and go home.

Lakota considered her suggestion seriously."I'm leaving nothing to chance. We'll start at Jakarta, the old port at Sunda Kelapa and then Jaya Ancol. They call Jaya the dreamplace. It's like an upside-down Disneyland. From there, we'll catch a steamer to the Arctic for polar summer. There's nothing like seeing ice floes in the middle of wildflowers and the sun in July is hotter than the tropics." Lakota's voice was hypnotic. "Heat gets inside of you, transforms you into a being of pure energy. You'll be more than human, know your cosmic insignificance yet be assured of a place in the grander scheme." He held Day's wide-eyed gaze. "You and I are forged links on a chain from time's beginning forward into the future. Nothing can break us apart. Am I scaring you?"

A little.

Day looked out at the endless, black sky. She wasn't in another busy city with another Paragon man. She was in Heaven with an angel who played the music of destiny. Staring into Lakota's wine-dark eyes and listening to his spellbinding voice, she was transported on a spiritual yet intensely visceral hegira.

"You're not scaring me, Lakota," Day said. "I love hearing you talk even when I don't understand a word you're saying."

Lakota threw back his head and laughed. "You're the real thing, Day, honest, questing, compassionate, beautiful. You have Teton blood somewhere in your lineage. I'm sure of it."

Beautiful. Lakota had called her beautiful. And tonight, content on his porch, stomach full, warm, and secure, Day *was* beautiful. She sighed, her lashes fluttered, and she drifted into daydreams. Soon the hammock's lulling sway sent her off to real dreams, if there was such a thing.

Chapter 26

Day opened her eyes and looked around. The horizon shimmered a radiant pink as the sun crested the line of hills. Where was she? What was this beautiful place? Oh, God. She was still on Campbell Mountain after spending the night in the hammock on Lakota's porch.

Day threw off the scratchy blanket and looked for her shoes. Papa would be worried; she had to go to the museum; Grace Nakamura might have discovered she had snuck out and fired her. The phone vibrated. Beanie probably, returning her call and waiting for the dish. Day dug into the pocket of her shorts and checked the screen. So many missed calls and messages, the two most recent from Nakamura. With growing anxiety, Day dialed voice mail and listened to Nakamura's surprisingly pleasant words. "My presentation was excellent. If I'm not mistaken, we shall be allotted a small increase in our operating budget next year. Not in Personnel, you understand, but I may be able to manage a new computer for you." With a sigh of relief that Nakamura was still at the conference and had no clue the office was unmanned, Day left a message for Papa and texted Beanie:—*I'm still upstate. TTYL.*—

Swallowing the knot in her throat, Day hopped off the hammock and was amazed that her muscles were neither sore nor stiff as she bent to tie her sandals.

There was no bedroom or bed in the cabin and Lakota, shirtless and still in the jeans he'd worn for the shoot, lay asleep on his stomach, a mound of blankets cushioning his long, lean body. His coil of hair had loosened and fell, dark and thick, against one shoulder and the muscles of his back pulsed rhythmically. How good it would be to lie down next to him and feel that golden smoothness against her skin. Day splashed her face with water from the bucket beside the sink and headed for the outhouse. She was on her way to the cabin when Lakota appeared in the doorway pulling on a white T-shirt.

"Good morning. We never made it to the sweat lodge," he said.

Day tried to calm her racing heart. Papa, Beanie, and the person she was going to marry, *what was his name?* were all waiting back in Belmont. But Day had done it again, leapt into the devil's mouth for a magnificent, dazzling, sensational man she'd never find the likes of again. She hadn't changed at all. She was still a starry-eyed adolescent searcher stuck in dreams.

"Thank you for dinner last night, Lakota. Everything was wonderful and I enjoyed working with you, but I really must go. You should have gotten me up."

Lakota gazed down from the top step. "Couldn't do it," he replied. "I liked having you on my porch all night." He walked over to her. "Let's sit in the sweat lodge for a while."

"No, that's okay." Lakota's nearness was making her tremble.

He picked specks of blanket lint from her arm. "The repellent oil is magic against mosquitoes, but it clogs the pores. You need to wash it off."

"You don't have a shower."

He laughed. "I have a sweat lodge. Trust me; a few minutes and you'll feel a lot better. It's like being reborn."

Day had to get back to the city. She couldn't stay, dare not stay, not a single moment longer. "I can't," she said. "I have to go to the office."

"By the time you get home, shower, change, and drive into the city,"—he pointed out with calculated logic— "the museum will be closed."

Lakota hadn't hidden her car keys or tied her to a tree. But even though he was stretching the truth a bit, something told Day not to argue the point. She reached down to refasten a loose strap on her sandal prepared to follow him to the sweat lodge, to the ends of the earth.

"Leave the shoes," Lakota said, scooping Day up in his arms and carrying her a short distance to a mud-covered hovel that looked like a cave. "Time to sweat," he said, gazing at her with dark intensity, his voice quivering.

He's as jumpy as I am.

"Is that it? The sweat lodge?" she asked when he set her down.

"Crawl inside and hand me your clothes," Lakota said. "Dip some water to wet the stones and sit. There's a blanket to wear when you're ready to come out."

Day regarded the tiny opening, about the size of Shappa and Makawee's dog flap. A faint aroma, like sage and cedar wood emanated from its depths.

"Where will you be?"

"I can go in next," Lakota replied. And then his eyes melted into hers. "Unless you want company."

Naked with Lakota in a tiny, fragrant burrow warm as a caress. Day was so ready for that. But it was wrong. She was engaged. Not married though, not yet, and everything about this trip, the misty lake, the hammock, the soft, yellow sunlight slanting through the pines; the whole scenario was unreal, a dream to carry her through life. Not to mention the man. Day looked at Lakota. Longing, hope, and vulnerability warred on his face. It was the vulnerability that did it.

"Come in with me," she said.

The sweat lodge was just tall enough to stand in and softly lit by the glowing circle of rocks at its center. Filaments of spice-scented smoke hung between the curved walls like a tranquil fog.

"Sit there, in the north," Lakota directed, indicating a spot to the right of the entrance. "It's the traditional women's place. I'll sit in the south facing you."

He shucked his T-shirt, and every cut and rolling muscle of his torso gleamed in the smoky light.

"You have to get undressed," he said levelly, his hands on his belt buckle. "God lives in those stones and when we pour water on them, he rises up as steam, enters our bodies, and gives us some of his divine nature before being absorbed back into the earth and sky."

Lakota's eyes bored into Day as he unbuckled his belt and stepped out of his jeans. She gulped at his magnificence and girth, and turned away to undress. Nervous as a virgin, she undid her bra and lowered her panties. Dropping down quickly, Day wrapped her arms around her knees, hiding as much nakedness as possible.

"Don't do that," Lakota breathed. "You're

beautiful."

Beautiful. Again that word on his lips.

Day followed Lakota's lead and curled her legs beneath her. What did Lakota see when he looked at her, she wondered, this enigmatic man who was himself beautiful in every way? Could she possibly be the lovely creature reflected in his eyes?

Lakota poured a stream of water onto the stones and they sighed like living beings. Immediately, Day was engulfed in a thick haze of vapor that whispered across the surface of her skin perfumed and soft as flower petals. She threw back her head and inhaled another scent, sweet grass and the dust of a desert plain. Day trembled as wavering animal shadows, coyotes and prong-horned elk leaped into her heart's field of vision. An eagle, talons curled, plummeted from a jagged cliff like a gyre, so close Day felt the whoosh of its golden wings.

"Oh!" she cried, flinching.

"What did you see?" Lakota asked. Only the fire pit separated them, but his words came from a great distance, from another world.

"I'm not sure," she whispered, afraid the exquisite vision might flee with the harsh sound of her voice. "A canyon, I think, and the valley below it. Animals are grazing, bison maybe, birds and smaller creatures, lizards, and ferrets with raccoon eyes. The colors are like jewels. It's magical."

"Are there people?"

To her amazement, Day realized there were people.

"This is crazy," she said. "But yes. They're dressed in animal skins and shaggy headdresses." She suddenly tensed. "What's in this haze? Am I hallucinating?"

"Maybe," Lakota answered, the outline of his form a boulder in the shadows. "But the *Oyate,* my ancestors, the Buffalo Men, lived in the Badlands a long time ago. I think that's who you see. They show themselves when they feel safe, when they trust the one reaching back to them from the aftertime."

Lakota wet the stones a second time. Day waited for the gentle swirl of mist and smoke but the steam that billowed up and encircled them was foul and choking, and the stones hissed like a cauldron of snakes. A pair of bestial yellow eyes emerged from a hail of snapping sparks.

"What is that?" she cried out, afraid.

"Don't move," Lakota warned. "It's Black Bear come to test my loyalty."

Lakota seemed to gather into himself, body straight and bronze as a yearling oak, hooded eyes staring through Day into the infinity of generations. A mere handbreadth across the fire seconds ago, Lakota was no longer present. In his place, a huge black bear growled. For a brief moment, Day's spine contracted and she wanted to run from the devouring beast. Then the air cleared and the comforting snuffle of Shappa and Makawee could be heard outside the lodge. Lakota broke his trance and asked if Day was okay.

She smiled tentatively. "I think so. You went someplace for a while. Where?"

"I was with you," Lakota answered. "But not here. We were together in the before time." He offered Day his hand. "Your blood was pure then; so was mine. It isn't now and that makes Black Bear angry."

"Who's Black Bear?"

"My totem animal and a pain in the ass."

Lakota rose and brushed sand onto the fire. "Black Bear hates that I'm mixed." He pulled Day up and held her, smoothing his big, rough hands across her naked back. "Time to cool off."

She gasped at the swell of his desire on her naked belly. But she didn't resist. "That won't cool me off," she said.

Lakota lifted her so easily that Day felt like a zephyr and ducked into the rising morning, running wildly through waist-high poppies and drifts of yellow jessamine. In a field of wheatgrass, he laid her down and loved Day with the restrained ferocity of a hunter, touching her in places no man ever had before, his mouth on every part of her, murmuring words she didn't understand that sang in her soul.

Again and again, Lakota claimed Day's body with his until the air grew thick and feral and the sun peaked, high and hot above them.

Chapter 27

Day and Beanie sat on the front porch.

"So then he said, 'Come with me,'" Day explained.

"And you—ah, came?" Beanie asked.

It was a command performance for Queen Beanie. *Don't stop no place, don't go home,* Beanie had responded to Day's message. *Come right here or I'll kill you.*

Dutifully, Day had complied, remembering to slip her engagement ring back on seconds before mounting her cousin's front steps.

"Oh yeah. I came," Day answered. "We both did, so many times I lost count. He never, you know, stopped. "

Beanie was wide-eyed and overflowed with questions. "Outside on the grass? Was it soft? The grass, I mean, not him. He had to be like a rock. Did it hurt? Him, not the grass. How long? Not his thing; that must have been—Shit!" Beanie lit a cigarette. "I'm getting confused. This is better than porn. How many times?"

"I don't know how many times we made love or how long we were out there. I lost track and I'm sore all over. But it wasn't like that," Day answered. "We didn't only make love. We talked and talked. Lakota told me about Black Bear, his jealous totem animal, and about sunrise over Kilimanjaro and the market in

Rouen, and Rome at night when the Coliseum lights up like a giant birthday cake. He says there's a *penzione* on the Viale in Rome where, if you sit on the balcony just before dawn, you can hear Julius Caesar tossing dice into the Tiber. I told him it was the Rubicon not the Tiber and that throwing dice was a metaphor."

"Metaphor? Geeze." Beanie snorted. "You sure know how to kill a mood."

"He likes that about me," Day said. "That I'm not phony or pretentious or anything."

Beanie's expression changed from eager interest to wariness. "You don't buy none of that shit, do you?"

Day shrugged. "Maybe not. My judgment's not always the best when it comes to men."

"You think?" Beanie rose and tossed her cigarette over the railing. "Let's go inside. I'm cold."

It was hot on the porch, but Beanie wore a sweater, holding it around her shrunken frame with tiny, bloodless fingers. She looked shriveled and very ill, but the doctor proclaimed that chemotherapy and radiation were going to work. Vinny believed it and passed on the good news to everyone. Beanie never said much. If you asked how she was, she got cross and said, "Fine. Now shut up."

Inside, Beanie sat irritably under a blanket and reached for a pack of cigarettes. She pulled out one and immediately threw it onto the coffee table, muttering under her breath about, "goddamn taste buds" and "a stiff shot of gin." She harangued Vinny to "Get these goddamn kids as far away from me as possible. Drown them if you have to," and the boys scattered without protest. Then she subsided into brooding silence. Day said nothing; there was nothing to say. The best way to deal with Beanie's illness was to be close and quiet. Vinny turned off the TV and took a beer into the backyard. Beanie blew him a kiss and sat quietly with Day until she suddenly blurted, "Fuck me!"

"What is it?" Day cried, alarmed.

"I'm a meddler; worse, I'm a dumb, stupid, head up my ass, no business in anybody's business stick-nose meddler. I should have never told you to sleep with Big Bear."

Day swallowed a grin. "It's not your fault, Beanie. I wanted to sleep with Lakota and I did. I'd known I would since the minute we met."

Beanie held her head and moaned. "I pushed you so you'd get it out of your system. I want you to stay in Belmont and not take off for–" She grimaced. "—where the buffalo roam."

"Stop that," Day admonished. "If it's anybody's fault, it's mine. Lakota is awesome and I think all that smoke in the sweat lodge got me high. But see?" Day waved her re-ringed fingers. "I'm still engaged. I'm still going to marry Bobby."

Beanie glanced from under lowered lashes. "For real?"

"For real," Day said. "I've already told you that Lakota's not the marrying kind. At best, we might have a great time for a few months and then I'll miss Renzo and want to come home. And I am so over that leaving and coming back nonsense."

Beanie grunted something that may have been approval or pain, and Day stopped talking about Lakota.

"You feeling any better, cuz? You look okay," Day lied.

"I feel like fuck," Beanie replied sullenly. "Why you changing the subject?"

"I'm not. It's just that I'm running late to meet Bobby at Ombre and he hates that."

"Don't you ever get sick of that place?"

"Bobby likes it. And the view of the water is spectacular."

"Nice as the Rubiyat?" Beanie cracked a half-smile and then started wringing her hands.

"Rubicon. You sure you're okay? Want me to call Vinny?"

"I'm great," Beanie answered. "But one tiny little thing just so I'm sure you stay strong."

Day sighed. "Go ahead."

"I had an affair after Mikey was born."

Day's jaw dropped. "Get out!"

"Hand to God," Beanie swore. "Me and him used to walk the woods behind Orchard Beach and he'd read me poetry while I took off my clothes. He said my stretch marks were elegiac, whatever that means."

Day kept the doleful meaning of the word to herself. "Who was he? What happened?" she asked.

"Just a guy, different like yours—skinny, cute, not from around here. But then life happened and I ended it because I was being a jerk risking a good husband, and at the time, my three kids."

"Do you still think about him?"

Beanie's eyes, small and shiny as pebbles in a river, darkened for a second. "Nah; not until just now. Well, hardly at all." She blinked. "And you'll forget all about your hunky photographer once you and Bobby settle down."

Day felt constrained to mention that Beanie's affair

had taken place long after she and Vinny had been settled down for years.

"I'll cop to that," Beanie said. "But the point is, I wised up. I was mad for the sex and the whole danger/stranger thing, but it's over and I'm glad."

"How come you never told me any of this before?"

"You was never around long enough," Beanie accused. "And I was ashamed. Believe me, that ain't a good feeling."

"And you're telling me now because?"

"Because…" Beanie looked up at the ceiling. "Because I got to get this out before I, no, before you–"

"Before I mess up again?" Day volunteered.

But that wasn't it. Beanie wanted Day to do the right thing so she could die in peace. No matter what Vinny and the doctors said, Beanie knew the truth. A year would be a gift but Beanie doubted she had that long.

The air between the cousins grew heavy and dark. Day's eyes started to well and she jumped up before Beanie could notice.

"What time is it? I have to go."

"Right. Your date," Beanie said. "But just a minute, okay? I got one teeny tiny sermon to lay on you. I'll keep it short, I promise." Beanie wrapped the edges of her too-big sweater around her and spoke as if choosing each word. "Your iron man, La-ko-ta," she pronounced the syllables carefully. "He's like–ah, let me see–he's like a dozen Dandy Donuts."

"What?"

"Just shut up and listen, okay? Fresh out of the box, them donuts look great and taste like heaven. The first bite, you think you never had it so good. But damn if they don't go dry and gluey quicker than Vinny can chug a Bud. And they're murder on your system, am I right?"

Day nodded. "Yes, so?"

"So you're better off with plain old bread," Beanie continued. "It tastes good and don't never go bad." She rested a pale hand on Day's arm. "My Vinny may not be anybody's idea of a hero, but he's always around, know what I mean? He's great with the kids, works all day in the truck and still has a little leg left over for me at night." Beanie's hold on Day tightened to a grip. "Well, when Vinny and me used to-when we used to– Never mind. Anyway, all that wild shit with your wild man lasts for today but it's tomorrow that counts." The pressure of Beanie's tiny hand was almost prehensile as if she'd channeled all the strength of a failing body into her fingers. "You and Bobby got a million tomorrows ahead of you," Beanie went on. "That's what makes up a life."

Day rubbed at the red finger marks on her skin ""I understand, Beanie. Thanks."

"And don't let no man tell you how to be. You're Deanna Maria Danese from the Bronx. If you got to change anything about that for a guy, he ain't the right one."

"I know," Day nodded. "I'm not running after Lakota. I'm marrying Bobby and staying right here with you."

Chapter 28

Day worked on composing wedding vows. She disliked spouting personal, moony stuff in front of people, but Bobby wanted to, "pledge our love," as he put it, preferably with a microphone to the entire neighborhood.

"Write my speech, babe," he urged her. "Tell everybody you're my horse and I'll ride you till the day I die. Just kidding," he added, seeing the expression on Day's face. "But I can't write for shit. I showed my mother a bunch of stuff straight from my heart and she pissed her pants and said it was gay."

Day spent lunch hours at her desk to come up with credible vows, something about being blessed to spend the rest of her life with Bobby Leone, a good friend and good provider who was also…ah…um…good. What else? Bobby was handsome and dressed nice. Was he a good lover? Day stared at the screen. Well, his idea of foreplay was just that, an idea. His dibs and dabs to get her in the mood were perfunctory and ended before they began. That was actually fine with Day, who just wanted to get the sex over with and go to sleep.

She deleted what she'd typed and started over. *Wedding Vows,* Day wrote in underlined caps. Ten minutes later, she studied the words on the screen. *Thank you, Bobby, my mate for life, I'll love you forever and be your wife.* Day sighed and pressed

Delete. She could have written an epic poem about Lakota. Bobby Leone was a limerick.

No matter where Day was or what she was doing, Lakota intruded, on her thoughts, her actions, her life; Lakota and Enchanted Gardens. The restaurant, if not on the verge of collapse, was certainly sliding toward it. Papa claimed things would improve over the holidays but the holidays, not to mention Day's February wedding, were fast approaching with no significant upturn in sales. Bobby kept telling her to chill; he was working on a deal with the bank and by next summer, Day would be pregnant, anyway, with better things to worry about. But she imagined the Carciofolo boys lurking behind every corner, and it turned out she wasn't far from wrong.

****

One Saturday while Day was working in the restaurant, Carmine Carciofolo, the community Don, walked right into Enchanted Gardens like he owned it, wearing a pinstripe suit and silky white-on-white tie. With a courtly bow, the Cobra took cordial note of the recent and recurring absence of the presence of the *po-leeece* occasioned by the regrettable defection to a rival establishment and subsequent retirement of dipshit Hank the Cop. That was the way Carmine talked, Brit Box with a Bronx flair. The establishment in question to which Mr. Joseph Danese's disloyal former friend had fled, Carmine believed, was Flaming Vesuvius, but he couldn't be sure. "All these pizza jernts look alike."

Carmine declined Day's routine courtesy of a seat in the back room and a cup of espresso, but helped himself to a soda from the cooler and hiked cheerfully and rather gracefully considering his girth, onto a stool.

After flicking invisible specks from the counter, he allowed as to how Hank the Cop's absence was most unfortunate for Mr. Danese since ruffians and thieves were known to prowl Belmont after dark, and occasionally, Carmine crossed himself remorsefully, in broad daylight.

"Why just last Easter," he explained, "my dear friend Rocco Randazzo, you know Rocco, drives a Cadillac Escalade? Poor Rocco met, in that very same vehicle, with an unfortunate accident. Luckily, he sustained only minor injuries—a head gash, broken collarbone, and cracked ribs, nothing serious. But the car?" Carmine's downturned mouth and watery eye signaled utter distress. "Total destruction. *Che lastima*." A crying shame.

Day's legs gave out under her. With trembling fingers, she gripped the stool next to Carmine's. "What are you saying, Don Carciofalo? About serious accidents?"

He smiled beatifically. "Nothing, nothing, Miss Danese. I'm sure my other dear friend, Joe Danese, and his precious Buick are completely safe and will in no way meet such a fate as the unhappy one of Rocco Randazzo." Carmine paused demonically. "Nor should you."

Day recalled several monthly entries in Papa's ledger: *CC $500*, and asked the question straight out.

"You want more money, Don Carmine?"

He opened his smooth, pink, innocent palms. "No, no, Miss Danese. What do you take me for? I had a little chat with my good friends at Farenga Brothers and I merely wish to presume upon your company, upon your kind and may I say, beautiful company, to discuss a small matter of importance considering your father's persistent refusal to remove his head from his ass."

Day swallowed. The Don flashed several gold teeth.

"Joe must settle up before Farenga settles the score. *Capisci?*" Carmine pulled a silver Mont Blanc pen and a small, well-thumbed notepad from his breast pocket. "Now, you mentioned money." A throat-clearing cough. "As President of the Benevolent Friends of Belmont, I have been charged with the difficult task of restoring to its former glory our esteemed and gracious community, which has of late been going to shit." He uncapped the pen. "Donations help the work. How much shall I put you down for?"

Day knew exactly what the Cobra wanted. "How much does Papa owe?"

"Ah, Miss Danese," Carmine drawled, licking his finger and flipping pages. "Each time you leave us, you come back smarter than ever."

The Don named an amount that was a good deal more than Day anticipated. She balked politely. Carmine shrugged and mentioned fees, sales tax, and a service charge of unfortunate but necessary pay-offs.

He tapped his pen on a check mark next to Joe's name. "So little. Mr. Danese should pay more but see? I give a discount."

Papa's page was a warren of cross-outs, arrows, and red lines. The note, *Paid by BL* was prominent next to several sums and Day guessed Bobby had paid those. She wrote a personal check, handed it over, and tried not to grimace when Don Carciofalo kissed her hand.

That night, Day confronted Papa. "We need to talk."

He frowned. "Something wrong? Albina sick again? You and Roberto fight? The job?"

Day took the key from its hiding place under the paperweight and unlocked her father's desk.

"*Ue!*" he cried. "How you know I hide the key there? No touch!"

"Sit down, Papa. I have to ask a few questions."

Joe's expression turned obstinate. "And I no have to answer."

"Yes, you do."

Day told him about Carmine Carciofolo's visit. Joe frowned. "I paid what you owed," she went on, shaking a handful of invoices in his surly face. "And I paid all these other bills too, four, no five, of them: property insurance, the damn electric bill—you got a turn-off notice." She threw the bills back on the desk. "Luis told me the payroll taxes were in arrears and the penalty was huge."

"*Mascalzone,*" Joe muttered.

"You're in trouble, Papa," Day continued. "And in danger. The Carciofolo boys torched Randazzo's car. Think of what they'll do to the Buick if you keep making Farenga mad. And to you too."

Joe paled and rubbed his chest.

"I'm sorry, Papa. I don't want to add to your stress, but if Enchanted Gardens isn't at least breaking even, why not retire? Bobby wants to tour Italy for our honeymoon. Come with us. We'll drop you off in *paese* and pick you up on the way home. You always tell me how beautiful it is there."

Joe apparently heard only one word. "Retire? You crazy?" His eyes turned blank; his face hardened. "You mama and me, we build this restaurant together. I never retire. I die and you do what you want."

Papa had begun to talk a lot about death although his doctor would say nothing to Day beyond, "Tell Joe to rest and take his pills."

"The restaurant is too much work for you," Day argued. "You're beating a dead horse."

"Dead horse? Enchanted Gardens win Triple Crown; good food, good people, good living."

"It's not a good living, Papa, if you can't live on it." "

Joe slashed his hand through the air. "*Basta,* enough. I no listen no more. The restaurant she my business. You go upstairs and mind yours."

****

When Day wasn't rewriting her vows for the thousandth time, or pondering Carmine Carciofolo's taunts, she worried about the restaurant, Papa's heart, and Beanie's worsening condition. Day's salary at the museum wasn't enough to pay her bills and Papa's bills, but she had to do something. Her father was wasting energy on a losing enterprise and Beanie was just wasting away. Day felt powerless to help either of them. The best respite from stress was supposed to be a placidly empty mind. But now, whenever Day was about to dissolve into a puddle of worry, she filled her head with images of Lakota shirtless and strong, engulfing her in steel arms and breathing husky endearments. The sun reminded her of his glowing skin, the night sky of his quiet calm, and the summer rain, sliver against the streetlights, of Lakota's shining hair bracketing her face when he lay her down and claimed her.

At the museum, Day finished the Hecate County

article and sorted through Lakota's pictures. He had emailed her a photographic account of the day in two separate files, one labeled *For the Newsletter* and the other *For You.* Lakota had taken Nakamura to dinner at Nobu and whatever he'd said about the shoot convinced her he'd done it alone. Day almost felt sorry for lovesick Grace Nakamura as she saved Lakota's stunning compilation of bucolic landscapes in the *For the Newsletter* file and emailed them to Nakamura. The pictures in the *For You* file were even more stunning and mostly of Day. In awe, she gazed at her likeness rocking in the hammock shoes off, hugging the dogs, and perched on the hood of the Jeep, legs shiny with insect repellent. The last two photographs were magical. Taken at Ohanzee Wahkan, they were mostly close-ups of Day's serene face haloed in the misty light. One was a shot of her and Lakota in the Jeep, their arms entwined, relaxed, spent from love-making, and utterly happy. Day was about to email the *For You* batch to herself, then decided it was better to send it with a note to Beanie. Bobby had an unfortunate habit of snooping.

Filled with wonderful Hecate County memories but still hungry, Day went to lunch. When she returned, a young girl was seated at her desk behind a nameplate reading, *Miss Midori.*

"Yes?" the girl asked Day with a smile. "Can I help you?"

"That's my desk," Day replied politely, retrieving her nameplate from the bookshelf. She pointed. "If you're the new secretary, your desk is over there."

"I am not a secretary," Miss Midori said stiffly. "I'm the new Assistant Editor."

Day froze. *What?* Then she noticed a box on the

floor, its top taped closed. The shopping bag she kept folded in her bottom drawer was beside it, a miscellany of Day's personal items sticking out the top; tampons, hand lotion, and a half-eaten bag of potato chips resealed with a paper clip. A sliver of fear pierced her stomach, churning her lunch of falafel and honey cake into sour mush. Midori's cheeks turned bright red. She pressed the call button on her desk phone and Nakamura flew down the hall.

"What are you doing here, Miss Denise?" Nakamura demanded. "Did you not read my text?"

"I, no, I," Day stammered. "I just got back from lunch."

"You shall have to pay for that lunch since you are no longer an employee of the museum. You've been fired."

"Fired?" Day cried. "I don't understand."

But with a sudden sinking feeling, she did understand. Nakamura was waving a sheaf of printouts. The jury of one had found Day guilty and sentenced her to death. '

"I misjudged you, Miss Denise," Nakamura said tightly, slapping the *For You* file on the empty desk. "It pains me to make errors. You are the cause of my pain."

Day glanced at the pictures she had emailed to Beanie, or *thought* she had. Obviously, she'd sent Beanie the newsletter pix and her boss the damning ones. The shot of Day and Lakota embracing in the Jeep was prominent. Nakamura had enlarged and separated it from the others.

Day paled but controlled her tone. "I thought Lakota explained why he took me to Hecate County. He was only thinking of you. Please, can we just sit down and talk about this?"

"There is nothing to talk about, Miss Denise," Nakamura replied stiffly. "The subject is closed. You have not worked out."

"How? In what way?" While there was no law in any book anywhere that gave a boss the right to fire an employee over a man, that's exactly what Day's boss was doing.

Nakamura's usually bloodless face turned scarlet. Her small, dark eyes narrowed to slits. "I work with Loco, not you. Loco and I are colleagues, partners, friends. How dare you presume to take my place. As if you could, as if anyone could."

Miss Midori mewed and sank so deeply into her chair that only the top of her head was visible.

"Sit up straight, Midori," Nakamura commanded, crumpling up the photographs. "You have work to do. Start by throwing out these abominations. And you, Miss Denise," Nakamura ranted on. "You forced Loco to become a victim of your treachery and wasted his time with your silly flirtation. Don't bother to deny it. I've seen you cajoling. As if a man of his caliber could ever be seduced by someone crass as you while I–" She seemed to realize she had gone too far and clamped her lips shut.

"It wasn't just flirtation, Mrs. Nakamura," Day muttered, furious, all hope lost.

Day gathered up her possessions and was nearly out the door when Grace Nakamura shot a final arrow.

"Let this be a lesson to you in your next job," she taunted. "Not that you'll ever get one in any museum or in any institution that does business with this one. I'll see to that."

It was vindictive, uncalled for, and unfair. Day boiled over and slammed down the box. Miss Midori jumped.

"I'm leaving," Day retorted. "But once and for all, my name is not Denise. It's Danese, three syllables, Dah-nay-zay." She took a step closer. Nakamura backed up. "Lakota pronounces it perfectly. When we spent the night together in his cabin, he told me it was beautiful, as beautiful as me."

Day drove home in a trance and parked in the loading zone. Just let the new cop try to give her a ticket. Upstairs, her whole body was shaking. She dug for her phone and punched in Lakota's number. He didn't answer. Standing in her coat and scarf, mind blank to everything but an urgent, crying need, she redialed, praying Lakota would answer. Day needed to hear his voice, those deep cadences that enveloped her like a warm blanket, needed to connect with him, even distantly, even for a few moments.

But as ever, Lakota, the elusive chimera, wasn't available. Maybe he didn't exist, maybe Day had conjured him up, another Paragon dream, powerful, alluring, and too seductive to be real. She poured a glass of wine wishing it was something stronger, and was padding to the Jacuzzi when the phone rang. It had to be Bobby. He always called at the wrong time; no, he just always called. She answered without a hello. "Not now, Bobby. Call me tomorrow."

The voice on the other end made her head spin.

"Day? You just called me. This is Lakota."

Chapter 29

Lakota hadn't left for Indonesia; he was still in Hecate County. Day fired up the Forester and hit the thruway. The night sky was lowering and what Day had thought were stars turned out to be snowflakes. As they thickened, she slowed to a crawl, peering nervously through a curtain of white. Lakota had warned of a blizzard, said that they might be snowed in, and offered to meet her at Rosalie's with the snowmobile. But in Day's fevered imagination, her lover was always standing on the porch, arms spread wide in a seductive welcome. How often she had imagined running through the meadow, being lifted, spun around, and set gently down on the nest of grass and blankets that smelled of mint and pine bark.

Lost in daydreams, Day nearly missed the exit. She skidded along rutted switchback roads until reaching the one that led up Campbell Mountain. Heavy snow mounded on the trees like cotton batting and she would have missed the lay-by leading to Lakota's cabin if it weren't for his snowmobile barely visible under drifts of white. Day first smelled then saw the smoke from the cabin's chimney threading above the treetop. Setting the emergency brake, she put on gloves and climbed out into the arctic freeze. Christ, it was cold. Day pulled down her hat, wrapped her scarf tightly, and dug into the wind for the final trek through the woods.

Anticipation fueled her ascent. Day's cheeks flamed and her heart pounded as every trudging footfall brought her closer to Heaven. But minutes later, she had to stop and catch her breath. Ten more minutes passed before Day had to pause again and get her bearings. Dense woods loomed on either side of her, snow was sheeting and the trail behind was as indistinguishable as the one ahead. She no longer saw smoke and smelled nothing but the bracing, slightly alkaline tang of glacial air. Her toes were fast becoming numb, and her fingers were stiff as icicles. The coat she had worn to work was an unlined pea jacket and although she had remembered boots, they were ankle-high and at the moment, filled with snow. Damn, was ever a man so hard to reach?

A prickle of doubt crawled up Day's spine. She had been walking steadily along the trail through the woods, or what she thought was the trail, and should be at the top by now. This was taking too long. Had she accidentally veered off the invisible path, actually parked at the layby or just pulled over at a snow-masked widening of the road? It was impossible to tell; everything looked white. Another quick glance around revealed nothing familiar, no recognizable terrain, only miles of stark, unrelieved blankness, eerie, ghostly, and forbidding. Day wondered if this was even happening? Maybe she had fallen asleep and was having a nightmare in the Jacuzzi as the water cooled.

"Where am I, Mama?" she bleated. "Are you there? Help me."

Taking a deep, painful breath, Day planted her feet firmly and willed herself to move, bending her knees, lowering her head and straining against the shrieking wind. After a minute more of bone-breaking torture, she wiped away ice tears, threw down her tote bag and sank on top of it, slapping numbed cheeks with frozen gloved hands and stomping feet she no longer felt. Panic crept in. This was no Jacuzzi wet dream; this was real. She was alone and lost.

The wind intensified and began to eddy stinging swirls of snow into Day's face. *I'm the little match girl*, she mused dismally. *Except I don't have any matches to start a bonfire and send up smoke signals. I'll die here and centuries later, archaeologists will find my corpse, beautiful and preserved. They'll call me the Ice Maiden and YouTube will run the video.*

Day struggled to her feet and slogged on. A few more steps, she told herself, not knowing which way led up to the cabin, which down to the car where she could at least turn on the heater and wave the phone around for a signal. The wind howled like mad dogs, louder and louder until it seemed as if the hound of Baskervilles haunted Campbell Mountain. In fact, Day thought she saw ghost dogs bounding toward her, kicking up sprays of snow. She didn't realize until they were almost upon her, barking excitedly, that it was Shappa and Makawee.

"Oh, my God! You guys!" she cried, hugging their warmth. "I'm so glad to see you."

Lakota, buried head to foot in shearling, wrapped his arms around Day and carried her to the cabin.

"You're frozen," Lakota said, setting her down by the fire and pulling off her shoes and socks. He rubbed her tingling skin with big, warm hands. "Sorry, there's no brandy. I don't use alcohol."

"Keep doing that and I'll warm up," she said,

shivering.

"No, you won't. First storm of winter is always the hardest one to take. Blood's not thick enough yet. Come on. Let's go."

He extended a hand and she took it. "Where?"

"To the sweat lodge."

He has to be joking. "That's outside."

"It's important you heat up fast and deep. The sweat lodge is the only way." Day's coat was by the fire. She reached for it. "You won't need that, or anything else," Lakota said. "Don't you remember?"

"Naked?" Day gulped. "Are you crazy? It was summer last time—a hundred degrees outside."

Lakota lifted her again in one swift, easy motion. "Let's go, tenderfoot. We can strip in the lodge."

He waded easily through the snow and then nudged Day into the small opening of the sweat lodge. Inside, it was exactly as she remembered, steamy, hot, and but for the bullseye of glowing stones, tenebrous with moving shadows. Day felt Lakota beside her, solid and close, and heard his steady breathing. Her own breaths, ragged and sharp, gave away the nervous desire warming her blood. Lakota's hand stroked the sleeve of her sweater.

"Can I help you take this off?" he said.

Seeing Lakota again, touching him, smelling the spice of his body, smoky and sweetly feral; it was too much. Day turned into him and he grasped her, his mouth roaming her, kissing and sucking and biting. Day reached under his shirt to feel the ridges of Lakota's muscles and bare skin, hot as her own now. He wasn't a figment of her romantic imagination; he was real and she was in his arms, consumed, beloved, wanted.

Lakota tugged Day's sweater and bra over her head and pinioned her arms, tasting her breasts, teasing her pearled nipples with his tongue. She moaned as he slid off her slacks and panties and lay her on the hard earth. His breath quickened.

"Day," he rasped, shucking his clothes and wetting the stones. In the hiss and flare of the fire, Lakota's deep animal eyes devoured her. "You're like *Woman Who Walks With Stars*" he murmured. "Brave and fierce and soft as a rainbow."

She pulled him atop her, opening to him when he entered her, filling her, the whole of her dying and reborn with each powerful thrust, the heat of him and the sacred stones searing her soul. They loved through the night, the scent and sweat of their passion filling the small cave, sinking through the stones to the before-time and rising with the smoke into the future.

****

Day awoke to Lakota deep inside of her again, rocking slowly, deliciously as the moon rose and lowered. They made love until the stones burnt dry and the water bucket emptied, and returned to the cabin, naked, barefoot, warm.

On the hearth rug, Lakota pressed the length of him against Day, flesh cleaving unto flesh, and whispered, his mouth at her ear, "I love you."

A shadow gripped Day's heart. Lakota saw and his eyes darkened. "You don't want me to say it."

He wasn't like the others, Day's so-called paragons, the ordinary men she'd imbued with majesty to justify her own weaknesses. Lakota was a true paragon. She didn't have to make him up, furnish him with false attributes. Day covered her face and felt him leaving her, felt a chill on her skin despite the blazing fire. When she looked again, Lakota was cross-legged on the blanket.

"Tell me," he said.

Day had to explain. She'd fled to Campbell Mountain to unburden herself to someone who wouldn't judge, who took her as she was and, she swallowed hard, *loved* her for it. Day studied Lakota for a long moment, his dark hair gleaming in the firelight, his muscles bunched with tension.

"I lost my job. Mrs. Nakamura fired me."

His jaw hardened but Day didn't let him speak. Nakamura wasn't the problem. Lakota deserved the truth.

"I'm engaged to be married."

He didn't move, not a muscle. Day laid her cheek against the hardness of his shoulder blade and spoke into the flames about her determination to end the pain she caused herself and everyone she cared for with her many escapes to imaginary meccas of perfection. Then she told Lakota about Bobby.

"I don't love him," she said."Not in the way I should. But I've known him since we were kids and he proposed and,"—she bit back tears— "He's steady and hard-working and wants what I want, a home and children. He'll never leave me."

Lakota reached an arm behind him and held her. "I can't promise you any of those things, Day. I–I don't want children."

"I know that," she said softly. "I didn't come here to force myself on you. I would never–that's not me." Despite the heat, Day shivered. "I'm scared I'll mess up again. My father's business is falling apart, and my cousin's cancer is getting worse. Sometimes I think my wedding is the only thing keeping her alive." Day began to sob. Lakota pulled her around to him and held her tightly. "I just had to see you one more time," Day confessed through tears. "The thought that in February my whole life is going to change, that I'm going to belong to somebody else while you'll still be in the same world, still eating and sleeping and taking pictures, but far away from me, so far we never could–"

Lakota stopped her words with a kiss. "It's all right, Day," he murmured, his lips roaming her cheeks, her eyelids, her hair. "I understand. We understand each other. That's why it's so good between us." He stroked her and kissed away the tears. "Don't be sad, we have this, we have now." He cradled her, his mouth warm and soft, moving across her body, loving her.

In the high, pale rays of the Arctic moon, they slept entwined as the room cooled. Toward morning, Lakota rose quietly and covered Day with a blanket. When she awoke, he was gone.

Chapter 30

February, Day's wedding month, was a disaster. For starters, it was a constant balancing act with Bobby. He wanted them to live in the new hi-rise with floor-to-ceiling windows overlooking the medical center, or a semi-attached two-story on the Parkway. Day said no to both. His third option, a crumbling Tudor off Shore Road, was huge and dark, and way over-priced. When Day said no to that as well, Bobby took offence. They argued, exhausting for Day who had to choose her words, and energizing for Bobby who picked up steam with every insult. By the time Day finally gave in, the house had gone to somebody else and Bobby, as usual, nursed his grudge for a few hours and then, miraculously, proclaimed Day a genius. Why hadn't he thought of it? They could live in his mother's house. It would make her happy and he had put a lot of work into the basement apartment. Bobby was so pleased with the idea that Day suspected it might have been the plan from the beginning.

Another disaster was Beanie. Her health was deteriorating and at the final wedding gown fitting, she looked emaciated, and nearly fell off the mirror platform.

"It's these goddamn shoes," Beanie grunted.

Beanie had chosen to walk down the aisle in a pair of open-toed bootie pumps that resembled something one might wear to an S&M rave—needle heels, three instep buckles, and a chain that wrapped around the ankle. Beanie claimed they were from a designer who went by the initials SH. "And it don't stand for stank ho," she snapped when Day remarked that the shoes didn't go with her elegant maid-of-honor dress.

Beanie countered that if she had to wear that goddamn shit-brown maid of honor dress she was goddamn going to goddamn accessorize it with sexy shoes.

"First of all, the dress isn't brown," Day replied. "The color is called autumn leaves. It's orangey-gold, earthy and—"

"It looks like the inside of Renzo's diaper when he eats my mother-in-law's lasagna."

The fitter's face was a Noh mask. Day decided to lift the mood. "The color is very pretty on you, Beanie."

That was a lie. Beanie made her *don't even* face, and wobbled in front of the trifold mirror while the fitter took in yet another inch at the bodice. The capacious folds of the skirt, meant to cascade from under the breasts like a waterfall, billowed unattractively from Beanie's skeletal frame. The long, narrow sleeves bunched and drooped, and the trumpet-shaped hem, slightly longer in back than in front to suggest a delicate train, trailed on the floor like discarded laundry.

"Can we fix the bottom?" Day asked the fitter.

Beanie hiked up the dress. "Yeah," she said. "Make it shorter to show the shoes." She stuck out a toe and then suddenly, without warning, grabbed her head with both hands and hissed through clenched teeth. "Jesus Effing Christ."

"What's the matter?" Day asked. "Your face is all red."

Beanie grimaced and folded into a crouch.

"Beanie!" Day kneeled beside her. "What is it?"

"I don't know," Beanie gasped, vigorously rubbing her temples. "I get these pains all of a sudden." She moaned, took several deep breaths, and then smiled feebly. "It's gone now. Help me up, cuz."

Day suggested they cut the fitting short. But after a glass of water, Beanie revived. She approved of the beribboned headpiece and offered to spring for dinner at Hunan Panda. Back in the car, however, Beanie begged off, complaining of dizziness.

"Let's go home," she said. "I'll feel better after a beer."

****

The next day, Vinny telephoned Day from the hospital.

"Beanie collapsed last night," he told Day tearfully. "Doctor says more tests but she don't want nothing done. Talk to her, yo. I'm a mess."

Day rushed over and tried but her cousin was adamant, vowing to do whatever the doctors wanted, tests, knife, even more of that goddamn chemo shit if they said so. But not until after the wedding. Beanie was going to walk down that aisle in a poopy dress and fuck-me shoes two weeks from next Friday or, "I sweat to shit, Day, I'll never talk to you again."

"How about if I postpone the ceremony?" Day suggested.

"How about I kick your ass?"

"I can get married in city hall, you know," Day explained. "It's legal"

"Ain't gonna happen," Beanie shot back. "You do that, and I bail, ugly dress and all. Luis can be your maid of honor."

"A big wedding was Bobby's idea," Day argued. "I never wanted it."

Beanie gave Day a queer look. "Like you don't want the pictures you emailed me? Good thing I trashed them." At the horrified look on Day's face, she retracted. "Geez, you're white as a sheet. Calm down. I made a copy and sent it back to you."

Day hung her head. "I'm never going to see Lakota again."

"I know, cuz. I know. But make sure to stash the file where Bobby don't look. It's kind of hard to explain."

Day hid her worry about the file of damning photographs and her guilt about dancing around while her dearest and best friend was so ill.

The honeymoon issue led to Day's third disaster. She balked at Bobby's booked tour of Rome, Florence, Milan, and Venice citing concern for Beanie's condition and Papa's failing business.

"I can't be away that long, Bobby," Day complained. "Beanie is in a bad way. What if anything happens to her while we're gone? And I'm needed at the restaurant. Papa can't cut it anymore, and Luis is barely holding on."

"Fuck Luis."

Bobby rocked back and forth on the balls of his feet like a prizefighter. His face hardened, his fists clenched. Too late, Day saw her mistake.

"No wife of mine works," Bobby growled. "I let it go until now, let the cops and firemen chat you up like some tramp. But from now on, you do like I say. And when we get back from the honeymoon in Italy, yes, I said Italy, you stay home, got it?"

Day's heart began to pound. She felt dizzy, desperate, and started to back away when suddenly, it hit her. This was ridiculous. She was worn out with worry and work and didn't have to put up with Bobby's harangues, didn't have be afraid all the time. A man who claims to love you isn't supposed to tear you down every chance he gets. If this was how married life was going to be, Day didn't want any part of it. No more choosing her words, picking the right time, hiding in plain sight. Day squared her shoulders and stood up straight.

"I see," she said evenly.

Her engagement ring slid off easily but Bobby wouldn't take it from her. Day dropped it to the floor, turned, and walked away. The ring hurt when it hit the back of her head.

Day waited for the other shoe to drop, for Bobby to grovel or enact his revenge. When nothing happened, she tasted a few sweet drops of relief and drew up a list of cancellations; dress, cake, hall, travel agent. But then Bobby made his move. He enlisted Beanie.

"Bobby's a wreck," Beanie said over the phone. "He don't eat, ain't slept since you gave back the ring. Just tell him sorry. The wedding's next week, for God's sake. I can't wait to wear my shoes."

For all Beanie's conviction, her voice sounded weak and Day hated disappointing her.

"I don't know, Beanie," she sighed. "We fight a lot."

Beanie aimed for humor. "Tell you what. Get

married and if it don't work out, get divorced."

"He wants me to give up everything and kneel at his feet," Day said.

"No, he don't. That's just Belmont bullshit. Look, ain't no secret Bobby has a hot collar but he told me he'll postpone the honeymoon and you can work with Papa Joe whenever you want. So lighten up. The guy loves you. That ain't no secret."

Beanie's last few words came out strangled. She started coughing and couldn't stop. Vinny took the phone.

"Please, Day. Don't do this to Beanie. She lives for your wedding. It's the only thing that keeps her going. She–I—me and the boys–we can't take it anymore."

In the end, Day couldn't either, and the wedding went off as Bobby planned except for the honeymoon, which was canceled until…nobody said it, but until whatever was going to happen with Beanie happened. Or didn't. The groom's mother who'd failed her audition with the Amato Opera Company back in '01, sang Ave Maria in a squeaky vibrato, good for a few titters, and Bobby never took his eyes off his new bride, allowing Day to dance with her father but nobody else.

Beanie entered the hospital for a battery of tests and was informed she had to undergo another operation to remove, according to her, "a little something growing where the other little something used to be." In truth, her cancer had metastasized and she was given months, with luck, a year.

Chapter 31

After the wedding, Bobby's view of Day shifted from a much-desired prize to *Who the hell do you think you are?* The vigilance of Day's dating days became a way of life as she not only had to be careful with him but with everyone else as well. Bobby had a network of spies reporting her every move, where Day had gone, what she'd done, and who she'd done it with. He grudgingly approved visits with Beanie, but Enchanted Gardens was off limits, too full of cops and firemen and "that lowlife Luis." Day found it easier to stay at home in his apartment, now theirs, rather than submit to leading questions and lengthy caveats. Handling Bobby went from habit to art form.

Day spent as much time as she could with Beanie but didn't tell her how much she hated married life. Her cousin was fighting the toughest battle of her life and didn't need to know that Bobby ping-ponged from temper tantrums to evangelical rages. "Do it or burn in Hell," was a frequent cry.

Day learned to negotiate the tricky terrain and managed to keep her mercurial husband relatively content. But at the half-year mark, something turned Bobby dangerous. She was alone in the house scrolling listlessly with the remote when Lakota called. He was between planes at JFK and could they meet on the steps of the museum for a quick coffee? He was leaving that evening on a year-long assignment and wanted to say goodbye given that he'd taken off like a jackrabbit the last time. Virtually imprisoned, drowning in Bobby's rules, Day didn't hesitate to come up for air. *Have to sign release papers at the museum. Be right back* she wrote on the post-it stuck to the refrigerator. In hindsight, she should have taken the time to make up a better lie.

****

Lakota was waiting on the Seventy-Seventh Street steps with two cups of coffee and two donuts in a white bag, chocolate for him, jelly for her.

"You remembered," Day said, licking powdered sugar off her lips.

His eyes were like leatherwood honey, dark and promising. He flicked his thumb across her cheek. "A little smear of jelly."

Day wiped with the back of her hand, then wiped again at a falling tear. "You'll be gone a whole year?"

Lakota nodded. "It's a rise and fall of British empire piece for Royal Geographic. They took over half the world, so–"

Day sucked in a deep breath. "Sounds exciting."

He put her empty coffee cup and half-eaten donut in the bag and took her hands. "I called on the chance you weren't married yet. But now you are, I'm still happy I did."

"Me too," she said, eyes brimming. "It makes it less like a dream and more–more–"

"More real?"

"Yes. It happened, it was beautiful, and then it ended."

Lakota kissed Day's palms, first one, then the

other. The feel of his mouth made her tremble.

"I guess this is the real goodbye," she said.

"My people don't say goodbye. We say *tayamaniye*, walk proud." He took her in his arms and released her; a thousand emotions played on his face. "Walk proud, Day, wherever you go."

"You too, Lakota."

She watched him cross the street and disappear into the park.

****

Day drove back to Belmont telling herself to be strong. Now that she and Lakota had made a proper break she would work harder on her marriage. Bobby flew off the handle and was too possessive but he wasn't an ogre. She had to stand up for herself and make him listen to reason. They had only been married a short time; things were sure to settle down. But when Day pulled into her street, all her well-intentioned resolve fled. It was only mid-afternoon but Bobby's Firebird was parked in the driveway and he was in it.

Fighting panic, Day lowered her window and shouted with false heartiness, "You're home early. Shall I park behind you?"

Like a bolt of lightning, Bobby was glaring down at her. He reached in and grabbed her throat. "God damn bitch! Fucking whore!"

Everything in Day went numb; hands, face, toes. She didn't feel the pain as Bobby yanked her violently forward and back, assaulting her.

"Stop, Bobby, please. What I do?"

"Do? You fucked that fucking buffalo. Ask me if I give a shit?" *Slam, shake.* "Go ahead. Ask me!"

Day struggled to breathe. *Buffalo?* That's what

Bobby called people with dark skin.

"I'm signing papers at the museum," he mimicked. "Fucking liar. You think I'm an idiot? You weren't goddamn signing papers. That's not what I saw."

Blood pooled in Day's mouth. "I don't know what you think you saw. I was saying goodbye to a coworker, that's all."

"Don't tell me what I think, you cheap piece of shit."

"Please. You're hurting me. It was nothing."

"I'll give you nothing."

He balled his free hand and drew back. Day cringed. He was going to punch her, break her jaw, crack her skull, probably kill her. But the blaring horn had attracted attention.

Somebody hollered, "What's going on out there?" and Bobby jumped into the Firebird and skidded off.

Day sat trembling for a very long time, wiping her face with wads of tissues. Police came and silenced the horn. They asked if she was all right and she answered no, then yes; just a nosebleed. They were from the precinct and might say something to Papa.

After a few minutes, Day exited her car and went inside. Her marriage was over; no more playing games, making do. Bobby *was* an ogre. The next time he beat her, she'd end up in the hospital, and the time after that, in the cemetery.

Day's nose wasn't broken. She had a bruise on her forehead and a chipped tooth but two days later when Day accompanied Beanie to chemotherapy, her face had nearly healed. She held her cousin's hand in the tiny hospital cubicle as soft music played. Usually, Beanie dozed but today her eyes were wide open and trained on Day.

"What gives?" Beanie asked. "You look like hell. Worse than me." Her gaze was keen, calculating. "Wait a sec. You preg? Were you packing before the wedding? Shit! You're knocked up and it ain't Bobby's. That it? Holy Mother Mary! No way can you pass off a red-skinned, black haired–"

"I'm not pregnant, Beanie," Day answered. "Just tired. Marriage takes a lot out of you."

Beanie's face was puffy. Most of her hair was gone and today she was wearing her purple Tina Turner wig. She gave it a tug.

"You think I don't know what being married is like? I had my first kid while I was still in high school, remember?"

"You had already dropped out, remember?" Day reminded.

"Yeah, well, been a long time. Junior's a teenager now." She settled back and fixed Day with a conspiratorial look. "Make me forget why I'm here. Tell me what's bothering you so's I can fix it."

"Bobby expects me to cook like his mother but I'm not good at that. If I get take-out, he says I'm lazy or worse, trying to poison him. He's ah, very picky."

"That ain't the word, but go on," Beanie prompted.

"God forbid I ask his mother to show me a few recipes," Day continued. "I'm not supposed to talk to her. She thinks I'm a moron, anyway."

"She's the moron. Anyway, it's good she don't like you." Beanie was enjoying herself.

"I can't even talk to Papa or go to the market alone. Bobby has to go with me. And he put a tracker on my phone and took my car keys. I have a spare set, but I'm still afraid."

Beanie's eyes narrowed. "Afraid?"

Day had said too much. "Figure of speech. I'm not afraid of Bobby."

But she was.

****

Day tiptoed around her husband. Bobby said nothing about what had happened in the car but like Beanie had advised, "Clear the air. If you leave an elephant in the room, it's going to take a dump."

To keep Beanie and her illusions alive, Day suggested to Bobby that they invite the Siragusas to a barbeque in the yard on Sunday. She defrosted burgers and made salads. Bobby started drinking after breakfast, however, and by noon, he'd finished the second of many bottles of wine and by evening, when Day brought a tray of paper plates and cups out to the grill, he was stone drunk.

"Let's christen our first married summer," Bobby said, loosening his belt buckle.

Day's radar pinged.

"For luck. A fuck for luck, a good luck fuck," Bobby leered, slurring his speech. "On account of it's our first party as man and wife." His eyes went dead; he lumbered toward her. "You are my wife, aren't you?"

It wasn't a question. Bobby grabbed Day and ground against her. She wriggled and pretended to smile. "Get off, Bobby. Your mother can see us from the window."

He planted slobbering lips wherever they fell, Day's neck, cheeks, shoulders.

"Nobody's home." Bobby sneered. "It's just you and me, babe."

She steered him toward a lawn chair. "Don't kid around. I invited Beanie and the boys to the barbeque. Sit and relax. I'll put the burgers on."

"Don't tell me what to do."

From the corner of her eye, Day saw Bobby lift his arm, but the hard shove caught her off guard, knocking her against the grill, upending it. The grate slid off; the grass ignited. Licks of flame danced across the lawn like a pack of firecrackers.

Day scrambled to her feet. "The grass is burning! The house is going to catch fire."

Oblivious to the danger, intent only on Day, Bobby advanced. "Let the whole block burn down. I don't care."

Terror gripped Day. Bile rose in her throat. Dizzy and disoriented, she reached out to her husband of less than a year to keep him from getting any closer to her.

"Bobby," she managed to croak. "Stay where you are. Don't."

"Baa-bee," he mimicked in falsetto. "Dooon't."

Day looked around gauging her best escape. Should she make a dash for the sunroom and the alley, or run through the hedge into the street? Her mother-in-law had to have heard the noise unless she really was alone with this madman. Before Day realized, something hard hit her and everything went black. She came to slowly, face down on the bed, her shorts dangling from one ankle, her legs pried cruelly apart, and instinctively knew what was coming. Bobby's hand was clamped to the back of her neck.

"Bobby," Day choked. "I can't breathe."

"Shut up!"

He unzipped his shorts and tried to ram himself

into her from behind. He was soft and failed. Damning that stinking buffalo with his stinking braid, Bobby flipped her over but failed again and, grunting a slew of swear words, staggered out of the bedroom. Day waited until she heard the Firebird's engine then crept to the bathroom. Trembling, she shed her bloodied clothing and lay in a ball on the shower floor. The water's spray needled her skin painfully but Day soaped everywhere Bobby's foul hands had touched. Her image in the glass doors reflected a loser in a gang fight, a mottled, lumpy piece of rotting fruit, Dayzilla, the grotesque Bride of Belmont. Gradually, the pinkish pool at her feet cleared as Bobby's vileness washed with her blood down the drain and into the sewer.

Wrapped in a robe, Day peeked out the front door. Bobby and his car were gone. Repulsed by the bed, she lay on the couch, made some excuse to Beanie, and tried to think. She had to get out, but where? Papa's? Beanie's? What would she say to them? How could she tell them that Bobby Leone had turned from touchy guy to violent monster? Better to stay where she was until Bobby came home, which he surely would, sorry, begging for forgiveness, making promises he wasn't able to keep. Day knew that now. Bobby Leone had always been a bully. She'd bide her time until she was presentable then file for divorce. In the meantime, he'd better not touch her again.

Chapter 32

Day had forgotten to close the shades. A needle of sunlight hurt her broken face and she turned her head into the couch cushions. Her tongue felt thick and floury, her lips dry. With a groan, Day cautiously swung her legs over the side and crumpled to her knees. When the room stopped spinning, she half crawled, half walked to the bathroom, catching sight of Bobby sprawled on the bed, mouth open, fetid breath poisoning the air. In sleep, Bobby Leone looked innocent, hugging the pillow like a child, long butterscotch eyelashes shadowing pink cheeks. There was a smear of blood on his shorts; another on his T-shirt. Her blood.

Day curled her fingers into talons and raked his chest.

"Huh, what?" Bobby's eyes shot open, red-rimmed and terrified. His hands flew to his genitals. "What's wrong? Why you hitting me?"

"You creep!" she cried. "You fucking creep!"

Bobby sat up, scooching away from her, bracing against the headboard. "What I do? Did we have a fight? Whatever it is, I'm sorry, all right? It's my fault."

Day regarded her husband scornfully. "You don't remember?"

He rubbed at his face and hair. "Let me see. The barbeque. It didn't happen. I wasted all the food. Is that why you're mad?"

Day crossed her arms. "You hit me, you miserable fuck. You were drunk and you hit me." She leaned forward, her face inches from his. "Look at me! Look at what you did!"

Bobby crumpled and started to cry. "Aw, geez, babe. Oh God, oh shit, no." He rocked and moaned. "I didn't do that. I couldn't."

Tenacious, unrelenting, Day bent closer. "Then you tried to rape me. You threw me down on the bed and tore my clothes."

He slid her a confused look, but also a sly one. "Rape? Come on. That doesn't sound like me. I never forced you in my life. I never forced anybody."

Day stared at him, eyes fierce. Did he really think….

Bobby put a hand to his heart. "I must have been drunk. It was the booze, not me. I swear. And how can I rape you? You're my wife." He ventured a shamefaced shrug. "You can't rape your own wife."

She boiled with disgust. "But you did, you son of a bitch. And when you couldn't get it up, you hit me."

Bobby blinked. "What are you saying?" he asked affronted. "I always deliver. And if I tried to lay a hand, it was the beer, not me." He sat a little straighter and kissed his fingers. "Word of God, I'll never again touch another drop on my mother's life."

So that was the excuse. He didn't remember putting out her lights. Okay, maybe so, maybe at this moment. But give it a few days. He'd remember everything, including Lakota.

"We're through, Bobby," Day announced. "As soon as my face is healed, I'm filing for divorce and moving out."

He jumped off the bed. "You can't do that," he pleaded, face stricken. "Think of Papa Joe and Beans. This will kill them. You didn't say anything to them, did you?"

"No, Bobby," Day replied through gritted teeth. "I was too ashamed. You make me ashamed."

His face crumpled. "Don't leave, Dayglo. I can't imagine acting the way you said, but okay, if I did, I apologize. It's over. It won't happen again." He reached out a tentative hand. "I love you so much, babe. I'll die without you."

Day walked out. Bobby followed. She shut the bathroom door in his face and he knocked, begged, pounded. Finally, he threw himself against it and slid to the floor sobbing.

"I'll never get mad again, Day. If I ever so much as raise my voice may heaven strike me dead."

Then die.

Day wanted out, away from Bobby, away from everything he represented, everything she thought she wanted. He was a dangerous tyrant and she was a fool.

"Please, Dayglo," he whined. "You're my horse, my thoroughbred. One more chance. That's all I ask."

Day opened the door and glared at Bobby's abject form huddled at her feet. "No."

Very gingerly, he rose and caught her hand. "Then at least say you'll forgive me. I'll go away. I'll sleep in the store and won't bother you. Just tell me you don't hate me."

Day's body throbbed with pain, but her brain had exploded with too much content and shut down. The only thing that came to mind was coffee, hot coffee.

Would it sting the cut on her lip? She could use the plastic straw she kept in the utensil drawer for Renzo. Would the hot liquid melt it? Maybe iced coffee then. No, that wasn't the same. She craved a steaming cup of coffee, the steam and scent bathing the open wounds on her face. On some level, Day knew that these inane, incongruous ruminations disinfected the rage that had sustained her throughout the night. Right now, she needed twaddle to get through the rest of the day, clean up the yard and wash the wet clothes on the shower floor. Then more twaddle the rest of the week to keep her from septic madness.

Day moved into the kitchen and filled the carafe with tap water, measured coffee, and turned on the machine. Bobby hovered. When Day sat at the table, he fetched two cups, two napkins, two spoons, the milk, and the sugar bowl. He poured and moaned when Day winced at her first painful sip.

"Shall I get you an ice cube?" he asked pitifully. "Why don't you lie down and I'll bring it to you in the bedroom."

She glared. "Shut up."

****

Day told Papa she'd fallen on the sidewalk; it looked bad but it was fine. Joe whipped up a raw egg with sugar and Marsala wine, the Italian cure for everything from hangnail to snakebite, and he insisted Day see the doctor. She drove to Beanie's house and found Vinny, Jr. on the front porch texting. The shades in the master bedroom upstairs were drawn.

"Where is everybody?" Day asked Junior, hoping nothing was wrong.

"Dad took Mikey and Anthony to the batting

cages," he answered. "Ma's putting Renzo to bed. Hey!" he whooped, catching sight of Day's face. "What's the other guy look like?" His smile faded almost instantly. "Ma ain't been so good."

Day walked into the house. Beanie's kitchen was cluttered and dirty; dishes in the sink, a lidless jar of peanut butter with the knife still stuck in, pizza boxes half full of moldy crusts.

"One of these days, I'll start cooking again," Beanie muttered apologetically, shuffling into the kitchen with a Harley Davidson kerchief on her bald head. She wore a bathrobe over heavy sweats although the heat had to be cranked up to eighty. Her droopy eyelids widened when she saw Day's face.

"Holy shit. What happened to you?"

"It's nothing," Day said. "I fell. Looks worse than it is. How you feeling?"

"Where'd you fall?"

"Um, in the street." Day launched into a rehearsed story. "I tripped on the sidewalk and went down like a tree."

Beanie rubbed her chin and examined Day critically. "You tripped over something on the sidewalk you say? That's good, very good. Around here? Which sidewalk? In front of what store? I hope it was Flaming Vesuvius; hate that guy. You got a lawyer?"

"Lawyer? What do I need a lawyer for?"

Beanie pushed her cousin into a chair, washed down a handful of pills with a slug of milk, studied the carton, and made a face. "I'd offer you coffee, but it looks like the milk expired." She tossed the carton into the trash. "You need a lawyer, dumbass, so you can sue."

"Why would I sue somebody in Belmont, even Flaming Vesuvius? Besides, it happened in the city."

Beanie let out a whoop. "Fantastic. The city is rich. Money will go into six digits."

"I tripped over my feet, Beanie," Day pointed out, as if she really had. "It was my own fault."

"Bite your tongue," Beanie responded, alarmed. "It's never your fault, okay? *Never*. Did you take pictures? I bet you ain't took no pictures. Junior," she hollered, "where's my phone? You seen my phone?" Beanie tossed the cluttered counters and searched in cupboards. "Damn kids. Bobby's bound to know a guy. Get his number and say you broke an arm and can't play the violin no more. That has to be good for a couple of mill at least."

"I don't play the violin, Beanie."

"Sure you do, with the Bronx Philharmonic. We got one? Never mind. Make something up." Beanie prattled on and Day decided not to interrupt. There were two patches of color high on her cousin's cheeks and Beanie was acting like her old self, spouting words from one of her favorite detective programs, figuring the angles. Day nourished a glimmer of hope. Was it possible Beanie would beat the disease?

****

With time, the marks on Day's face crusted over and eventually faded. Sunglasses and make-up did the rest. In little over a week, she looked almost normal again except for a numb, soul-softening emptiness that wouldn't quit. Lakota was a turned page and her marriage was in ruins despite Bobby's hangdog eagerness to make amends. Day hadn't filed the divorce papers yet or told her father what really happened.

Beanie gleefully bought the lie, but Papa was suspicious, not of Roberto, such a nice Italian boy, but of *her*. Joe didn't trust his errant daughter, who tended to solve problems by creating more.

He badgered her until demons poked her with what-if pitchforks. What if Bobby dropped his pussycat act and went back to boxing gloves? What if he locked her in, took her out for walks on a leash, fed her bread and water? That was far-fetched, but habits of a lifetime aren't easy to break. Day's bones, however, were.

Damn it!

Just when she had stopped running after delusions and settled down, the old insecurities were kicking up, urging her to turn tail and run. She should ignore them, file divorce papers, move out of Bobby's apartment, save Papa's restaurant, and walk proudly like Lakota said. She still had Beanie, who was always ready to help, but this was Day's fight. She had to walk proud on her own.

****

One night, Bobby who had been staying upstairs with his mother, walked into the bedroom where Day was sleeping and switched on the light.

"I'm running out of patience, babe," he said, sitting on the bed. "What are you going to do?"

He'd been drinking and the irritation in his tone sent up a warning flare. Instantly on alert, Day told him they could talk in the morning.

"Do you want me to leave?" he asked. "Stay upstairs and never come back?"

Day kept her tone even. "This is your place, Bobby. I should be the one to leave."

He obviously hadn't expected that answer and

blinked. "Okay then. If you think you should go, go. Running is how you roll anyway." He jabbed a thumb at his chest. "But I'm a man. I got my pride and I'm done hanging around like an unclaimed suit. We make this work, or we trash it."

How ironic that Bobby was the one delivering the ultimatum.

"You broke my jaw," Day said tightly.

"So you say. I don't remember."

Her robe was on the floor. Day picked it up and put it on. She needed to be dressed for this battle, protected, armored.

"I think you're setting me up," Bobby accused.

"What?" Day tied the sash, feeling as if he'd struck her.

Bobby backtracked. "Wait. That didn't come out right. I know you're not into that other guy. You can't be, not somebody like that."

Her overnight bag was in the closet. Day pulled it off the shelf and opened the zipper. Bobby watched from the bed.

"I don't remember doing what you said but if I hit you, I promise I won't again," he repeated. "Okay? Good enough?"

Day started stuffing clothes into the bag.

"I'll start there," Bobby went on. "With that promise. You start by letting the whole thing, whatever you think it is, drop."

She gave him a withering look, but Bobby's face was implacable.

"That's it, Day," he continued. "That's all I got. What's done is done and I'm not going to keep apologizing for something I don't remember." He got under the covers and leaned back against the headboard. "Like you said, it's all mine, anyway—this bed is mine, the house is mine, you're mine." Bobby smiled and tapped the mattress. "So get in or get out."

Day zipped up the bag. "I'm going to Papa's," she said. "I'll have his lawyer draw up divorce papers. Sign them and we're history."

She was steeled for an argument, but Bobby curled on his side and smirked. "Suit yourself, Dayglo. Turn off the lights on your way out."

Chapter 33

The lights were still on at Enchanted Gardens. Luis opened the side door.

"Papa Joe's upstairs," he said, glancing at Day's suitcase. "Why don't you come in for a minute?"

"Papa okay?"

She followed Luis to the back. "The dishwasher is still on the blink," he said, filling the sink with water and liquid soap. "Your father takes his meds but he's, you know, worried about this place. I offered to buy it, but your husband offered a whole lot more."

Day watched the suds rise. "He's not my husband anymore, or won't be as soon as the divorce comes through. I'm moving back upstairs."

Luis nodded thoughtfully. "'Bout time. The guy's scum. He cheats on you."

Day was surprised. "Bobby?"

"My wife and I saw him in Atlantic City with some redhead, before and after the wedding. And he fools around with the woman in his store who does the alterations."

If I'd only known, Day mused as she helped load the sink. Bobby had been a player in high school. What made her believe he'd reined it in?

"Bobby's always on the prowl," Luis continued. "Papa Joe knows but figured marriage would be the cure." He gave Day a quick once-over. "Just don't tell him Bobby hits you."

Day nearly dropped a stack of pans. "Who told you that?"

"Everybody in Belmont wanted to believe Bobby had changed. But when you started showing up with bruises—" He shrugged.

Day's cheeks flamed. "I knew he had a temper, but nobody ever told me how bad it was."

"Mostly it's us guys who know. The women—" He shrugged again. "They're like scared to say anything. And, anyway, you ran off. We hardly saw you."

"Does Vinny—" she began.

"Vinny knew but he didn't tell his wife. Beanie would have said something if he had. And, anyway, like I said, we all believed Bobby was different after you two got married. He doesn't talk to me, doesn't like me, but even I could see how happy you made him."

Day was shocked and angry at herself for not picking up on the signs. How desperate she must have been to change her ways, fit in, and make Papa happy. *Don't let no man tell you how to be,* Beanie advised but Day had gone and done just that, mess up for a man and then mess up the mess-up. She stacked the pans and said nothing.

"Don't beat yourself up about it," Luis said kindly, folding his apron. "Bobby's smart. He'll charm your ass faster than he drives that Firebird, but when you're not looking, he'll throw it into reverse and backass mow you down."

****

Papa took Day's return philosophically. When it came right down to it, he seemed happy to have his Deanna back home. Father and daughter tiptoed around the actual reason for her return. Joe hinted at infidelity and Day admitted that was part of it but declined to talk about the beatings. She told Vinny about the divorce but kept it from Beanie, who had been discharged from the hospital, probably for the last time. Vinny asked Day to help out with Renzo, and it was easier to bring the baby home with her. As for Bobby, he laid low. If Day saw him or caught sight of the Firebird rounding a corner, she ducked into a store.

Early one morning, Vinny Junior called. "It's Ma, Aunt Day. She's, I don't know. Can you come?"

Day rolled out of bed, grabbed Renzo and her car keys, and sped to the Siragusas, forgetting to shift into third, wondering why the engine was dragging and whining. At Beanie's house, Day parked crookedly and snatched Renzo from the car seat. Vinny, Jr. sat on the front steps, his face ashen.

"What happened?" she cried.

Junior wrung his hands. "Something ain't right, Aunt Day. Ma's breathing funny. She ain't eat or drink nothing."

"Did you call the ambulance?"

"She won't let me, says to leave her alone."

Vinny buried his head and wept.

"Call your father and take the kids to Nonna's," Day said.

"Renzo too? He don't like her."

"Yes, Renzo, too." Junior stood but didn't move. "Go on, hurry," Day urged. "What are you staring at?"

He colored and turned away. "You ain't dressed."

Day suddenly realized she was barefoot, braless, and still wearing only panties and a T-shirt. Cheeks red, she ran up the steps two at a time, calling to Mikey and

Anthony to go with their brother.

Day found Beanie curled in bed, wasted body thin as a comma under the sheet.

"I'm here, cuz," Day whispered.

Sounds escaped from Beanie's lips, gentle exhalations followed by feathery coughs. "I'm okay. You didn't have to leave work and come over."

The few words precipitated a stronger coughing, dry and sharp.

Day crouched on the floor beside the bed. "I don't go to the museum anymore, cuz. I was fired, remember?"

"Oh, yeah. How's Renzo? Are my kids-?"

"Everybody's okay. Junior has them. Vinny's on his way."

Beanie grimaced and let out a moan.

"You want a shot?" Day asked.

"No shot." Only Beanie's lips moved. "Don't want Vinny." Her eyes fluttered open. "I want you."

Day rested her cheek on the pillow. "What can I do?"

"You have to figure that out for yourself now that the pumped-up little fuck I made you marry is gone." A hint of a smile lifted the corner of Beanie's mouth. "You kill him yet?"

Day returned the smile. "So you know."

Beanie rolled her head from side to side. "I'm sorry, Day."

"Shhh. It's not your fault," Day said, wiping flecks of blood from the sheet as Beanie started coughing again."Take a sip of water. You need to drink."

"Please don't touch me," Beanie said. "Hurts everywhere."

Day laid her head on the pillow and was quiet for a moment. Then Beanie's breathing quickened.

"What is it?" Day asked.

Beanie seemed to will the words from her mouth, pushing them out with great effort. "Okay to mess up."

"What?" Day repeated, not sure she'd heard right.

"Indian guy. He's the one. I know it now." Beanie's lashes fluttered. "Don't beat yourself up about it. Go get him."

Day's chest tightened. "I'll let you beat me up," she said. "That's your job."

A deep groan escaped from Beanie's lungs. "I'll take that shot in a minute, but first I have to tell you something."

"Okay."

"Before it's too late."

"Okay," Day said again, uneasily.

With effort, Beanie hiked up on the pillow. "It's about Renzo. He's yours."

"Shhh, Beanie. Lie back. Don't talk."

"No, listen. I'm giving him to you, we are. Me and Vinny signed papers." Every muscle in Day's body clenched. She couldn't move but her heart was beating like it would explode. "Now you sign and he's yours."

"I'm not signing anything," Day protested. "You'll be fine, you and all four kids."

"Stop being a jerk," Beanie whispered through cracked lips. "I ain't going to be fine. Best thing I can do for Renzo is give him to you. Best thing you can do for me is take him."

****

For two days, Day never left Beanie's side. She didn't go home to change but wore Junior's Knicks uniform rinsing it out at night and putting it on damp in the morning. It fit like a bedspread. Vinny came and went; at night, he lay beside his wife, cradling her gently.

"How you doing, cuz?" Day asked Beanie one rainy morning. "Want anything?"

No response.

"The boys are in school. Renzo's with Papa Joe. Vinny went to work."

A sound from Beanie; not words exactly, but an acknowledgement.

Day took a deep breath. "I'm sorry you got hit with bad luck," she continued. "I hope you get better but it's okay to go if you want to. The boys will manage, Vinny too after a while. And don't worry about Renzo. I'll raise him to be just like you."

Beanie's lips twitched.

"I know you think I'm going to mess up again and maybe I will," Day talked on. "But not like before. Never like before. You can take that up to heaven with you. Tell that to my mother when you see her. She worries." Day smoothed the sheet, careful not to touch Beanie. "I don't know how good I'll be without you, but I'll do my best. I'll remember to be myself no matter what." Day kept her tone light. "If I find myself slipping, I'll act as if…"

Beanie started to gag, as if preparing to expel an object caught in her throat. Her eyes shot open, she pointed weakly and worked her jaw.

"I don't understand," Day said. "What are you trying to tell me?"

Beanie licked her lips.

"Yes?" Day prompted, bending close.

Beanie's bone-like finger pointed to Day's jersey. "I know you like them dark," she said, the words barely audible. "But did you have to sign with the Knicks?"

Day grinned and launched into the tale of her nearly naked ride in third gear and Junior's offer of his precious Julius Randle jersey. "The funniest part," she went on, "is nobody notices. Not Vinny or the other kids. Not even your mother, and you know how she is. Anyway, when Bobby came by–"

Day stopped talking. Beanie had begun to breathe in odd, shallow inhalations that escalated into labored gasps.

"Beanie?" Day cried.

Beanie struggled feebly, not so much for air it seemed to Day, as to trap some essence of mortal life to carry with her into the next eternal one. Day held Beanie's small hand until the spasms quieted and then felt for a pulse. Remnants of life still flickered but they were intermittent and thready. Dry-eyed, Day kissed her dearest friend's cool forehead and waited for Vinny.

Chapter 34

Day made over the bedroom of her apartment into a nursery with pale blue wallpaper, a crib, and stuffed animals. She filled a bookcase with Renzo's picture books and her own childhood collection, *Frances the Hedgehog, Babar the Elephant,* and Renzo filled the house with baby smells and laughter.

At night, when the sudden quiet evoked sleeplessness and memories, Day sat beside the crib and gazed at Renzo's stubby feet, tiny, down-turned nose, and pointy chin so like his mother's. It was as if Beanie was in the room with them fondly approving, occasionally haranguing. Mama also visited Renzo. She and Beanie cooed over the crib and then talked about Day.

Maria: *Deanna, she never satisfy.*

Beanie: *I hear she gets that shit from you.*

Maria: *No curse, Albina. We in heaven now.*

Bobby took Beanie's death hard. At the funeral, he sobbed on Vinny's shoulder and asked if he could take Renzo once in a while.

"I'm his godfather," Bobby explained. "I love the little guy."

That wasn't exactly correct. Junior was Renzo's godfather, and Renzo lived with Day. But she gave the matter some thought. It had been a while since the divorce, and allowing Bobby to visit her adopted son might be a way to start mending fences. She asked Bobby to stop by the restaurant.

****

Bobby never showed. Weeks passed and Day decided he had forgotten all about Renzo, or didn't care to deal with her. But one evening, when Day was getting Renzo ready for bed, there was a noise at the door.

"It's open. Come in," Day shouted, expecting Papa.

Bobby walked through the open door and pointedly locked it behind him. "Expecting company?" he said nastily.

Old feelings of dread Day thought she'd buried, resurfaced. "What are you doing here?" she demanded.

Bobby held out his arms. "Give me my godson." He moved closer; his breath stank of booze. "I'm taking Lorenzo."

Day backed up, clutching Renzo. "Like hell you are."

An angry crimson flush crept from Bobby's neck to his hairline. "I had a talk with Vinny. I told him you're going to take off like you always do and raise his kid with some tomahawk lowlife." He reached for the baby.

"Get out of my house," Day screamed.

Renzo started to cry.

"Now see what you did," Bobby said. "Give him to me before—"

Day fled to the bedroom and laid Renzo in his crib.

"You're not fit to be a mother," Bobby shouted. Fists raised, he advanced, growling.

Day shoved him back toward the door, away from the crib. He tried to shove her aside, but she was a pylon, fueled by rage strong enough to support a bridge.

What happened next spun out in fast forward. A strange effervescence started to tickle Day's skin, a cool, bubbly sensation as if somebody had sprayed her with soda water. No, with champagne.

Don't you dare let that fuckwad touch Renzo, Beanie commanded. *I'd stomp the crap out of him for you but I ain't got no legs.* She giggled. *It's kinda cool.*

Bobby staggered forward. Day reached behind her and gripped the rail of the crib with one hand and dug for her phone with the other.

"I got this, cuz," she assured Beanie. "He won't get near Renzo."

Bobby gave her an odd look. "Who you talking to?"

"Nine-one-one," Day said loudly. "I have an emergency. Someone's trying to break into my apartment at–" She recited the address. Bobby glared. "I called the cops," Day announced. "They're on their way."

Bobby's face changed and Day knew he was envisioning tomorrow's headline in the *Press Revue*: *Prominent Local Businessman arrested.*

He left the bedroom and walked to the front door. "And I'm calling a lawyer. No tramp is keeping Lorenzo."

****

"I can't stay in Belmont," Day told Vinny the next day. "I'm afraid of Bobby. He says he's going to take Renzo."

"Bobby told me you have a new boyfriend," Vinny responded. "And some other stuff. But I paid it no mind. Yo, Beanie's dying wish was for you to raise

Renzo. We signed papers; it's all legal. There's nothing to worry about."

Day did worry. For the rest of the summer and into the fall, she walked around like a fugitive, looking over her shoulder, jumping at every noise. Bobby would call, leave scary messages, and hang up.

Watch your back, bitch.

Got eyes on you.

Let Renzo out of your sight to take a piss and he's gone.

****

"Day!" Luis barked one brilliant autumn day. "You there? Papa Joe's been calling you for ten minutes."

Day was in the back room, leaning against the open door, watching Renzo play in the yard.

"You in a trance or something?" Luis went on. "Papa Joe made soup. He says for you and Renzo to come eat."

"Not hungry," she mumbled.

Luis walked over and stood beside her. "Man, you been acting weird lately. You want to tell me what's going on? I mean, you know, we always talk."

She shrugged. "I guess I'm kind of restless."

Joe called from the front. "Deanna, *a tavola.*"

"Coming, Papa," she replied but didn't move.

Luis probed. "I know you, Day. You have that look. You in love again?"

She smiled. "What are you, the amazing Kreskin? I don't know about love but there's somebody a million miles away I'd like to see again."

Luis nodded sagely. "So call the guy."

But she couldn't call Lakota. He had six or seven numbers that changed all the time and even if she chanced on one that worked, Lakota might be out of reach in some jungle ashram or Middle East war zone. What possible message could she leave, anyway? "Hi. Remember me? We spent a couple of nights together over a year ago." Right. He was going to stop dodging bullets for that? And Lakota could have called her. She had only one number and that never changed.

Day watched Renzo roll his truck in the dirt and was wondering if it was too early for a beer when a voice instructed, *Get your ass to the cabin, cuz.*

"Luis? You say something?

I'm up here.

"Beanie?"

Yeah, it's me. I'm with your mother. Go get him.

No chase no man, Deanna. Make him chase you.

"Mama?"

This guy's different, Maria.

Mama and Beanie were chatting.

They all the same, Albina. He Italian?

Shit no. Far from it.

I no like.

He's hot.

You mean he gangsta?

Day felt as if her ears were being pulled apart by the two women arguing in her head.

He's home, Day, at the cabin.

"How do you know that?"

"I tracked him down. It's easy when you're dead. The foylage is beautiful upstate this time of year.

"Foliage."

Geeze. Will you stop it? I'm an angel now. Go after him, fuck your brains out, then make him kick Bobby's ass."

Albina! No curse. We in heaven.

Yeah, don't I know it. Harps and clouds but no sex.

After Renzo and Enchanted Gardens, sex was the subject uppermost in Day's mind and clingy as a limpet. At night, she touched herself, imagining Lakota's hands stroking her breasts and pearling her nipples. But it wasn't Lakota, and dreams were no match for the heat and power of a beautiful, thrusting body and bruising, hungry mouth. Night after night, Day bit her lips to keep from crying out, afraid to wake Renzo and afraid of the chill in her heart when, after she brought herself to climax, she lay back in the big bed alone.

****

"Take a day off," Papa advised Day. "Go to a beauty parlor. Your hair, she look like, what's that dog? Portuguese Man of War."

"It's not that bad, Papa," Day said, flattening her mass of thick curls.

"Listen to Papa Joe," Luis butted in. "And mow those brows while you're at it."

"Give me a break, guys," Day protested. "I don't have time."

Both men stared. Luis eventually shook his head and walked away. But Papa gave no quarter.

"You got plenty time, Deanna. No have to spend every minute with Renzo, and the restaurant run okay without you."

No busy was a euphemism. It was lunchtime, peak hours, and Enchanted Gardens was empty. In the absence of diners, the back room was now used for storage and littered with pizza boxes, cases of soda, the old console TV, and Renzo's toys. Day and Luis often brainstormed ways to reverse the restaurant's waning fortunes, like his Wacky Wednesday sidewalk man and her gluten-free options. But nothing helped sales. Joe advised patience. Enchanted Gardens would bounce back; people always wanted reasonably priced Italian comfort food in a clean, friendly environment. Yet, as Day stacked giant cans of plum tomatoes under the empty tables in the back room, she wondered where everybody was.

Chapter 35

It didn't take Day long to find out why avoiding the Daneses and Enchanted Gardens had become par for the Belmont course. One morning, she found deep gouges on Papa's car and hers with four flat tires. Then somebody threw a brick through the restaurant's front window, broke in, trashed the place, and unplugged the walk-in so everything spoiled. Day suspected the Farenga brothers' fine Italian hand and paid Carmine Carciofolo a visit.

The Don was in his office at the Benevolent Friends of Belmont finishing a sausage and pepper hero Day had the foresight to send over in advance. She'd also shown respect by calling ahead for an appointment. Carmine stood and bowed when she entered and hurriedly removed the napkin from around his neck.

"Ah, *la bella* Signora Leone. No, *scusi.* You're Signorina Danese again." He wrapped the remainder of the sandwich. "Thank you for this splendid repast. Please. Have a seat. How may I be of service?"

Day remained standing and got right to it. "Somebody vandalized our cars last night and broke into the restaurant."

With a pinky fingernail, Carmine dug a tiny bit of something from a back tooth. "Yes," he said sadly. "I had a word with my sister about the, ah, incident, but you know how things are with family."

"So it was you?" Day accused.

Carmine shrugged innocently. "Yes and no. Joe Danese is a dear friend but blood is blood."

Day didn't like the sound of that. "Please, don't talk about blood, Don Carciofalo."

"My sister is a Leone by marriage. Bobby is my nephew," Carmine said. "Somebody want pizza they go to your papa. They want trouble, they come to me."

"So Bobby wanted trouble?" Day asked the obvious question.

Carmine put a finger to his lips. "Keep this quiet, but once in a while, he asks me for a favor. How can I say no?"

Day fell into the chair muttering. "The bastard. I expected something like this from him. No wonder the restaurant is always empty."

"Bobby wanted a little of this and a little of that." Carmine weighed his upturned palms like scales. "I took care of it peacefully so nobody gets hurt."

Day may have spent a lot of years away from Belmont, but she'd grown up there. Everybody knew that Carmine the Cobra worked in stages; a warning not taken was followed by a mishap that could have been accidental, followed by a bigger mishap, followed by your head face-down in the *vitello tonnato*. She knew her ex-husband too. Bobby wouldn't stop at a break-in. There was more to come.

Carmine made a gesture of helplessness. "I don't like violence, Miss Danese. Negotiate; that's the ticket. One hand washes the other. If your father sells Enchanted Gardens to Bobby Leone, Belmont will get a nice new cleaners and your father will keep all his teeth." He smiled. "Coffee?"

Day stiffened. "Don't you dare go near Papa," she said through clenched teeth. "I'll–"

Carmine cut off the threat. "Please, Miss Danese. I shall use my influence to make sure nobody touches Joe. You, my dear, are another story. Bobby Leone wants more than a new cleaning store. The boy is out to break you. Take my advice; pack up the Siragusa baby and run."

****

Where to hide? Hecate County? It was small, far away, and nobody had heard of it, at least nobody in Belmont. Day considered asking Vinny and Luis to keep an eye on Enchanted Gardens until the heat was off and calling Marge Coots for a short-term rental. But how short-term? Bobby's grudges consumed him and regardless of what Carmine had said about protecting Papa, Day was worried. The wiser option was to stay home and buy a gun.

Day did an online search for *New York City handgun license* and found there were five different kinds of applications to choose from, each one with seven or more pages to fill out and requiring reams of attached documentation, an FBI background check, and a personal interview. She thought of asking around the neighborhood, but word was sure to get back to Bobby, and in any case, she would have to take shooting lessons, which would also get back to Bobby. Day wracked her brain. Hire a bodyguard? Adopt a pit bull? Nothing was guaranteed. She'd just have to stay close to Papa and watch her step.

Day's life became a Netflix top ten; heroine in peril skulking around corners and peeking through blinds, bad guy in a darkened longshot, hero ten minutes in, getting out of a car boots first. She worked full shifts at the restaurant and trailed her father like a duckling. If she broke out to the playground with Renzo, Vinny and Luis kept her apprised of Firebird sightings, and at home, Day sheltered behind a gulag of locks and chains.

Papa had no idea that Bobby had been behind the break-in. Joe wasn't feeling well. He paused frequently to feel his chest and then ridiculed Day's concerned questions. The doctor admitted Joe's heart was enlarged. It wouldn't shrink by itself and there was just so much pills and rest could do. Unless he worked less, exercised more and ate a bland diet, Papa was on borrowed time. Day was well aware that words like *bland* and *exercise* weren't in her father's lexicon, but she nevertheless initiated a *Let's Get Healthy Together* campaign of salads for dinner and a family gym membership. It didn't last long and annoyed Joe so much, his blood pressure shot up. Hearty suggestions like, "Let's cut back on the pasta," were turned aside with inattentive grunts, and oblique hints like, "It's a perfect day to put on sneakers and go for a walk," had no effect at all.

As with most things in Day's life, destiny made the final call. One Saturday, she dropped Renzo off with Vinny to make a grocery run. Day always kept one step ahead of Bobby by varying the market. This week, it was Shop-Rite, next week it might be Acme, and so on. By now, she had memorized the aisles and shelves of every grocery store in the Bronx and moved quickly. She was in the check-out line with a full cart when the phone rang. It could have been another Bobby hang up and she almost didn't answer but it was Luis.

"Papa Joe had a heart attack," he said, his voice breaking. "Ambulance took him to Montefiore Hospital."

Day abandoned the cart and ran.

****

Joe's bay in the ER was empty. His black pants, short-sleeved white shirt, and stained apron were folded on a chair, shoes neatly aligned underneath. A nurse swept back the privacy curtain.

"They took him up to Cath," she announced, handing Day a plastic drawstring bag. "Put his stuff in here and wait in CCU."

Dazed, Day zombie-walked down hallways, through double doors and up an elevator to the Cardiac Care Unit. The first thing she saw when the doors opened were three gurneys lined against the wall. Two were empty; Joe was in the third. His usually carefully combed-over hair was sticking up and out and his cheeks were flushed, but he looked normal, not pale or in pain, just normal, even healthy.

"Hey, Papa," Day said. "You gave me a little scare."

Joe tried to sit up. "Deanna, take me home."

Before Day could say another word, two attendants politely intervened and wheeled Joe away.

"I'm his daughter," she said, following them. "Where are you taking him?"

One of the attendants pointed to a room. "Wait in there, please."

Day waited what seemed like hours until someone in scrubs informed her that Joe had suffered a heart attack and she could see him through an ICRA viewing window. She spent that night and the next two alternately staring at her father through a pane of glass and making phone calls. Vinny and Junior came, Luis and his wife, Officer Hank, Mrs. Navona from the bakery, and a string of Joe's Belmont friends and business acquaintances. Day panicked when she spotted Bobby in the hallway, but he headed for the elevators before she could bean him with her water bottle.

On her third day in the hospital, the kindly doctor, looking as haggard as Day felt, said that Joe likely wouldn't recover but she could go into his room and sit by the bed. Day held Papa's hand for another day, her heart overflowing, begging him to open his eyes, move a finger, anything, until her mother's voice said, *Lascialo, let him go.*

Papa heard it too. He called Maria's name before joining her in Heaven.

****

Day fell apart, seeing no one, talking to no one. After days locked in the apartment, not eating or sleeping, she awoke one morning to find Beanie at the foot of the bed.

"Is Papa with you?" Day asked. "Let me talk to Papa."

"He's busy," Beanie answered. *"Get a grip and go pick up my kid. Your kid. Renzo misses you."*

"I can't," Day answered tearfully. "Without you and Papa, I can't do anything."

Cut the crap. Me and Papa Joe are here, your mother too, and a shitload of other people you'd be surprised. Fucking Elvis. Can you believe it?

"I'm a mess, Beanie, a failure. Renzo is better off with Vinny."

Beanie was silent, neither agreeing nor disagreeing.

Then suddenly, she was gone.

"Beanie?" Day cried. "You still here? Don't give up on me."

The disembodied tip of a cigarette glowed near the ceiling. *Ain't that what you're doing, cuz?*

"I just need time," Day pleaded.

Smoke floated in the air.

Okay. Here's the deal. One more day to pity party, then if you don't move your fat ass outta here, you won't ever see my skinny one again.

****

Day thought about taking a shower, cleaning the house, stocking up on milk. Instead, she sped north on I-87 and talked to the trees.

"This is just a distracting drive. I might stop in Rainwalker Ridge long enough to watch the moonrise over Campbell Mountain, but then I'll go right back to Belmont and get Renzo."

She picked up a donut at Rosalie's. Everything reminded Day of Lakota, from the Jeeps in the parking lot, to the tall pines, the spicy fall-scented air, and the freedom of open spaces after weeks in hospital corridors. And yet, although, unlike Papa and Beanie, Lakota, wasn't dead, he was a dead end. If she ran into him right now walking out of Rosalie's with a cup of coffee, he'd smile and start spouting Oglala claptrap about former lives and destined incarnations. Then he'd check the time of his next flight and disappear. Well, she wasn't a beforetime/aftertime Oglala globe trotter. She had one life, and she'd live it with Renzo in Belmont. But not right this minute.

It was a swimmingly gorgeous afternoon with a dazzling blue sky and orange, yellow, and red leaves falling like confetti. Day rolled down the windows and cruised the open road at seventy-five miles an hour. When she skidded into the first switchback up Campbell Mountain, she slowed to watch a yearling fawn graze. At the second switchback, Day kept climbing, and at the third, hit the brakes and screeched to a stop. Lakota's black Renegade was parked in the layby hitched to a horse trailer with a lowered ramp. Day's palms began to sweat. She pulled alongside and peered through the Jeep's window: books, maps, a CD labeled *Songs of the Pyrenees*, and a dream catcher hanging from the rearview mirror. Those were Lakota's things. He was here. She hadn't turned south back to Belmont and Renzo, but kept on going north to Lakota.

Don't fuss at me Beanie, Day said in her head. *I'm not giving up on either one of them.*

She took a moment before getting out of the car. She hadn't showered or bothered to change before leaving home, nor paid much attention to herself since Papa's death. Her face in the visor mirror was gaunt and pale. A hasty smear of blush made her look clownish; eye shadow worsened the effect.

"What am I doing?" Day muttered aloud, wiping everything off with a tissue and slapping shut the mirror. It was probably Mal at the cabin anyway. And if the universe was aligned just right and Lakota was actually home on this one lucky day out of three hundred and sixty-five to answer a few questions, he wouldn't. Day could almost hear Lakota's raspy voice. "Sorry. Back of Beyond called and I have to leave you to photograph dragons." Nevertheless, heart racing, Day locked the car and started up the overgrown path. The universe didn't work that way, but maybe there was something to destiny.

At the edge of the clearing, Day peered through the branches. Two horses were tethered to a porch railing. One was huge and brown, the other small, mottled gray and delicate, with a smudgy chocolate nose. They stamped the dry earth and flinched at flies. The cabin door was open, the interior dark and unknowable. Day took a step forward, scanning for Lakota's dogs. Her foot snapped a twig and out they shot, barking raucously. She crouched down with her arms out.

"Shappa, Makawee. You remember me."

Engulfed in a whirlwind of doggy love, Day was knocked flat on her back, licked, and tail slapped. The mare took note, nickered and twitched its velvety ears.

"Hello," Day cooed to it softly. "You're beautiful."

"Her name's Kohana," a voice said, a voice she'd never forget. "It means swift. She's pure Appaloosa."

Tall and easy, long hair streaming like a thundercloud, Lakota approached from behind the cabin. His boots were caked with mud, T-shirt sweat-stained and torn. He carried a branch in one hand and shook it lightly. "Black walnuts. Pretty rare this late in the season. Want one?"

Suddenly, it was obvious to Day why she'd come. Brain in mourning, body paralyzed with grief, it wasn't answers she wanted but healing. Her heart understood that Lakota was the balm she needed to ease her pain. She accepted a walnut and bit into a morsel of bonfire smoke, cinnamon sugar and mulled wine.

"It's delicious," she said. "May I have another?"

Lakota's eyes roamed her, long and slow. "You're here."

Day drank in Lakota's rough scarred face, wide,

mobile mouth and eagle's beak of a nose and inhaled his scent, leather, pine tar, and raw earth. Their eyes locked; Shappa's and Makawee's heads swiveled back and forth.

"The dogs are curious," Lakota remarked.

Day swallowed the lump forming in her throat. She had never fainted before but, oh my God, after all this time and all that had happened, to have Lakota inches away looking at her with deep, spellbinding eyes.

"What you been up to?" Day asked in a feathery voice.

"The usual. I was in Kat with a film crew, Katmandu," he explained. "Drank something called *tsampa* with a Rinpoche, that's hot buttered yak tea. Got sick as a dog while my friends climbed Everest."

"Really?" Day's breathing was ragged.

"Really." He smiled crookedly. "I tried my hand at a little rappelling in Reykjavik. Iceland's great; puffins, fjords, the most unbelievable sky. It was twenty below the whole time and then I sweat off ten pounds shooting a spread in the Mellah. That's the Morocco's Jewish Quarter." He stopped and frowned, suddenly looking ill at ease. "But you'd know that."

He tossed the denuded walnut branch to the dogs. Shappa killed it with a shake. Makawee tugged it from Shappa's mouth and they chased around the clearing. Day watched, understanding that she and Lakota were both on edge. She had to say something to break the tension.

What came out of her mouth was a quip. "I drank hot buttered rum in the Bronx once."

Instead of laughing, Lakota's frown deepened. "What's wrong, Day?"

She swallowed; her eyes welled. "My father died."

Lakota said nothing for a long moment but his face was tender. "Oh, Day." He took her hand. "You ride?"

"Me? Never been on a horse in my life."

Lakota untied both mounts and held the mare's bridle. "Kohana's gentle. Come on."

"Me?" she said again, feeling stupid. "Up there?"

Lakota gave Day a leg up and showed her how to handle the reins. Then he attached a lead line to Kohana's bridle, mounted the gelding, and headed into the woods.

"Oh," Day gasped, bouncing. "I'm falling off!"

"Hold on to the pommel." Lakota ventured a small, lopsided grin. "Grip with your thighs; you do that well." He picked up the pace. "I have to finish brush hogging then we'll go back to the cabin and relax. You can stay, can't you?" he added, a little uncertainly.

"What's brush hogging?" she asked, concentrating on staying upright. "Do you groom pigs or something? Is it complicated?"

His smile broadened. "Nothing between us will ever be complicated."

Chapter 36

Indian summer had descended on Campbell Mountain like some exotic angel, all russet robes and golden wings. Day mentioned the splendid scenery but Lakota snickered. Oglala called October's blaze of warmth and color *Anishinaabe*, a time to attack the white man under cover of smoky campfires and the autumn haze. Day experienced a twinge of awkwardness. They were different to the point of farce, she and Lakota. Hers was a world of pizza and parkways, yet she clopped along a dirt trail on the way to brush hog with a Paragon man from America before Columbus. If she were smart, she'd climb down from Kohana, say *Ciao*, and live her city life. But she wasn't smart enough to dismount, so she gripped with her thighs and just like Lakota had predicted, the rest of the day was uncomplicated.

Lakota let the horses graze while he maneuvered a tractor through sweet-smelling pastureland, Day beside him, the noise and the scent of hay drowning any further city mouse/country mouse musings. When the work was done, Day managed saddle and reins like a pro as they rode back to the cabin. Seated on the quiet porch with a cool glass of birch tea, however, Day's tongue loosened and she began to speak of Beanie and Papa and her divorce from an abusive, revengeful ex-husband. Lakota listened without offering platitudes or advice but Day was nevertheless consoled.

As twilight approached, Lakota returned the horses to Ewan Campbell's stables and Day watched him walk the narrow balloch back to the cabin, dragging his shirt over his head and pulling off the strip of rawhide that tied his braid. It was getting dark; the car was at the layby and she should get going. But the sweat glistening off Lakota's muscles and the waves of dark hair falling to his shoulders riveted her gaze.

"We need to hose off before we eat," Lakota said, mounting the steps. For a moment, he stood with his hands at his sides, his face both grave and tender. Then he drew her into an embrace. "Let me touch you."

Day thrilled at his strength and hardness. She moaned as his mouth found hers. His palms smoothed across her breasts and down her hips and buttocks. All sorrow and tension fled and passion rose with the moon as Lakota shucked his jeans and Day stepped out of hers.

"I'm covered with burrs and sap," she said nervously, naked but for her underwear. "I'm filthy."

Lakota unhooked Day's bra and slid down her panties, caressing her hips and legs, pressing his face into the softness of her belly, his mouth into the mound of her sex. Day shivered and clung when he gathered her up and lifted her, wrapping her thighs around his back. Together they rocked, heedless of the loons screaming over the waters down at Ohanzee Wahkan, deaf to the hooting owls and ululating coyotes.

They loved the night long, on the cool deck slats, the porch swing, wrapped in blankets before the fire. The next morning, they rode again, the dogs in delighted pursuit. Day felt as if she'd been born on

Kohana. She stared in wonder at Lakota's broad, straight back and the proud set of his head when the mare stopped to graze. Whatever the gulf between them, she would never, could never, give him up.

"Can we stop here?" Day called out. "It's hot."

She slid down Kohana as Lakota had taught her, pulled off her boots, and dipped bare toes into the icy waters of a stream. Lakota soaked his T-shirt, wrung it out, and put it on again.

"Let's stay here all day," he said. "When it gets dark, I'll show you Venus and the Pleiades."

"Maybe next time," she answered, swirling her feet. "I have to get back to Renzo."

Lakota squatted on his haunches. "I thought you divorced the guy."

"No, Renzo's Beanie's baby. Well, my baby now. I thought to give him up after Papa died but I could never do that." Through the soft buzz of cicadas and the whisper of falling leaves, Day told Lakota more about her adopted son and how much she loved being a mother. "The next time I come here, I'll bring Renzo with me," she added. "He's crazy about animals, especially dogs and horses."

Something in the air shifted. "I have to work," Lakota said abruptly. "I'm supposed to be in London right now, Germany next week, Marseilles by December."

"Oh," Day said, disconcerted not so much by Lakota's traveling but because she'd intended to question it and hadn't.

"You'd love Christmas in Marseilles," he added hastily, possibly sensing her dismay. His usual slow drawl quickened. "They decorate the boats with lights and carolers sing on every corner. The whole city turns into a party."

Day blinked. "Renzo likes boats too." Lakota picked up a handful of pebbles and started skating them across the water. "Why do you never talk about family?" she asked softly.

"You've met Mal," Lakota responded.

"I don't mean that. I mean about family in general, having kids of your own."

He let the few stones in his fist drop. "Children are all right," he noted tightly. "But I don't want any."

The sting of Lakota's acrimony hit her like a slap. He stood, brushed off his pants, and loomed above her, solid as a tower in black jeans, black T-shirt, and black, unreadable eyes. "Now you know," he said with cruel finality, pulling her roughly against him.

Day tried to shrug away but Lakota tightened his grip. "Look at me," he commanded. "I'm forty and ever since I was little more than a boy, I've been on my own. I chose the life I have and I'm too old to change now, even if I wanted to. I can't and won't bring up a child if I'm never going to be around or, worse, drag him after me from place to place. I never lied to you, Day. I want you with me but only you."

Anger erupted. "I know that, Lakota. You've told me a hundred times about freedom and our fated union in the before time and after time." She released herself with a violent shake. "What makes you think you can drag me around the world but not my son!"

Lakota's face darkened. Day watched him struggle for control. "You're a grown woman who can do what she wants," he said, his mouth a flat line. "You have no ties."

"I have Renzo, you son of a bitch!"

Furious, Day sank back to the ground and started tugging on her boots. "Renzo is the one part of me you won't accept. You're telling me to come with you but leave my heart behind."

For a second, she struggled then gave up and stomped barefoot to Kohana. Arguing was pointless.

"I love you, Day," Lakota said, following her. "I don't want to hurt you. But I'm not a family man. I had my chance and I–" He halted, seeming unwilling to say more.

She turned to face him. Was Lakota going to finally talk about his son? She had never mentioned the baby he'd abandoned, never asked him to explain why he'd given it up.

Lakota dug his hands into his back pockets and gazed out over the stream. "Someday when I can't lift a camera bag anymore, I'll return to the mountain to stay," he said wistfully. "Maybe you'll stay with me, Day. We'll sit by the fire in winter and you'll tell me how well Renzo's doing in college or law school."

A tiny spark of hope fluttered in Day's heart. "Why don't you come back to the city with me tonight and meet Renzo?" she asked, imagining for a moment the stir that a six-foot-three, black-booted, long-braided, half-breed would cause with the contingent on the bocce court.

"I can't," Lakota said.

And there it was.

Day jammed on her boots and scrambled, grunting onto Kohana. Lakota didn't offer to help. They rode to the cabin in single file, Day in the lead wishing she felt more like an avenging Furie than a bumbling fool who once again had blown it.

* * * *

"There's some coffee left," Lakota said in the cabin's kitchen after he had stabled the horses. He filled two mugs and carried them to the fire. Day sank onto the pile of blankets, their love nest.

"Do you have to go?" she asked, drained of all but hope.

"Come with me," Lakota repeated. "We can grab a plane to Newfoundland before dinnertime."

For a moment, Day hated him. But then she saw the pain in Lakota's face, the longing and helplessness there that reflected her own.

"How long will you be gone this time?" she asked.

"I don't know. It depends on the job."

Day cracked a tough little smile. "What if I ask you not to go? What if I ask you to give it all up and stay with me?"

"I asked you first," he said. "And I believe I've been turned down."

Day sighed. They had come full circle and another impossible idyll was about to end. Black walnuts and brush hogging aside, Day had known this truth the minute Lakota had taken her in his arms. She'd eventually have to make her peace with losing Papa and Beanie; now she'd have to deal with losing Lakota as well. But she wouldn't be alone; she had Renzo to love and Enchanted Gardens to keep her busy.

"Meet me in a month," Lakota urged in a tone that was steely but not cold. "I'll arrange to pick you up in Paris right after the first of the year. We'll miss Christmas in Marseilles but there'll be others and the delay will give you time to–to–" His looked away, his brow furrowed.

"To get rid of my son," Day finished.

Lakota neither confirmed nor denied. Day courted outrage but it didn't come. What was the point?

He gazed into the flames. "I might be able to make it back between assignments," he said. Day shivered. He draped a blanket across her shoulders. "You must be hungry. I'll make us dinner."

"I need to go home to Renzo," she said, letting the blanket drop and pulling on her scattered clothing.

"At least stay until morning," Lakota said. "Or come back with your son after I'm gone and stay as long as you like."

After I'm gone.

Day shook her head. Lakota too began to dress.

"I'll follow you into town," he said, zipping his bag. "The road's dangerous at night."

Outside, the air was frosty. The moon peeked through the pines; the dogs curled together in its cool light.

"How did you know I was in Hecate County?" Day asked as they walked to the layby. "That I'd drive up the mountain today and find you here?"

Lakota kissed her, his mouth sweet and evanescent as the wind. His eyes glittered like black gemstones.

"I was on a stopover at Lesage on my way to Prudhoe Bay when something drew me in the opposite direction." Lakota shook his head. "Not something— you." He stowed his pack in the Jeep and helped her into the car. "This is for you," he said, dropping something into her upturned palm—a deep red stone glimmering with mica.

"It's beautiful. What is it?" she asked

"Sphalerite. I found it while we were brush hogging. Miners call it Ruby Jack. They polish it and sell it for jewelry. But to my people, it's a blood oath."

She ran her finger along the stone's many intricate whorls. "Is it like a talisman, a promise to–"

Lakota didn't let her finish. "Promises are words. You and I are more than words."

Day cupped both hands around the stone and clasped it to her chest. "I don't want to hear about dimensions or mystical eons, Lakota. Talk to me about this life, about where we are right now."

His face was serious. "There is no now, Day, only *woniya* and *wanagi,* life. I'm Oglala; we're a people of the land. But the *wasichu* cursed us to wander. I suffer under that curse, more so because I'm part white. I have no home, no kin that are mine alone, no lineage. I exist in *wichapi* and *makha*, in *pheta* and *mni*. I am *maniyetu, hehaka* and *matho*. I am all things and all creatures and you are always by my side."

Day didn't know what the beautiful words meant, only that they were sacred and taking Lakota away from her.

Chapter 37

Back home in Belmont, Day embraced motherhood, and worked hard to provide Renzo with everything a boy needed for a happy childhood and glorious future. She also planned to foil Bobby, keep his grubby hands off Enchanted Gardens, buy it herself, and turn it into a success. But this time, no damn the torpedoes, full speed ahead. This time, she'd have a strategy.

Day drew a line down the middle of a sheet of paper and began to write her plusses on one side, minuses on the other. On the plus side: *don't pay rent, eat at the restaurant,* and *Vinny covers Renzo's health insurance.* On the minus side: *the bank owns Enchanted Gardens, I have no savings,* and *nobody to help me out.* Day chewed the eraser. She enjoyed plenty of companionship, Luis and Renzo, Vinny and the boys, and Beanie, who kept floating around insisting that sex was okay but falling in love was a straight line to heartache. Basically, Day was content and couldn't complain. Bobby was a "been there, done that," and Lakota, while not exactly ancient history, was too. Yet, on warm nights when the air vibrated with music and couples boogied on the sidewalk, Day forgot all the bad things and longed for the heat and challenge of a good man, specifically the one that got away.

****

Time passed quickly and on the one-year anniversary of Joe's death, Day attended his memorial mass. Everybody wiped tears at Luis' tender speech. Officer Hank, retired and pounds thinner without all the freebies, called Joe his best friend, and Mrs. Navona's affectionate words left Day scratching her head. Had she and Papa been lovers? Way to go, you old dog. Day sat with the Siragusas but kept shifting nervously looking for Bobby. Thankfully, none of the Leones showed up although some gremlin inside of her craved to see Bobby's new wife, a nineteen-year-old he'd imported from Italy along with, according to the gossip, her entire family. Bobby's overseas sojourn had afforded Day a respite from worry and threats but now that he was back, word on the street was that he'd set his sights on Enchanted Gardens again.

The restaurant was limping along. Luis had learned the secret of Papa Joe's sauce and his siracha meatballs weren't bad. But even with garlic knots and a free soda, nobody lined up. The Belmont tide was changing from a residential neighborhood with specialty shopping and take-out, to Bronx's Restaurant Row. Tourists from the upstate counties, and from Connecticut and Jersey across the river, threw twenty dollar bills at lattes, and waiters with name tags served your slice with a side of truffled arugula. Day's bottom line for saving Enchanted Gardens meant turning it into a gourmet mecca with elegant decor, proper wait staff, and linen tablecloths. But her grand plan required barrels of cash, not to mention time away from Renzo. He cried bitterly when she dropped him off with Luis' wife in the morning, and by the time Day mopped up and collected him after work, he was asleep. Missing her baby was a constant fear but a greater one was that Renzo would stop crying one day and forget her. Soon, he'd be strutting around on sturdy legs, talking in complete sentences, and ready for kindergarten. Could college be far behind?

Weeks and months hobbled along in a grueling routine. Day fell into bed exhausted and woke up the same way, ate quickly between oven and counter, and threw on any old whatever since a chef's apron hid ratty T-shirts and baggy jeans. As Day's pennies and customers dwindled, she realized she had better stop racing around plugging holes and start building a brand new dyke.

"I'm buying Enchanted Gardens," Day announced to Luis.

"You win the lotto?"

"The bank owns the building. We pay rent but it's a hassle for them. The second floor is vacant and there's all sorts of rules and licenses and paperwork you have to stay on top of in a place like this. Plus, the bank lost money foreclosing on Papa.

"Okay, so?" Luis questioned dubiously.

"So I'll borrow enough money to offer them fair market value plus extra for renovations."

Luis went back to washing dishes.

"I'm going to turn Enchanted Gardens into a high-class restaurant with waiters and a bar and music."

Luis said nothing.

She leaned over him and turned off the water. "It's a good investment. Belmont is booming."

"What you going to use for collateral?' Luis asked. "That hunk of crystal you always wear around your neck?"

Day fingered the sphalerite and wondered if she was being an idiot again and whether her plan was just wishful thinking or worse, the fantasy of a madwoman. Her dreams tended to turn out badly and so would an ambitious venture into upscale dining when all she knew was pizza. But she had to try. Renzo was growing up and she was growing old. Allowing Enchanted Gardens to wither away until Day was forced to close its doors for good was unthinkable. It might come to that, but at least Papa would know his Deanna went down fighting.

****

Day dressed carefully, spritzed on a little *Espoir*, and drove to several Bronx banks. All the loan officers bit their cheeks to keep from laughing at her business plan. The last one praised all six-pages, told her she was wasting time, and to forget about owning a restaurant and have dinner with him instead. Papa's doctor and Mrs. Navona wrote generous checks to help out, but Day needed a lot more. In bed at night, she noodled with her magnum opus, made spreadsheets, researched equipment costs, crunched the numbers until they shredded. There were so many angles to consider or avoid; greasing official palms, handouts to fast-track permits, demolition to replace the old strip-mall design with a villino-in-the-Apennines vibe, the exorbitant cost of landscaping the back garden for alfresco dining, live music, and a mirrored bar, not to mention, the liquor license. Neither Day nor Luis were cooks, and her chef had to be Cordon Bleu and wear a toque. She'd be the hostess and welcome diners at the front door in a black dress and heels. Seating would be roomy and plush, and tables set with fine china. Day's bottom line was staggering but it was that or nothing; compromise was not an option.

She considered putting the bite on Carmine Carciofolo who'd been known to finance a few projects. But his interest rate was staggering and if you didn't pay on time, well…it would be hard handing out menus with two broken legs. There had to be somebody who understood the lure of Belmont and possessed the savvy to recognize a profitable investment. Somebody rich, acquainted with Day's dogged willpower and diligent commitment to hard work, and willing to take a chance. Now where could she find somebody like that?

****

Day's hatred of Bobby Leone had passed through her like a kidney stone, leaving her scoured and empty. According to Vinny, her ex was a changed man, under the thumb of a new wife and looking to move to the ritzy Riverdale section of the Bronx. Good for the bum, Day thought. That meant he was raking it in and had plenty to lend. But she wasn't stupid; Bobby Leone also had volatile DNA. Day vividly remembered Bobby's verbal and physical assaults and his threats to steal Renzo. But he'd been mostly MIA lately, her tires hadn't been slashed, and the Firebird no longer passed by Enchanted Gardens at a murderous crawl. And if Bobby was dancing in cash like Scrooge McDuck, maybe, just maybe, if Day had the guts to make a pitch, he'd rhumba a little her way. She fingered the sphalerite hanging between her breasts. It was heavy and sometimes interfered with sleep but just knowing it was there, a reminder of Lakota's love, gave Day the courage to take one last, enormous step.

Chapter 38

Bobby's Firebird was parked in front of his house and another car was parked in the driveway under a cover. It had to be the new Mercedes Maybach, the talk of Belmont that according to Google, cost over two hundred thousand dollars. All the better, Day thought as she set the hand brake on her battle-scarred stick-shift; that meant Bobby couldn't plead poverty. She studied the entrance to the basement apartment she had fled in fear two years ago, and rehearsed the speech she had prepared. The prospect of dealing with Bobby Leone made her dizzy but among his few positive attributes was respect for someone who did the research, presented it efficiently, and didn't waste his time. Consequently, Day had anticipated Bobby's questions, written them down, memorized the answers, and thrown away the paper. Basically, she was going to explain that she'd run the numbers and if Bobby gave her the cash to buy Enchanted Gardens and transform it into the Lutece of Belmont she would guarantee a return on the investment plus six percent in five years. She planned to tout their long acquaintance and her extensive knowledge of the food business in New York City, but steer clear of mentioning their marriage.

She turned off the engine and was about to open the car door when two women emerged from Bobby's apartment. Both were tiny platinum blondes wearing spike heels and carrying what looked like expensive designer bags. They could have been sisters although, as they got closer, one was clearly more than a decade older. So this was the Sicilian bride and her mother, Day thought. The gospel according to Joe Danese held that Neapolitan women barked worse than they bit, ladies from the north, *le donne del alt'Italia*, knew how to mind their business, and Sicilian females were the devil incarnate. Perfect, Day concluded with satisfaction. Now Bobby had someone else to spend his animus on and from the two fashionable munchkins' dressed-to-kill swagger as they headed toward the shops on the boulevard, they already knew what had taken Day a year to learn. Getting as good as he gave might take Bobby down a peg and put him in a magnanimous frame of mind when his docile first wife asked for a handout.

Day took a deep breath and rang the stupid *O Sole Mio* bell.

The tune had barely begun when Bobby yanked open the door growling angrily, "I said no American Express card, okay? The Visa is all you get."

Day could hardly believe her eyes. It was Bobby Leone all right but not the man she had married. The many months since the divorce had not been kind to this creature in too-small cargo shorts, too-tight muscle T-shirt, and heavy gold chains. Day's ex-husband had changed drastically. The former six-pack hid behind a paunch and the muscular, tanned arms were flabby and white as pancake batter. A five o'clock shadow covered Bobby's cheeks and his dirty blond curls were just dirty.

"Dayglow," Bobby said, grinning. "Long time no

see." He gave her the two-finger flip from his eyes to hers. "You no see me but I see you being thrown out of a few banks. Poor kid." Bobby turned and strutted down the hallway. "Shut the door and get yourself a beer. I'm in the back."

He looks different but his personality is the same, Day reflected as she followed the barefoot Quasimodo past a series of dirty, disarrayed rooms. The expensive cherry wood floors were littered with shopping bags from Fifth Avenue stores, and the blue velvet upholstery on Bobby's beloved couch was hidden under layers of women's clothes with the tags still attached. The kitchen sink overflowed with unwashed dishes, the stove was crusty with layers of dried something or other, and bottles of nail polish, wads of lipstick-stained tissues, and an open box of tampons cluttered the table where Day had served Bobby coffee every morning. The heated sun porch, however, was unchanged; wicker, empty beer cans, piles of laundry. Unaccountably, this pleased Day.

"This is where they let me hang out," Bobby said without a trace of embarrassment. "I leave the rest of the place to my ladies but they're going to need more room. I'm buying a house."

"I heard," Day said. "Saw the car, too. Congratulations."

Bobby popped a light. "The Yonkers store is doing great and I'm opening one in Staten Island next year."

"Good for you," Day said, encouraged by Bobby's friendly bragging.

He gestured to a chair. "So let me guess. Enchanted Gardens is up to the oarlocks in dirty water and you want me to bail her out."

Day continued the metaphor and dove right in. "I'd like to keep the restaurant afloat for Papa's sake." Day wondered if she should add, "and for Renzo's," but decided to leave that can of worms unopened.

"I see," Bobby commented flatly. "Go on."

Bobby's hair was greasy and his fingernails needed trimming. Day wondered why one of the wealthiest men in Belmont, who was supporting his fancy wife and her fancy family, had let himself go to seed. It didn't add up but she wasn't here to speculate and settled into a rattan chair.

"Since you've been following me and know my loan applications were turned down," she began.

"Leone the Lion doesn't follow," Bobby interrupted. "I have people for that."

Yeah, same old Bobby.

Day moved a few lines down in her speech. "I've never asked you for anything."

"You asked for a divorce."

Wrong direction. Day forgot the planned presentation and switched gears, remembering that sword-falling flattery sometimes deflected Bobby's anger. "I did. We both made mistakes but yes, I'm the one who bailed."

His eyes narrowed slightly.

"I could have given it more time," Day continued. "I knew you cared about me."

"I still do."

Better, Day thought, but not enough. Spread the butter. "You've moved on, new house, new stores, new wife. I'm still figuring it out but I don't have Papa and Beanie to lean on anymore. How'd you do it, Bobby?"

He chugged the beer, crushed the can, and held it

between his knees. "It wasn't easy, babe. You came at me hard, right between the eyes."

Which is where I still have the scar from one of your punches.

"I'm sorry about that," Day managed to respond. "Here, let me take that can to the trash." She dropped the empty beer can into the wastepaper basket and resumed her presentation. "You and I used to be such good friends."

Bobby looked down at his hands. Was he remembering how they walked home from Mt. Carmel together all through middle school? How Day had shared Bobby's pleasure when he finally reached her height? How he'd cried in her arms after his father died? Or was Bobby remembering Day in Lakota's arms on the museum steps? Day feared she might have strayed into UXB territory again but when Bobby looked up, his face was tender and Day went for it.

"If you still care about me even a little, please help me."

A long moment of silence while Day's dream hung between them.

"What do you need?" he finally asked.

Day expelled a huge sigh of relief. "I want to buy back Papa's building, fix up Enchanted Gardens, and run it as a real sit-down restaurant. But I haven't got enough money."

He chuckled. "Don't even, Dayglo. You haven't got a dime."

She pretended abashed amusement. "Yes, all right. I'm broke but if you give me a loan, I'll work hard and pay you back with interest in five years. See? I have it all mapped out."

She handed him her business plan, the same one the banks had rejected.

He took the folder but set it aside, studying her instead, almost like Lakota did, but dispassionately, head to toe and back again. Men, even inadequate ones like Bobby Leone, have this speculative way of appraising women as if considering their naked worth. Day had read somewhere that males were visual in matters of mating while wealth and position attracted females. But the affair with Lakota had confirmed Day's belief that women were as rapaciously sexual as men when it came to love. If it weren't for Renzo, she'd be camping out with Lakota in a swamp right now just for the extraordinary pleasure of waking up every morning beside his muscular body and beautifully sensual face.

"–are really a trip."

"What? Did you say something?" Bobby had been talking while Day was mentally paddling down the Okefenokee.

"I said you really are a trip, Day. Putting the touch on the guy who broke your nose."

Was he making a joke or threatening? Hard to tell as his tone was expressionless.

"Like I said," Day continued, "I want to move on, support myself, and you know, be proud."

Bobby got another beer from the kitchen. "Fifth one today," he said, chugging at the open refrigerator. "I have to cut down, get back in shape. My wife's a lot younger."

"I saw her," Day responded. "She's-ah, blonde."

"She's a good kid," Bobby noted. "You were too, Dayglo, but your head was in the clouds. Nobody ever gets through to you." Bobby peered in the refrigerator and moved things around. "There's never anything to eat in this house. My wife won't let my mother cook for me anymore so we eat out." He removed the top from a plastic container, sniffed, and grimaced. "Christ, what is this? Looks like my screen saver but it stinks."

Bobby's belly jiggled as he walked back to her and all of a sudden, Day was overwhelmed by pity for the man she'd cared about since they were both in diapers. Bobby's big dreams of power and success hadn't brought him peace; neither had hers. But Day was ready for a new, less grandiose dream, building Enchanted Gardens into a restaurant that served more than pizza and earning enough money to send Renzo to college. That was all she needed to be happy.

Somewhere between the kitchen and sunroom, Bobby had found a candy bar. "Suppose I buy the building and let you run the restaurant for me," he said, biting off a chunk and chewing.

Day had been afraid of that. "No, Bobby. Enchanted Gardens has to be mine. I have to own it."

"Not a problem," he replied. "Maybe you will someday. I don't know anything about restaurants but you grew up in one. Make it work, pay me back my investment plus a profit." Bobby paused impishly; Day held her breath. "And I might sell it to you."

"Might?"

"Businesses are unpredictable, babe. Most of the new ones fail in the first two years. And what if you get itchy feet, take off and leave me holding the bag?" He licked chocolate off his fingers. "Again."

Dammit. Not home-free yet.

"I don't do that anymore, Bobby."

"Yeah, well." He locked eyes with Day. "Vincenzo tells me you love the guy."

The blood rushed from her face. "No–he–I–Lakota's out of the picture. There's no chance that he, that I–"

"Maybe there is and maybe there isn't," Bobby declared. "But even money's a bad bet. I like odds in my favor." He finished his beer. "I'm looking to branch out, diversify my portfolio. A restaurant could work so me and the wife will always have a place to eat." He gave Day his empty beer can. "But Enchanted Gardens without Papa Joe? Toss this on your way out, will you, babe?"

She stood stupidly, holding the can that she felt like crushing against his head.

"The door locks by itself," Bobby added.

Day set the beer can upright on the floor. "You know what? I don't need you. I'll get the money for Enchanted Gardens on my own. It will be the hottest place in the Bronx; reservations only but you and your wife are welcome anytime."

Bobby stared up at her, up and down actually. "You were always the best-looking woman in Belmont, Day."

"Fuck you."

"Yeah, and the horse I rode in on." He picked up the beer can and Day's business proposal. "This looks good but you didn't ask for enough. I'll have my lawyer call yours in the morning. You got one, right?"

Chapter 39

Bobby wrote a huge check and Day was able to use it almost immediately; Leone money was good as gold bars. Day hired contractors, drew up plans, argued with Luis about the pros and cons of an open kitchen, put on a Julia Child mask for trick-or-treating with Renzo, and cooked Thanksgiving dinner for Vinny and the boys, forgetting to take the giblet package out of the turkey and dodging remarks about having the nerve to run a restaurant. Mikey and Anthony refused to touch the bird so they took Day's sweet potato casserole and salad, but not the stuffing, and trekked over to Enchanted Gardens for siracha meatball sandwiches. Day focused on work and shook off everything else, whizzing through life on jet fuel so that it seemed that no sooner had she finished morning coffee than it was time to go to bed. She had to swallow spoons of Renzo's Benadryl to calm down enough for sleep, and woke up groggy, clutching her clipboard, hoping Papa was proud of her, and missing Renzo, who spent most of his time with Luis' wife.

Day heard little from Bobby. The contractor he hired, a grandfatherly man, paid the exorbitant bills, gave advice and did whatever she wanted, no questions asked. On April first, Day received an invitation to Mr. and Mrs. Robert Leone's housewarming party.

"Is this a joke?" she asked Vinny.

"It's going to be a block party, the biggest bash New York City has ever seen and that's going some," Vinny explained. "Carmine the Cobra is closing off the street in front of the Friends of Belmont, and Bobby and his wife are riding down Arthur Avenue on a Cinderella chariot, white horse and all. He's got two bands, a Jumbotron, and the Borough President."

"What if it rains?" Day asked.

"It wouldn't dare."

Bobby had moved with his entire family, wife, mother-in-law, mother and sisters, out of Belmont. He never checked up on the progress of renovations, and Day rarely saw him in the neighborhood.

"I guess Bobby's not the same guy he used to be," Vinny said. "We were on the outs after your divorce but now he's, like, mellow, don't yell or nothing, does whatever the wife wants. He's still hooked on you though."

Day denied any such thing.

"He gave you Enchanted Gardens, didn't he?" Vinny argued.

Day made a face. "The restaurant isn't mine. I can maybe buy it after I pay off the loan."

"What about the guy?" Vinny asked tentatively. "You know, the one—the one, ah, the one—" Vinny struggled for a way to describe Lakota.

Day rescued him. "We had a thing but it didn't go anywhere. Work takes him all over the world and I'm staying in Belmont." She put her fists together to illustrate. "We were at an impasse and nobody gave an inch."

"Separate one-way streets," Vinny said, nodding. "You really liked him?"

Day shrugged. "We didn't know each other long but I guess you could say we fell in love. My father used to tell me love is like bread. It has to rise and bake slow otherwise it's just sticky dough."

****

Later that night, Day put Renzo to sleep and sought a comfortable position in her cold, stiff sheets. Had she and Lakota been sticky dough? To him, love was memory and an eternal connection. Day could buy that; the idea was romantic and sexy. But to her, love was an expression of reality, a union of heart and mind in the present, of being together and wanting to be together. She and Lakota had caught fire and blazed, but then, presented with a small change to his routine, a simple change that would make everybody happy, Lakota dug his heels and balked. He had to know that fires must be fed or they die, and theirs wasn't even embers anymore, unless you counted the heat of her dreams.

An unwanted tear formed at the corner of her eye. Lakota had warmed her heart with a lyrical litany of Native American words, *wichapi, makha.* She couldn't remember them all, but for sure the word for sacrifice wasn't one.

****

The renovations took forever. Day dragged Enchanted Gardens through the spring season selling slices and minimal takeout food from a window on the street. By summer, when traffic was heaviest, the demolition crew arrived and she had to close down. Citing work pressure, Day told Vinny she wasn't going to attend Bobby's housewarming party.

"You should," Vinny argued. "He's putting on a show for you. The least you can do is watch it and—"

"But I'm not. I'm happy for Bobby. I wish him well."

"If you want him to sell you the restaurant, you better start acting as if."

Day took Vinny's advice. She went to the housewarming and complimented the food, the music, Bobby's wife, and even manufactured a catch in her voice when she left before the Mayor's speech. Vinny reported that Bobby kept an apartment above his fourth *On the Go Cleaners* in Manhattan and rarely went to his new house. He must have slipped in occasionally, however, since his bride of less than a year was pregnant. Day was relieved. Bobby pinned the sonogram to the Firebird's visor and forgot about Renzo. Day was happy for Bobby, but it was happiness tinged with sorrow. She had her own baby and could do as she liked with Enchanted Gardens. But neither was truly hers. That was the way of things, Day supposed. The honey of life drips from a thorn.

****

"Magnificent," Day exclaimed, spanning her arms in Enchanted Gardens' almost completed new kitchen. "This restaurant is going to be an institution."

"Nobody wants to eat in an institution," Luis grunted. "Who goes to the school cafeteria for a good meal?"

Day gave him a look. "We did it, Luis. The grand opening is right around the corner and you've been going around with a flopped soufflé face."

Luis hiked onto one of the stainless-steel prep station counters. "Everything looks great, Day, but that's enough. It's time to stop."

"Stop? They just put up the new sign, and the piano

is on its way, and–" She frowned. "What is it? Tell me."

Luis scrunched his cheeks. "You know I'm not a big Bobby Leone fan but every time he stops by, you ask for more money."

"So? You said yourself the place looks great."

Luis sighed. "It does and I know you want to buy it, but the contract says you can't until Bobby makes back everything he put in, and at the rate you're going that'll take twenty years."

He was right, of course. Day was aware she was spending far more than the original loan amount, but Bobby was always gleefully accommodating, peeling off hundred-dollar bills like playing cards. It was Bobby's suggestion to knock out the second floor and install a dining balcony. He also offered to level the Optimo store next door for a parking lot and hire Andrea Bocelli's son for opening night.

"All the way from Italy?" Day had gulped.

"Why not? I'll fly him over in my private plane."

"You don't have one."

"Give me time."

Day was so starry-eyed she would have taken all of Bobby's outlandish suggestions if it weren't for the delays they'd cause. She was anxious to be in full swing before the Christmas holidays, and in mid-November, she sent out notices for a week's trial run to be followed by another week of intense evaluation and adjustment before Enchanted Gardens hit the ground running on December first. Luis' sister, who'd had taken a course in Mixology, was hired to tend bar. Vinny, Jr. and a couple of girls pinched from Flaming Vesuvius made up the wait staff, and Vinny's brother,

Sal, a hospitality student at New York Tech, was made sous chef. The chef was CIA graduate Vito Carciofalo, Carmine's brother, recently paroled and in need of employment. An excellent cook, Vito took the siracha out of the sauce, duplicated all of Joe's dishes to perfection, and his lantern-jawed, six-foot presence in the kitchen assured Enchanted Gardens' safety. Day took on the dual role of hostess and general manager.

Business during the trial week was erratic. Day fiddled with the prices and set up a slate menu board on the sidewalk. That helped. She balked at early bird seating, insisting that Enchanted Gardens was a class act, but agreed to half portions for children. Everybody from the chef to the wine steward, who used to run an on-line liquor business until his conviction for tax evasion, argued about the music. Day wanted Mozart, the Siragusa contingent lobbied for Kanye, and Luis for doo-wop. They compromised with Sinatra naturally, and alternated classical with Beyonce and Lady Gaga, but no Kanye. Chef Vito, who had a sliced ear, scars from eyebrows to chin, and fierce gold teeth, learned to stop ducking out of the kitchen and scaring the shit out of diners. Luis' sister remembered to chill only the sweet wines, and sous chef Sal didn't shout "Fuck me!" every time he cut himself. For her part, when Day felt as though she couldn't move another muscle, she called on Beanie, who was always good for a push.

"The big boss don't tell me nothing," Beanie proclaimed. *"But you got what? Fifty, sixty years left to live your dream? Get off your fat ass, make the restaurant a winner."*

Enchanted Gardens opened to the general public as scheduled on December first, no brass band, no buy one-get one, just a welcome a drink on the house and a never-to-be-forgotten meal in elegant but comfortable surroundings. It went well. At closing time, Day hugged the staff with grateful tears in her eyes and offered a few notes. The place was too hot, crack a few windows and lower the heat in the main dining room. Chef Vito's specials were superb but there were too many of them; one was enough. Vito said no deal and begged Day to stay out of his kitchen. He knew what to do with leftovers and she knew fuck-all about cooking. And for the love of God, stop filching the cocktail shrimp.

Day didn't need a Benadryl to get to sleep that night, drifting off almost immediately into the usual Lakota dreams. Months had passed since she'd waved goodbye and watched the Jeep Renegade diminish in her rearview mirror. They had been months of loneliness, longing, and hard work culminating in gaining a restaurant but losing a life with the man she loved. Lakota phoned a few times from distant aeries with unpronounceable names, but their conversations were unfulfilling, characterized not only by poor reception but by empty pauses, unasked questions, and strangest of all, small talk. He claimed email and texts were unreliable, better to write care of the Royal Geographic Society in London which Day did, enclosing a photograph of herself mounted on an old sway back from the Pelham Bay stables. *Holding on and gripping with my thighs*, she'd scribbled along the bottom. Lakota hadn't replied to the joke or anything since. The man who had called Day *weayaya*, his red-beaming sun, was out of reach and probably out of love.

****

Renzo kept Day going. As his second birthday approached, he was no longer a baby but learning to speak his mind in a complete sentence and run without falling. Enchanted Gardens was finding its footing as well. Nightly post-mortems revealed that the sound system was a success but the new, discreetly posh sign Day loved was practically invisible and needed to be replaced or glitzed up with neon. Mrs. Navona's daughter-in-law signed on as pastry chef, attracting a cohort of fans who filled the tables early. The word was out; on weekends you couldn't get into Enchanted Gardens without a reservation.

One snowy morning, Day checked her mail. Like always, there was nothing from Lakota, no crumpled envelopes with strange-looking stamps, no email. His texts were brief and rare. The last one had been sent months ago, informing Day he was leaving chilly London to warm up in the tropics. She stared at the impersonal weather report and finally composed the reply she had been afraid to send until now. *Your love made me strong but our shared past has no future. We are better apart. Toksaakhe.* Day knew the phrase translated into something like *See you later*, but to Oglala, it meant goodbye.

On Christmas Eve, Enchanted Gardens was fully booked for three sittings of *La Vigilia,* the traditional seven-course fish dinner. Day dropped Renzo off for an overnight with Vinny and hurried back to the restaurant. After the first two sittings, she ran upstairs to her apartment for a quick break and was kicking off an uncomfortable but sexy pair of heels Beanie would have lusted after when the phone rang.

"There's a guy down here asking for you," Luis

said.

"Who?"

"Beats me. Tall mother. Looks like Sitting Bull."

Day's chest tightened, and for a moment she couldn't breathe. She faced a long night plus a week of arguments with Chef Vito before deciding on the food for the restaurant's first New Year's Eve champagne buffet. It had taken every ounce of courage to break it off with Lakota and she couldn't chance seeing him again and raking up all the memories and futility.

"Day? You there?"

"Yes, Luis. Sorry. Give our guest a glass of wine and tell him I stepped out."

"Stepped out?" Luis responded. "It's crazy down here. The place is filling up for the last go-round. I can't fit in any more tables, and Vito says you practically ate all the shrimp and you better get down here before he makes you start shucking clams."

Nervously, Day darted to the full-length mirror. She'd shopped at the fish market earlier, helped clean endless tubs of whiting, cod, and eel, fed and bathed Renzo and cut his toenails, an excruciating, exhausting experience, driven to Vinny's, and then put in six grueling hours at the restaurant. It all showed. Day's face was flushed, and her hair frizzy. The customary hostess outfit, long black skirt and white blouse was past its freshness date, and somewhere along the line, she'd lost an earring. Day unhooked the remaining silver hoop and rummaged for another pair, changed from a skirt into tuxedo pants, and was sliding hangers willy-nilly, searching for a blouse when she stopped abruptly and sighed. She was doing it again, fussing like an insecure dilettante because the man she'd cut loose was downstairs. If it was Lakota. Okay, it was; had to be. There were no tall mofos that looked like Sitting Bull in Belmont. But just because Lakota Campbell showed up like the second coming after perfunctory conversations, stilted messages, and months of crickets, it didn't mean she had to go all breathy and adolescent.

Day's break-up message couldn't have been more to the point—they were history and Lakota had taken the blow dead-pan with no more response than a single question mark; no *Dear Weayaya, Let's talk*; just one testy euphemism for wtf, and nothing since. So why was he here? To plead a case? That wasn't Lakota's style. To say he'd changed his mind about Renzo? No. He'd made that point clear. There was another reason besides a sudden hankering for pasta and whatever it was, Day vowed to be polite but stick to her guns.

Day's heart beat erratically and her stomach knotted as she tore through the dresser. Where was the damn silk blouse? What had she done with the comfortable shoes? *Beanie,* she whimpered. *He's here, cuz. What should I do?* Beanie didn't answer, or maybe she did. Day slipped back into the same sexy heels, pasted on a welcoming smile, and forced herself to breathe.

Chapter 40

The scene that greeted Day was so comical it almost calmed the jitters. Vito's head floated wide-eyed in the pass-thru and Luis and his sister stared with open-mouthed amazement at the dark-clad, lone drinker at the end of the bar perusing the menu. Lakota, sensing Day's approach, turned and gazed fixedly as she walked toward him, smiling tremulously. His hooded eyes, deep and appraising, never wavered, and her outstretched arm began to tremble.

"Lakota," she said, her voice breaking. "Welcome to Enchanted Gardens."

He nodded and lifted the sphalerite pendant. "Day," he said simply. "I see you still have the crystal."

Lakota's touch, her name on his lips; she blushed.

"How's your son?" he asked.

That broke the mood. Indignation replaced Day's wobbly composure. How dare he ask about Renzo after ignoring his existence?

"Why are you here?" she said, her tone unyielding.

"Your last email," he replied. "I thought I'd better cancel Iquitos and see what I'd done to rile you up. I'd already left London and was flying over the Canadian Rockies when I read it." He cracked a broken smile. "Close enough to the Bronx for a small detour."

Day heard nothing after the word *cancel*. The shell holding her upright cracked.

"How long can you stay?" she asked.

"Long as it takes."

She felt her face light up, couldn't tone it down, couldn't help herself.

Luis' sister bent over the bar. "More cranberry juice, sir?"

Lakota waved over his glass. "No thanks. I'd like dinner. I hear the food here is pretty good."

Day led him to a table. Vinny's brother popped out from the kitchen and pumped Lakota's hand. "Hey, man. Nice to meet you. Smokin' boots."

Day chuckled. "This is Sal, one of our cooks. Sal, meet Lakota Campbell."

"Lakota. That's Sioux Indian, right?" Sal shook hands. "I'm a Sioux too, a Sioux chef." He giggled nervously. "Get it?"

"Get out of here, Uncle Sal," Vinny, Jr. said, elbowing him aside and filling Lakota's glass with Sangiovese Brunello. "Compliments of the bar. I'm Day's nephew, Vincent," Junior said, bending close to Lakota. "She's my aunt. My mother used to talk about you. She told us—"

"Vinny is our head waiter," Day said pointedly as Junior grinned inanely. "Right now he's supposed to take your order."

"Oh, sorry." Junior hastily took out a pad then, at Day's cautionary glare, put it away and began to recite the night's specials.

"Have the kitchen bring me whatever you think I'd like, Vinny," Lakota said. "Day, why don't you join me?"

"I'm working," she responded coolly.

Something flickered behind Lakota's eyes.

Disappointment? Amusement? So much time had gone by, wasted time filled with unkept promises and long pauses. Day was sure Lakota hadn't come to Enchanted Gardens to win her back with an eloquent argument about the divinity of their relationship fated since time immemorial and destined to last into eternity. But why else?

"I get off at eleven," she hastily amended. "Can you wait?"

His tone was level. "Twelve hours on a plane from London to Vancouver to Newark, another hour in traffic, and two hundred dollars with a tip to get to the Bronx. Do what you have to. I'll wait."

Day tried to seat diners and answer their questions but she kept hovering over Lakota's table. He ate slowly, too slowly, asked to see the chef, and Day drummed her fingers while he and Vito talked about restaurants in Rome, and the damn orecchiette at Ciro's, and the damn crust of the *pizza margherita* in Naples. Day waited impatiently as Vinny brought another bottle of Pellegrino and Lakota toasted the baby squid salad and Sal sang the first verse of "Octopus's Garden." When Lakota kissed his fingers over Mrs. Navona's daughter's caramel cheesecake, Day shooed everybody back to the kitchen and, under several pairs of inquisitive eyes, led Lakota up to her apartment.

It didn't take long. Almost as soon as she closed the door, Day drew Lakota's mouth onto hers. The feel of him, his bulk and strength, probing tongue and stroking fingers, his realness after months of stargazing and empty daydreams, was exhilarating. Lakota lifted Day in his arms and carried her to the bed.

An hour later, sated, skin slick with sweat, hearts

beating, they lay together, legs entwined, Day's head on his chest. Lulled with contentment, she was finally able to speak. "I hardly believed it when Luis told me you were at the bar."

Lakota rose on one elbow. "You knew I'd come."

The familiar conviction irritated her. Here was more of that destiny palaver; the beforetime, the aftertime, souls fated through eternity.

"I knew nothing of the kind," Day retorted. "We haven't seen each other in months. What makes you think–"

Lakota placed two fingers on her lips. "I don't have to think. I know. You're my blood, my body, my soul. And I'm yours, have always been yours. Nothing can change that."

She didn't want to hear it. She wrenched away, wrapped his discarded shirt around her nakedness, and left his side. But Lakota's familiar scent on the cloth, clean and smoky like a fire of pine boughs, made her cry out.

"Come here," he said.

Day stayed put, head down, hands hanging. But the bed springs creaked and she knew Lakota was pulling on his jeans and coming over.

"I love you and I've hurt you," he said softly. "That's the last thing I want to do. I'm sorry."

"You're always sorry," Day accused, not daring to face him. "That's what you do. You hurt me and hurt me and hurt me!"

He tried to turn her toward him but she resisted. "I don't want that kind of love," she sobbed. "Go away."

His fingers tightened. "I can't do that. If that's what you want, *you'll* have to go away."

Despair descended on her like a shroud. "I can't either," she confessed miserably. "But this thing we have between us, it's not natural. People who love each other want to be together but you've made me into some kind of epic heroine. I'm not Penelope and you're not,"—she wiped her nose with the hem of his shirt.—"You're not what's his name? That guy who cleaned the Augean stables."

His mouth twisted. "Hercules?"

"Yes. No. I don't know. But he was the husband and he abandoned his wife, and she waited and waited for him to come back to her. She got old waiting."

"I'll always come back to you," Lakota said, his hold on her arms more gentle now. "Where will I ever find another woman who makes historical allusions when she's mad at me?"

He gathered her in his arms. Day rested her cheek against his heart.

"It's not working," she said. "Maybe we could have found a way but not now that I have Renzo. He's my son and I won't leave him to follow you around the globe, and it's not fair to drag him away from his father and brothers. Besides," she said, her tone sharp, "Renzo doesn't matter to you. You don't love him and you don't want him."

Lakota released Day so swiftly she stumbled. His face was thunderous. "Don't tell me what I want and don't want. Don't tell me who I love."

"Then why?" Day implored. "Renzo is just a little boy. Why can't you take pictures here or go off once in a while then come home to me and Renzo, and eventually our own children?"

"I don't want children," Lakota said flatly.

Day took a deep breath and plunged ahead. "I know. You had a baby and gave him up for adoption when his mother died."

The glow from the restaurant's bright new sign shone through Day's bedroom window illuminating Lakota's haunted eyes.

"Everybody in Hecate County gossips about the big Indian kid who got a girl pregnant and took off," he said. "I figured you'd find out sooner or later."

It was difficult to gauge what Lakota was feeling. His voice was hollow, his face empty, soulless.

"I don't blame you for what you did," Day said. "You were young. You didn't know any better. But with Renzo–"

Lakota grabbed Day again by the shoulders.

"Listen to me. I love my son more than my life. I didn't give him away or leave him to be adopted by strangers. His blood is mine, and every time I see him, I–" Lakota's voice broke.

"What are you saying?" Day asked. "I don't understand. You *see* him? When? Where is he?"

Lakota was shaking; the muscle in his jaw pulsed. He seemed to reach deep within himself for calm, but it came with a kind of reluctant surrender. He sat Day on the bed and squatted before her, his big hands shaking. "My son is probably at the cabin right now running the generator too long, overfeeding the dogs, and wrecking hell out of my car."

The words were meant to be light, but they rose from Lakota's throat like sandpaper.

Day blinked. "What? He's with you?"

Lakota rose and paced, hands in his pockets. "Mal isn't my brother. He's my son. There were rumors but

276

nobody knows for sure. I named him Koda, Little Bear, and brought him home to my dad and stepmother when he was just a baby." He extended one arm, palm up, fingers curled as if holding a ball. "He was so tiny. His head rested in my hand and his feet barely reached my elbow. God, I was so proud and happy. I wanted to keep Koda, but it was no use. I gave him to my father and stepmother. They're the steadiest, most caring people I know. They took Koda to Scotland for a while and returned to Hecate with their baby, Malcolm Cody Campbell. If anybody guessed he wasn't theirs, they mostly kept it to themselves." Lakota spoke his final sentence like a curse. "I went away too, joined the service, became a photographer, and left my family alone."

A million questions swirled in Day's head, each one different yet all pretty much the same. "Does Mal know?" she asked.

Lakota shook his head. "No. And it's going to stay that way."

Day was suddenly chilled. She hugged Lakota's shirt but there was no warmth to be found anywhere in the room.

"You have to be free, don't you?" she charged sadly. "Nothing can tie you down, not even your own son."

"I'm tied to you," Lakota said.

Day sighed at the futility of it all and let him hold her.

"Let's not talk about it," Lakota murmured into Day's hair. "Be with me tonight. Let me love you now."

They lay on the bed and Day drew Lakota close.

Now, she thought. *You're here now. Tomorrow you'll be gone.*

Chapter 41

Over breakfast the next morning, Lakota told Day he had an upcoming shoot in Peru and then a Middle East posting as soon as government clearance came through.

"I'll be back in the spring; summer for sure," he said. "You'll be here, won't you?"

"Where else would I be? This is my home."

His dark eyes seared a path to the center of her skull and down to her belly. "Will you let me in?" he asked.

Day hardened against the melting sensation, against her lover's beautiful face, ancient with wisdom and young with desire. How was she going to survive without him?

After breakfast, they stepped out into a raging snowstorm. Lakota cleaned off the Subaru and Day crawled along almost empty streets to the Bronx Park East subway train that would take him to Penn Station. In less than an hour, she'd be driving back alone, chilled to the marrow without Lakota's warm presence beside her. Day dreaded saying goodbye, dreaded the whole leaving ritual, the antiseptic hug and kiss, the disconsolate wave. She couldn't do it; she'd fall apart.

The cars on East 180th Street were buried under snow and nobody was waiting on the station platform. Day stood beside Lakota and knew in her bones there'd never be another for her, knew too that she had to take this man as he was, love him for who he was, and leave their future to the stars. An oncoming headlight shone through a scrim of snowflakes thick as batting. Seized with panic, Day watched the train clatter toward them and whoosh to a stop.

"This is it," she said, looking up at him.

Tall, and solitary, Lakota gazed at her for a moment.

"Believe, Day," he said, grasping her hand and pressing it to his lips. "That's all you have to do. Believe in me, in us. The rest will follow."

He stepped into the waiting car, the doors hissed shut, and the train glided onward, dwindling to insignificance. Day walked to her car already mounded with fresh snow. She had Lakota's love but not the rest, not the happy ever after. Was that enough to last a lifetime of goodbyes, strained letters, and stilted phone calls? She would have to believe it was, just like Lakota had assured, and work at believing it like she worked at the restaurant, and at raising Renzo. Both were hard jobs and worth the effort.

A man in a Santa Claus suit shouted Merry Christmas. Day grinned and waved back. Vinny and the boys were expecting her for pancakes and presents under the tree and she quickly cleared her car's windshield with a gloved hand. It was good packing snow. After breakfast, she'd take Renzo back to Enchanted Gardens and build him a snowman.

A word about the author...

Maria Paoletta Gil, herself born and raised in Belmont, has worked many jobs including personal chef, tour guide, real estate agent, drug counselor, newspaper reporter, dog walker, English teacher, and administrator with the City University of New York. In addition to writing romance novels, she reviews Bollywood films and Korean dramas for American audiences. www.mariapaolettagil.com

Thank you for purchasing
this publication of The Wild Rose Press, Inc.

For questions or more information
contact us at
info@thewildrosepress.com.

The Wild Rose Press, Inc.
www.thewildrosepress.com